FIRST LANDING

ROBERT ZUBRIN

ACE BOOKS, NEW YORK

FIRST LANDING

An Ace Book / published by arrangement with
the author

PRINTING HISTORY
Ace hardcover edition / July 2001
Ace mass-market edition / August 2002

Visit our website at
www.penguinputnam.com
Check out the ACE Science Fiction & Fantasy newsletter!

ISBN: 0-441-00963-8

ACE®
Ace Books are published by The Berkley Publishing Group,
a division of Penguin Putnam Inc.,
375 Hudson Street, New York, New York 10014.
ACE and the "A" design
are trademarks belonging to Penguin Putnam Inc.

PRINTED IN THE UNITED STATES OF AMERICA

10 9 8 7 6 5 4 3 2 1

For my daughters,
Rachel and Sarah,
explorers of the new world

ACKNOWLEDGMENTS

The author wishes to acknowledge the assistance of many people who helped in the creation of this book. These include: Jonathan Vos Post, who contributed many valuable ideas to the initial development of the story; Greg Benford and James Cameron, who provided useful advice for the refinement of the plot; Brian Frankie, who provided input on the rock-climbing scenes; and Laurie Fox, Susan Allison, and Kevin Anderson, all of whom helped the author sharpen the final manuscript for publication.

Most of all, I would like to express my thanks to my wife, Maggie, without whose loving support the writing of this novel would have been impossible.

CHAPTER 1

THE *BEAGLE* WHIRLED SILENTLY THROUGH THE VOID. Round and round she looped, suspended by centrifugal force at the end of a mile-long tether from her long-expended propulsion stage. Lit by the sun on one side, and an eerie red Marsglow on the other, she looked more like a big tuna can riding on an oversized plate than a daring ship of exploration. But brave explorer she was, and the plate her shield and only protection against the incandescent blast of her imminent Mach 30 entry into Mars' atmosphere. A technological marvel, her inner workings included over ten thousand mission-critical electronic circuits. As she approached her trial by fire, all but one were working perfectly.

ABOARD THE <u>BEAGLE</u>, APPROACHING MARS
OCT. 26, 2011 14:22 CST

"Oh, Houstonnn, we've got a problemmm," Luke Johnson drawled in a Texas accent with a singsong pitch.

Beneath the *Beagle*'s primary electronics console, Major Guenevere Llewellyn overheard the comment and set her mouth in a grim line. He could say that again. She rubbed her hands on her grease-stained NASA flight suit and stared up at a world of wires and fuses, circuit breakers, capacitors, switches, voltages, currents, resistances, temperature readouts on pyro bolts—and a clock with twenty-seven minutes left on it.

As she tinkered furiously, Gwen muttered half to herself and half to her anxious crewmates. "It doesn't make any sense. Why aren't the pyros firing? We've got plenty of power, and three redundant circuits for delivering the ignition spark."

Shortly after launch the better part of a year ago, when Mission Commander Townsend had separated the spacecraft from the upper stage, the burnt-out booster rocket had remained connected to the *Beagle* by a mile-long tether, dangling like a long counterweight on a string. After firing a small rocket engine on the Hab module, Townsend had set the craft spinning; at the end of its tether, the whirling upper stage produced enough centrifugal force to provide the crew with sufficient artificial gravity for their long journey to Mars.

But if Gwen couldn't disconnect the tether in time, the *Beagle*'s Mach 30 aeroentry would be uncontrollable, and the ship would be burned to a crisp.

Stumped, she tried to think of any malfunction that could have caused the breakdown. "The pyros are a new type, designed to prevent inadvertent ignition by static discharge. Maybe this close to Mars they got too cold, chilled below their ignition temperature. If I shunt over some extra power from the life-support system, that might warm them enough to light."

"Worth a try, but better hurry," Colonel Townsend said. "Do it."

Gwen swiftly threw some relays, switching the surplus LSS power into the pyro prewarmers. In seconds, however, it was obvious that the move would be ineffectual.

The flight mechanic crawled out from beneath the control panel and faced the mission commander. He wasn't going to like what she had to say. "Colonel, there's no choice. I've got to go EVA and pull the manual release."

"Major, no one is going EVA around here until I give the order. That's a last resort. Now try shunting the backup power from the RCS actuators to the pyro ignition system."

Gwen sat down at her control station. She knew it wouldn't work, but arguing with the bomber-jacket-clad ex-fighter jockey would waste precious time. If she made quick work of it, there would still be time for the EVA. Barely.

"Aye, aye, sir." Gwen sat down at her control station.

Townsend gave her a grin and a thumbs up. *That's not going to do it, Colonel.* Townsend flipped the switch to de-safe her board. "Okay, fire on five. Five . . . four . . . three . . . two . . . one . . . Do it!"

On Townsend's order, Gwen hit the firing switches. There was no response. Townsend cracked his knuckles in an unconscious admission of stress. She could see he didn't want to let her go EVA, but he'd have to, and soon.

"Colonel, I've got to suit up." Gwen started to rise, but the colonel's hand shoved her back down into her seat.

"At my mark . . ." Townsend said, "fire again." She could see the sweat on his creased forehead.

Gwen hit the switch. "No go, sir," she reported. Twenty-four minutes.

"All right, shunt *all* the life-support power to the igniters. Switch to batteries for the lights."

The last alternative to EVA. Gwen's fingers flew over the power regulator controls. "Aye, aye."

The internal lights of the habitation module dimmed. Ruddy Marsshine illuminated the cabin interior.

"Fire!"

Gwen stabbed down on both power switches. No response.

"Try again . . . Fire! . . . . Fire! . . . Goddammit!"

The colonel is losing it, Gwen thought, startled by his uncharacteristic language. *Twenty-three minutes left.* "Colonel. This isn't going to work." She turned to him, trying to keep her own professional cool. "The only solution is for me to get out on the roof of the Hab module and release the tether manually. Now."

"There isn't time."

"Luke's got a Marsuit all ready. It's the only way."

Townsend drummed his fingers on the control panel while his chief engineer felt precious seconds ticking away. "All right then, Major. There's no time to verify with Houston, and I won't waste time arguing about who's best for the job. It's my prerogative as commander to approve your suggestion. Go for it."

"Yes, sir." Gwen leapt across the cabin toward the space-suit locker. Big Luke, the mission geologist, had her Marsuit waiting. Marked with her old army helo unit insignia, it was thinner, more flexible, and much easier to don than a standard spacesuit. Designed for field work on the Martian surface, Marsuits were not rated for space. But despite the qualms of the NASA safety mafia, everyone who had ever worked with them knew they were the best choice for fast EVA work as well.

"Don't try to play hero," Townsend warned. "Just stay cool."

Gwen took it on faith that Luke had checked out the suit correctly; there wasn't time to do it herself. Twenty-one minutes.

It took her seconds to strip off the NASA flight suit, revealing an athletic body clad in an Atlanta Braves T-shirt and cutoff blue jeans. The geologist helped her wriggle into the EVA gear, then strapped on an auxiliary cold gas jet pack.

The Marsuit fit like a second skin. "If my pants were as tight as this suit, they'd never let me into church back home," she commented wryly. Luke chuckled as she took the transparent globular helmet from him. "Okay, folks, I think I'll take a little stroll outside."

"By the book, Major," Townsend said.

As she crossed the cabin, Gwen could hear Townsend giving instructions to Luke and Rebecca Sherman, the excessively sophisticated ship's doctor and chief scientist. "I'm going to start programming in emergency maneuvers. You two, take your emergency stations at consoles two and three. As soon as Gwen goes outside, you watch with the multi-cams. If you see anything that looks even the slightest bit odd, I want you to scream. Is that clear?"

Professor McGee, the other egghead on board, was nowhere in sight. Probably off somewhere dictating to his journal. As mission historian, there wasn't much else he could do. *We'll all burn up in a little while if I don't get this done,* Gwen thought. *Not much of an ending to his story.*

"Okay, Major, it's your play. Good luck."

With a practiced hand, Gwen crossed her two red braids behind her neck, removed her Atlanta Braves cap, and clamped the helmet down to seal the Marsuit. Then she entered the airlock, closing the hatch behind her. Through the viewport she could see Dr. Sherman making double-sure it was dogged shut.

Gwen checked the airlock readouts. Praise the Lord, at least this system was in working order. "All secure in here. Commence pumpdown."

Twenty minutes.

"Pumpdown initiated." Townsend's voice was muffled inside Gwen's helmet. The lock began to hiss. Because the *Beagle*'s cabin atmospheric pressure was kept at a modest five pounds per square inch, no prebreathing was necessary, and the depressurization operation proceeded swiftly. As the pressure dropped, the Marsuit began to stiffen.

Gwen looked out the window into space as the hiss and throb of the evacuation pumps grew fainter. As she stared open-mouthed at the wild profusion of stars, with nothing to do but wait, a poignant memory of a long-ago clear night in rural North Carolina briefly possessed her.

She was twelve, looking out her bedroom window on a cricket-haunted night, the full moon hanging peacefully above her apricot tree. Pebbles rattled against her window. "Gwennie, let's go," whispered the boys from the neighboring farm. She climbed down the vine and crawled past the kitchen window, where she could hear her parents talking about her: "I don't know how Gwen's ever gonna get herself a boy if she keeps acting like one. Did you hear how she beat the tar out of the Nichols boy in the schoolyard last week?"

The kids had listened for a bit, giggled conspiratorially, then sneaked off into the barn, where they jumped out of the loft onto haystacks, yelling "Geronimo!" When it was Gwen's turn to leap, it seemed as if she hung in the air for minutes, her heart pounding, while the moon and stars spun around her.

It had been her first taste of weightlessness, of space. . . .

Finally, the hatch opened, and the last bits of air puffed out of the airlock, sparkling with instantly frozen specks of water vapor. They looked like gold dust in the harsh sunlight of outer space. *Time to stop holding your breath, girl.* Only eighteen minutes left. Gwen gingerly edged out onto the exterior white-painted skin of the habitat module, her magnetic boots clanging hollowly.

Up the ladder. Gwen made her way to the tether-deployment unit, slowly unreeling the umbilical safety line that would keep her attached if her magnetic boots slipped off the hull. *There's the windlass, just a few more steps. Uh-oh. The umbilical is too short.*

Sixteen minutes left.

There was only one thing to do and no time to argue about it. *Better not even tell Townsend.* Gwen detached the safety umbilical from her suit. *Okay, now take it easy.*

She grabbed the handholds onto the roof of the Hab. The unobstructed view of Mars from the slowly rotating spacecraft was spectacular, but it made her dizzy. Feeling like an ant crawling across the outside of a yo-yo, she paused, feeling nauseous.

Townsend's voice practically shouted inside her helmet, scratchy with static. "How's it going, Major?"

"Almost there, Colonel."

"Well, get to it. We've only got fourteen minutes before aeroentry."

Gwen scrambled forward and grabbed the windlass. *Made it.* "Ready to initiate manual release."

"Proceed, Major."

Gwen put her hands on the lever, braced her boots under the windlass baseplate, and pushed down hard. No give. *Dammit, is the stupid thing vacuum-welded?*

She tried again, but the lever still wouldn't budge. She considered trying to cut the cable, but discarded the idea. The spectra tether was over three inches thick. With her sheath knife as her only cutting tool, hacking the cable would take far too long. A secondary set of pyro bolts held the windlass to its baseplate. The bolts had refused to fire—but maybe they could be detached entirely.

Gwen took a wrench from her tool belt and hesitantly placed it on the bolt's hex. *If that bolt fires when I twist it, I'm fried. But if we don't get loose, we're all fried.* She put both hands on the wrench handle and braced her feet on the windlass. "Okay, stand by me, Jesus." Then she pulled with all her might.

The brittle bolt broke with a snap but no explosion. The force of the push hurled Gwen away from the windlass, but she caught a handhold and swung herself back to the Hab roof. *Okay. Now for the other three bolts.*

"What's going on up there, Major?"

"The manual release won't move, so I'm snapping off the pyro bolts."

"You're what?"

"Snapping the bolts. One down, three to go."

"Major, Gwen, try something else. If those bolts should fire—"

"No time, sir." She continued with her work.

"Major, this is an order—"

Gwen cut him off. *Okay, number two.* She braced, pulled, and got another snap. Catching her handhold, she swung back onto the roof. Ten minutes left. *Better hurry.*

The third bolt broke free with eight minutes remaining.

Then, confident, Gwen placed the wrench head around the final hex and pulled. But this time the bolt wouldn't give.

"Come on, break, damn you!" She had one trick left. Fully braced, she kicked down on the wrench handle with all the force she could muster.

Everything changed in a blink. The bolt snapped, the whole windlass tore free of the Hab module—and Gwen lost her footing. She grabbed for a handhold, but the *Beagle* was now separating from her at a velocity of fifty meters a second. She tumbled off into space.

Watching the ship recede into the distance, Gwen whispered "Geronimo," her voice echoing strangely inside her helmet. Then she fired her cold gas jets to negate her spin. For a moment, she hung weightless with the entire panorama of Mars, the diminishing ship, and a vast, star-studded sky surrounding her.

The spell lasted only a second before she realized that Townsend would feel obligated to maneuver the ship and come after her. With only six minutes left, the risk was too great. She switched on her suit radio.

"You're home free, Colonel; suggest you prepare for aerocapture."

"Major, where the hell have you been? Where the hell are you?"

"I've separated from the ship, sir."

Townsend's voice was hard and no-nonsense. "What's your bearing?"

Gwen looked at the ship, then in the opposite direction. "You'll find me in Pegasus, sir, but there's no time."

"Pegasus? Gotcha. Hang in there, Major, we're coming for you."

Gwen knew it was useless to argue. That colonel was a damn fool; he'd lose the mission to try to save her. She saw a retro flare on the speck representing the retreating ship, and felt a tear forming in the corner of her eye.

He'd never make it. Still, it was good to have friends.

CHAPTER 2

"ONE HUNDRED NINETY SECONDS TO ATMOSPHERIC CONTACT," Luke announced. Tension sharpened his normally slow, relaxed voice.

The computer chanted softly, counting down the numbers.

Colonel Andrew Townsend's computer screen flashed one dreadful message after another: ATMOSPHERIC ENTRY ANGLE INCORRECT FOR AEROCAPTURE.

SHIP ROTATION INCORRECT FOR AEROCAPTURE.

FLIGHT PATH ANGLE INCORRECT FOR AEROCAPTURE.

AERODYNAMIC ANGLE OF ATTACK INCORRECT.

PITCH INCORRECT.

YAW INCORRECT.

ROLL INCORRECT.

THRUSTER ORIENTATION INCORRECT FOR AEROCAPTURE.

Townsend grimaced: This was going to be a real mess. Gwen's voice crackled on the intercom. "Give it up, Colonel. You don't have time for this. Bring the ship around and save the mission."

No doubt about it, Gwen was a gutsy kid, but this self-sacrifice stuff was getting irritating. One hundred seventy seconds. Plenty of time—maybe. But now she was less than fifty meters to starboard, still chattering. "Colonel, you only have two minutes left. You've got to—"

He'd had enough. "Don't tell me what I've got to do, Major. I'll save you *and* the mission, so we'll do it *my* way, if you please."

Easy does it. Twenty meters away. *Better rotate the air-lock toward her; there won't be time for climbing around.* "Come on, Major, use your gas jets. We're close enough now."

The computer screen flashed, AERO ENTRY IMMINENT. FLIGHT VECTOR ELEMENTS ALL OUTSIDE SPECIFIED LIMITS. CONDITION RED. CONDITION RED.

Alarm klaxons began shrieking, shockingly loud in the Hab cabin.

"Colonel!" Luke barked from his temporary position as co-pilot in Gwen's absence. "We're going in too steep! The aeroshield's off-center. We're going to burn!"

The man was obviously hysterical, but he had a point. The Martian atmosphere was only six-tenths of one percent as thick as Earth's, but at the *Beagle*'s tremendous velocity, a too-steep angle of entry would burn them to ashes once their heat-resistant aeroshield gave way. "Calm down, Luke. We still have forty-five seconds."

"Colonel, Gwen's moving in toward the starboard lock," Dr. Sherman said, keeping her voice level. "If you can hold this orientation just a few more seconds, I think she can make it."

"Thank you, Doctor." Townsend made a mental note. *Dr. Sherman. She has a cool head on her shoulders, that one.*

The ship creaked and shuddered with vibrations as they encountered the first wisps of Mars' upper ionosphere. Where was Gwen?

"Only fifteen seconds left! Colonel, you've got to—"

"Shut up, Luke," Sherman interrupted. "She's almost— Oh no, now she's being pushed back by the wind."

No time left. Townsend stabbed the port retro, shoving

the ship one last time in Gwen's direction. There was a substantial thump. *Gwen, I sure hope you didn't bounce.*

"She's in the lock."

Townsend smiled, but only for a second. The klaxons were deafening, and every light on the control panel glared red. The vessel shuddered with the impact of substantial atmospheric entry. He grabbed the aero-control stick, and pulled back hard.

"All right crew, fasten your seat belts, we're coming about. Time to do some real flying."

A sudden lurch told Townsend that he'd been a second too late. All hell broke loose in the cabin as the *Beagle* convulsed into a wild spin. Townsend caught a momentary glance of several crew members tossed about like rag dolls; then they were gone from his peripheral vision. All that existed for Townsend now were some retros, a stick, and data readouts.

He fought madly with the controls, but the aeroshield's angle of attack was all wrong, and the *Beagle* tumbled in the thickening air.

Gasping inside the starboard lock, Gwen managed to close the outer door before the riotous spin started. The rotation slammed her back and forth within the lock until she wedged herself between the narrow walls. *Christ, we're out of control!*

If they were going to get out of this alive, the *Beagle* needed two sets of hands at the controls. Somehow, she had to make it back to the command console. She hit the emergency pressure equalization button and heard the *whoosh* as cabin air flooded the lock compartment. As her suit flattened with subpressurization, she undogged the inner lock door and pushed her way into the cabin.

What a mess! Debris was scattered everywhere; one computer monitor had been smashed by a flying object. Dr. Sherman clutched the back of her chair, swinging about as it spun in place, struggling in vain to pull herself into the seat. Luke Johnson sprawled on the floor, holding tight to one of the legs of the galley table. As Gwen watched, a badly bruised Professor McGee staggered into the cabin and bounced off the wall, caromed off a set of science consoles, then crashed fortuitously into his own chair, buckling himself in not ten feet from her, as if that had been his plan all along.

If that lubber can make it to his station, then so can I.

Gwen muttered a brief prayer, then scrambled across the deck, only to be hurled back to her starting point by a sudden 3-g force. For a moment the force varied in direction, then settled down to a near-constant vector, directly contrary to her intended path.

Well, at least Townsend seems to be limiting the tumble—that constant g-force means he's finally gotten the shield around.

But that left her with the problem of climbing across the deck inclined against 3 g's worth of pull. She set her boot magnetos on maximum and tried trudging forward again— no use, not enough traction. She stared across the deck at her control station, impossibly close, impossibly far.

Now something strange was going on. That idiot egghead McGee began climbing out of his chair, locking eyes with her. *Is he crazy?* Gwen thought. *He's gone down on the deck, holding the base of his chair. I don't get it. Jesus, he's stretching himself across the deck towards me! He's making himself into a rope ladder. Well, I'll be!* "Okay, Professor!" Gwen shouted through the chaos. "Here I come."

She shoved off the airlock outer door, feeling as if she were rolling heavy boulders uphill, and grabbed McGee's feet and hauled herself forward. She reached an arm up and grabbed his knee, then his belt. As she climbed, Gwen felt a surge of admiration. The man was holding two human bodies steeply sloped against 3 g's. It had to hurt like hell. "Now don't let go," she gasped in a whisper. "If you do, you'll crush us both when we hit the wall." *Just a few more seconds. Hold on.*

Gwen's arm reached the shaft of McGee's chair, and she

pulled herself up. "Well done, Professor!" She shot him a smile, then pushed away from his chair to reach her own. She flung herself into her seat and buckled in. Tossing off her helmet, she could smell burnt insulation in the cabin air. "Status, Colonel?"

"Glad to see you back at your post, Major. We're under control, but seem to be a bit deeper into the atmosphere than called for in the nominal flight profile."

Gwen glanced at the altimeter and recoiled in horror. Twelve kilometers! Way too deep within the atmosphere for aerocapture into a stable orbit. One way or another the ship was going down, and soon.

"ABORT TO SURFACE, ABORT TO SURFACE," the navigation computer bleated metallically.

Gwen checked the local navigation readouts: two thousand kilometers from the primary landing site. She was ready when Townsend hit her with the expected question: "Do we have enough airspeed to make it to the return vehicle?"

Their ride home, the Earth Return Vehicle, had been launched from Earth a full year and a half before the *Beagle* lifted off. The ERV had landed in a carefully chosen spot, sitting on its site automatically processing oxygen, water, and rocket fuel from Martian resources. Everything had been carefully planned for the habitation module to touch down nearby, for the crew to go find the nice welcome mat.

But plans made in comfortable conference rooms didn't always turn out as expected.

"Way too much," Gwen answered quickly. "The only way to slow down in time is to fly low through the canyon and thread the needle. Risky with all this irregular ground, and flying that low won't give us enough altitude for the chute to land us. Might be safer to abort to the south and hope that the backup ERV can be retargeted for a rescue mission."

"That'll be the day," replied Townsend. "Hold on tight, we're going in."

Oh brother, here we go, thought Gwen, wincing. *Where*

do they find guys like this? She watched the nav readouts as Townsend did everything he could to control altitude. Looking out the window, she could see the blinding light of the trail of ionized gas as the ship streaked like a fireball across the Martian sky. Their target was the landing radar transponder aboard the ERV near the north edge of the Valles Marineris—the greatest canyon in the solar system, deeper than the Grand Canyon and as long as the entire United States. If they didn't make it there, the crew would be hopelessly stranded.

Then the blazing plasma trail was gone. Gwen stared at the unearthly landscape rising on both sides as the ship streaked between mountains and through the canyon.

"SEA LEVEL," the computer announced neutrally—an odd phrase for a desert planet that had lost its lakes and rivers many millions of years ago. "ONE KILOMETER BELOW SEA LEVEL. TWO KILOMETERS BELOW SEA LEVEL."

Gwen's heart pounded with growing hope. "You're in the groove, Colonel. We're way below the surrounding terrain, right in the axis of the canyon. You've got one chance to pull out of this dive, sir, so make it good."

"Roger that." Townsend pulled the stick back into a climb.

Suddenly, in the rapidly approaching distance, Gwen spotted the tiny ERV glinting silver-red in the sunlight, the only man-made object on the alien surface. "Target in sight."

Townsend steered toward it, but he had sacrificed too much velocity just to fly the ship. Gwen waited for the inevitable order. "Pop the chutes."

She slapped her hand down on the control, releasing the drogue and main parachutes in sequence. When the main opened, a sudden shock slammed her against her seat; then all was strangely quiet except for a rocking motion as the ship swayed at the end of the chute's risers.

"Release aeroshield."

Gwen obeyed without comment, knowing they were

about to discover the answer to a key question: Do we have enough altitude to land, or do we smash? She regarded the control readout. "Too low," she whispered. Townsend nodded grimly.

Momentarily possessed by a bit of black humor, Gwen activated the ship's annunciator. "Attention all passengers. Prepare for crash landing. Free champagne if we make it down alive. Thank you for flying *Beagle* Airlines."

"Thank you, stewardess." Townsend laughed.

Gwen looked at the altimeter, all business again. "Time to cast off the main chute."

"No, we keep it. This is going to be a sails-and-engines job."

Or a wing-and-a-prayer job, Gwen thought.

"Arm landing rockets. Arm orbital maneuvering system."

She flipped switches. "Landing rockets armed. OMS armed."

"Arm emergency backups."

More switches. "Backups armed."

"Disengage all engine safety throttle limiters."

"Engine safety throttle limiters disen—What?" The order made no sense. The throttle limiters were a feedback control circuit to reduce propellant flow if the thermocouples detected engine overheating. They shouldn't be switched off. And couldn't be.

"I *said,* disengage the throttle limiter safety system! Can you do it?"

"Yes, sir." If he needed thrust, she'd give him thrust, but . . .

The computer continued its emotionless recitation. "TWELVE SECONDS TO IMPACT, TEN, NINE . . ."

There was one way to do it quickly. Gwen reached for Old Faithful, the sheath knife attached to her boot, and pried open her control panel. Which were the right connections? No time for subtlety. She grabbed a clump of wires and ripped them loose with a hard, two-handed tug. "Throttle limiters disengaged."

"Roger," said Townsend. "Firing."

He slammed his hands on the control panel to fire all landing rockets and emergency backups; then his hands danced across the OMS controls as he fired the ship's own orbital maneuvering system as well. The Hab module shuddered with the shotgun bang of the rocket systems kicking in. Seconds later, they rode through a massive jarring as the landing gear hit the ground.

Then everything was quiet.

Gwen turned around to look first at the mission commander, then at the crew. Everyone appeared dazed or in shock. Luke had lost teeth, and blood was streaming from his mouth and nose. McGee was clenching his jaw, rubbing an aching shoulder; Gwen looked quickly away from him, remembering what he had done.

Rebecca Sherman stared wide-eyed out the window, coughing quietly.

Gwen staggered over to her. At first she could see little in the thick, stirred-up dust, but then the view cleared to reveal the Martian landscape—with the vital ERV standing not a hundred yards away. She exchanged a glance of wonder with the doctor.

Before she could say anything, her thoughts were interrupted by the crackle of the radio. "*Beagle,* this is Houston Control. Please report on your post-aerocapture orbital status." Due to the long transmission lag, NASA was way behind the times. "We'll need to discuss a number of items before we give the final go-ahead for your commitment to land. Please prepare a detailed report on the status of . . ."

Gwen saw Colonel Townsend pick up his mike. *This should be interesting.*

"Houston Control, this is Mars Base One. The *Beagle* has landed."

A ragged cheer erupted from McGee and Luke. Gwen took another look out the window. It was true, it was there, right there, the ERV *Retriever,* their ticket home. From somewhere came an uncanny sound.

It took a second for Gwen to realize that the strange

sound echoing through the Hab module was her own voice, a rebel yell, the first and loudest ever heard on Mars.

Townsend's message had just come through to Philip Mason, the Chief of Mission Operations at Johnson Space Center. A somewhat overstuffed African-American manager who dressed impeccably in tailored suits and silk ties, Mason was confused to the point of hysteria. He looked around at the other staff members, as if they knew more than he did.

"What does he mean, 'landed?' That's not scheduled for another three days." He gestured to Craig Holloway, the young brown-clad ecogoth computer whiz, who in his own way typified the diverse workforce of the new NASA. "Craig, get that flyboy asshole to stop horsing around and give us his precise orbital elements so we can work out a nav sequence. By the book. And tell him to snap to it. We're going to have to go over a lot of things before anybody commits to a landing."

Al Rollins looked up from his console. Young as Holloway, but with close-cropped hair, white shirt, and pocket protector, Rollins was a more classic nerd. "Chief, we've got imaging telemetry coming in from the *Beagle*."

That sounded reassuring. "Put it on the main viewscreen." Mason self-consciously straightened his tie and picked up his microphone. "Ladies and gentlemen of the press, we have live pictures from the *Beagle,* which has now completed its aerocapture maneuver into a precisely targeted low Mars orbit." He smiled with proud confidence.

The viewscreen cleared to show a stark Martian landscape with a dusty Earth Return Vehicle in the near distance. As the Chief of Mission Operations stared in disbelief, he felt all the eyes in the room on him.

"Holy shit, I don't believe it!" he mumbled. "That flyboy asshole really is on Mars."

For one crisp moment, utter silence filled the room; then pandemonium erupted. Control operators jumped up on their desks and cheered, while those reporters who had not had the sense to smuggle their cellulars past JSC security shoved each other aside in a mad rush to the bank of available telephones. Mason felt his own spirits begin to rise. He was about to join in the cheering himself, when he felt a hand on his shoulder.

"Phil, I've got the report from the *Beagle*." Tex Logan was the last of the Apollo-era veterans still working in Mission Control. "The premature landing was caused by a failure of the tether pyro release systems. Major Llewellyn was forced to perform an emergency EVA, which upset the flight plan."

Mason looked at the old geezer in astonishment. "Complete tether release pyro failure? Are you sure?"

"Sure as taxes."

"But that couldn't have happened." That release system was triple redundant, Mason knew, with a ten-to-one over-design on the firing power.

"Nope." Tex's voice became grim and conspiratorial. "Not by itself, anyhow. Think about it."

Mason stared at the laconic old-timer, his lined face stern with unspoken implications. Sabotage? The thought was terrifying. Then again, Tex Logan was always coming up with bizarre conspiracy theories.

The two were joined by Darrell Gibbs, the nattily clad Special Assistant to the White House Science and Security Advisor. "So, gentlemen, what do we have?" the thirty-something politico inquired.

Mason turned to face the younger man. "Well, Darrell, Tex here thinks that we may be dealing with a case of sabotage."

Gibbs raised an eyebrow. "Really?"

"Gotta be," Tex insisted. "Either here in Houston, on-board *Beagle,* or somewhere at the Cape."

Gibbs smiled. Like most others in Mission Control, he was also acquainted with the older man's many conspiracy theories. "Tex, be reasonable. Who could possibly want to wreck humanity's first mission to Mars?"

"Now let me see," Tex replied, sliding into his drawl. "There's the Libyans, the Iranians, the Iraqis, the North Koreans, the Russians, the Chinese, the Europeans, the Japanese, the Mafia, the Colombian drug lords." He took a breath. "The crew's enemies, JSC's enemies, NASA's enemies, the Administration's enemies, the Trilateral Commission, the Bilderbergers—"

"Don't forget the UN one-worlders," Gibbs interjected.

"For sure. Then there's the Amber Room group, MI-5, the JACKAL, and—"

"The second shooter on the grassy knoll." Mason rolled his eyes and chuckled.

"There *was* a second shooter on the grassy knoll," Tex replied stiffly.

Gibbs put a friendly hand on Tex's shoulder. "Come on, old boy, lighten up. We've just successfully landed on Mars, for crying out loud."

The Chief of Mission Operations looked around and brushed a fleck of lint from his suit. NASA personnel from neighboring buildings were pouring into Mission Control. Champagne was flowing, and people were cheering, hugging, dancing on their desks like it was VE Day in Times Square. He'd never seen anything like it, and then it finally started to dawn on him. They'd done it! By God, they'd actually done it! This was the moment he'd worked for all his professional life. Tex was off his rocker. This was a time for celebration!

Mason grabbed a champagne bottle from Rollins, took a swig, and poured the rest on his head. "Yippee!"

With amusement, Gibbs watched the transformation of the normally straight-laced administrator.

But Tex had yet to join in the celebratory spirit. "Here you go, old man—have a beer! They landed safe. That's all that matters."

The Texan accepted a cool Coors from Gibbs and took a sip, but he still didn't look won over. "Yep. But they're still a long way from home."

CHAPTER 3

MCGEE PEERED OUT THE HAB MODULE'S DUSTY WINDOW at the spectacular Martian landscape. His abused arm throbbed, the ache of the sprain only slightly moderated by the anti-inflammatory and cold pack Rebecca Sherman had administered shortly after landing. But the awe he felt dulled the pain.

This moment was grand beyond measure, a historian's dream, the first landing on a planet that could someday be home to a new branch of human civilization. The pen of an epic poet like Homer or Milton, or a great historian like Herodotus or Thucydides, should be here to record the experience for future generations. Unfortunately, such men were not available. Instead, Kevin McGee was the inadequate man of letters on the mission, who would provide humanity with an account in workmanlike but ordinary prose. Still, he had to try.

He turned on his minicorder. Time to be brilliant, poetic . . . "Today is October 26, 2011. Our ship, the *Beagle,* after a voyage of ten months from Earth and passing Venus has at last landed on the red planet. Looking out the window now,

I see a cratered plain illuminated by the late afternoon Sun, backed by spectacular cliffs unlike any I've ever seen on Earth.

"Mars from space was a stupendous sight. It looked a little like the Moon, with most of its surface 3.8 billion years old, dating back to the violent era in solar system history when planets and moons were cratered by the impact of meteorites. But this is not the Moon—it's much bigger.

"Mars is a world like Earth, but bleached of the sweet blues and green of home. You can sense the violence of the place, its complicated terrain having been shaped by impacts, volcanoes, wind, water, and ice. As we approached, I could see the giant shield volcanoes along the crest of the Tharsis bulge, as well as runoff channels and ancient dry riverbeds that emptied into what looked like the basin of a long-gone sea in the northern hemisphere."

McGee stopped, discouraged by the mundane quality of his prose. He needed to say something deep. Suddenly he was struck by a new idea. "Mars had rivers and seas while Earth's oceans were still boiling. Within our solar system, Life's first opportunity to blossom would have been here, during an era when fast and furious meteors were bombarding its surface. All those craters—were they left behind as chunks of the living Mars were driven into space? Did the bombardment rip away the planet's life-cradling atmosphere too? Mars, was that the price that you paid to send your spawn aloft, perhaps to seed the Earth? If so, then . . . Father, we have returned." He smiled, satisfied at last.

"Very poetic, Kevin."

Startled, McGee looked up to see Rebecca Sherman, the *Beagle*'s doctor and chief mission scientist. She leaned over him and stared out at the same view, pressing close. McGee tensed in spite of himself. Tall and classically beautiful, Rebecca was sexually and intellectually intimidating even at a distance; at this range she was devastating.

"So . . . you liked it?"

"Well, I would say that it's both good and original."

For a moment, he was gratified by the remark; then Rebecca's condescending smile reminded him of the crushing subtext. *But unfortunately, the part that is good is not original and the part that is original is not good*—Samuel Johnson.

"Though the insight isn't new, I did like your metaphorical grasp of the Copernican principle suggesting the universal nature of life. Of course, that's what we've got to prove. But, if my colleagues on NASA's Mars Science Working Group shared half your intuition on that score—" She paused and looked out the window for a moment, then turned back to grin at him. "Then at least I would be dealing with a bunch of half-wits."

McGee chuckled along with her, only to be stopped by her raised finger. "But please, Kevin, can't you get the point across without bringing in such dreary medieval metaphors? Mars as martyr? You can do better than that." She turned to gaze out the window again. Stung, McGee pretended to do likewise, thinking of the beautiful doctor more than of the scenery.

Rebecca Sherman certainly had it all: exclusive prep-school background, Radcliffe B.A., Ph.D. from Cornell in exobiology on a Carl Sagan Fellowship, M.D. from Harvard Medical School, an international scientific reputation, not to mention liberal politics and a cosmopolitan sophistication. Rebecca could stop McGee's breath simply by combing her long brunette hair in his presence, all the while acting as if she were completely unaware of her effect on him. Never wore a spot of makeup, didn't need any. Few men could resist her when she flashed her smile. McGee dreamed about her nearly every night.

"Well, have you come up with anything?"

McGee hadn't realized that she'd been waiting for him to make another attempt at a profound quote; instead, he had wasted the moment in fantasy. Wisely, he decided to raise the white flag. "Sorry, I'm just drawing a blank. Everything I come up with seems either mundane or contrived. It's a grand moment, but I can't seem to get a handle on it."

Having won this battle of wits, Rebecca's expression

changed from subtle mockery to big-sister concern. She gave him an honest look in the eye. "Kevin, cobblers should stick to their lasts." She turned to face the window again.

Cobblers should stick to their lasts. What could that mean? Talk about what you know. He brightened. Forget about the Mars of the geologists; tell us about the Mars of the imagination. *Okay, coach, you got it.* He switched the recorder back on, and this time his blood warmed as he spoke, recalling the wonderful, fictional Mars that had inspired him in his youth.

"Edgar Rice Burroughs already told us about this place. Once there were canals here, and cities, capitals of mighty empires that had names like Helium, Ptarth, and Manator. I can now see one of the plains upon which thundering herds of six-legged thoats ran, ridden by their masters, the barbaric green-skinned Tharks and Warhoons."

Rebecca stared at him with a look at turns quizzical, then deliberately cross-eyed. For once, he wasn't intimidated by her. The Muse was singing in him now, and not even Rebecca could stop it. "I am looking at a pink sky, in which once the great battle fleets of the red men flew, commanded by their proud jeddaks, or daring and willful princesses"— McGee sneaked a glance at Rebecca; she'd definitely pass in that role—"seeking glory, fortune, love, and adventure beneath the two hurtling moons of Barsoom."

He took a breath, smiling to himself. "Ah, Barsoom, you were destroyed by the Mariner probes, which banished you into mere fiction. But now we are here to make amends. Once again, there are people on Mars, and before long there will be cities, and you shall be filled with new life, love, adventure, and unlimited potential. For those of us who dream will not be stopped, and the fact that we five pioneers are here proves that the human imagination is the most powerful force in the universe. We know your secret, Mars, we who dream by day. We know that you are not a rock, but a *world,* one filled with wonders waiting to be discovered and history waiting to be made by a new branch of human civilization waiting to be born.

"And so, Red Planet, prepare to live again! For the sight that meets my eyes now out this porthole shall someday greet the eyes of numberless immigrants, dreamers who shall fill you with Life as you fill them with Hope. Barsoom, awake! Your people are here."

He turned off the recorder and peered gamely at Rebecca, who gave him a sly look. "Any better?"

"Well, Kevin, it's all you," she replied, laughing softly. With a shake of her gorgeous hair, she glanced toward the bridge. "Hey, I gotta run. Keep working on it. I'll be back to check on that arm." As Rebecca hurried off, she held up her hand and said with a mocking smile, "By the way, I believe the word is *Kaor*." The classic Barsoomian salute. From Brontë to Burroughs, Rebecca was well-read.

Mildly humiliated, McGee consoled himself with the thought that over the months of flight he had occasionally beaten her at Scrabble. He had done so yesterday, as a matter of fact. Even so, somehow she always managed to win four games out of seven, thereby dooming him to do her chore duty for the following week. Was she hustling him? Probably. But McGee didn't mind. As the historian onboard, he didn't have a lot to do, and Rebecca used her liberated time to write magazine articles that she promptly E-mailed to every forum of public opinion from the *Weekly Reader* to *Newsweek* to the *Journal of Geophysical Research,* all for the purpose of mobilizing public support for a follow-up Mars mission.

But hey, McGee, aren't you supposed to be the writer here? And remember that Fremont novel about the Western frontier you promised yourself you would write during the boring outbound cruise? Nearly a year wasted, and you haven't written ten pages. Housework is your excuse for not writing. Admit it.

Not true, McGee told his nagging inner critic. *I'm doing it to have some degree of contact with Rebecca. Ah, Rebecca, goddess with the mind of an Einstein in the body of the young Kelly McGillis. And the heart of Joan of Arc, La*

Passionara, Bernadette Devlin. I am a mere historian; you are a maker of history.

A member of the old Mars Underground, Rebecca Sherman was one of a handful of people who had made the whole mission happen. She and McKay, Stoker, and the rest who realized that it is people with ideas who make history. It had been almost a decade and a half since Rebecca's first Mars Society convention, but she'd finally done it. In fact, McGee had seen her score the winning touchdown in her testimony to the Senate committee three years ago.

Did she notice him, sitting in the back of the room? He'd been there covering the hearing for the *Seattle Times*. McGee had given her good press; had she even paid attention? He doubted it. But, by God, she'd been perfect. Just the right mixture of brilliant reason, passionate conviction, girlish innocence, and womanly charm. In less than an hour Rebecca had turned three votes, two of which were clearly immovable. *You have magical powers, Rebecca; do you know that? I'll bet you do.*

But why did she have to keep him at such a distance? Of the *Beagle*'s crew of five, they were the only two at home in the world of ideas from Plato to Shakespeare, intellectuals who were passionate about real music and real poetry. On the long outbound journey, he and Rebecca had whiled away hours discussing opera, philosophy, literature. He couldn't imagine doing that with Luke Johnson, the mission's redneck geologist, or Gwen Llewellyn, the tomboy flight engineer, or Mission Commander Townsend, a test pilot who'd made the varsity. What did Rebecca really have in common with the others?

McGee's inner critic answered his question promptly and accurately—mutual respect, the kind that comes from being part of a team that had trained together for years, endured hardship and heartbreak, and beat nine competing teams to win the privilege and eternal honor of being the crew of the first human mission to Mars. In other words, the kind of respect that McGee could never have, since he was a last-minute addition to the crew, a mere replacement for a team member who should rightfully be here.

The geologist opened a nearby locker and pulled out a Marsuit. McGee called over to him as he checked out the suit, "What's the plan for the first sortie to the surface, Luke?"

"Can't you see I'm busy?" The geologist moved toward the control area, his overpriced fake cowboy boots clanging on the deck.

Disappointed and annoyed, McGee watched him depart. It had been this way since the crew shakedown simulation at the Devon Island Mars Arctic Research Station. Even at the top of the world, the team had excluded him from their camaraderie for the whole nine months there, treated him like a polar bear cub with rotten-herring breath.

Rebecca approached again, clipboard in hand. McGee ventured an inquiry. "Looks like they're getting ready to go EVA."

"*Perform* an EVA," she corrected.

"Whatever." He looked her straight in the face and summoned a demanding tone. "When? I've got a right to know."

For a moment, she dropped her condescending smile. "Yeah, well, I guess you do. Not till tomorrow morning. Townsend wants a full system checkout before we go outside. Which reminds me, I've got to get a full set of readouts on the status of the life-support system. Keep that ice pack on. Be back in a bit."

Feeling like a fifth wheel, McGee watched her exchange a few words with Townsend and then disappear into the lab. He switched his attention to the control section. There they were, Colonel Andrew Townsend, USAF, and Army Major Guenevere Llewellyn, the pair who would make the mission's life-or-death decisions, no input from the affected parties necessary. *Military thinking. How charming*.

Still, if the recent crisis was any test, the crew could not be in better hands. He stared at Townsend. The former fighter jock sat in the pilot's chair, wearing an old bomber jacket, half open, and a suitably decrepit military peaked hat. He looked like he'd just walked off the set of *Twelve O'Clock High.* McGee laughed to himself. "The target for today is Hamburg. Gentlemen, start your engines." *Well, it looks like you managed to get some real flying in, Ace.*

Next, McGee regarded the flight engineer, who was arguing with Townsend in hushed but animated tones. Suddenly, she shook her head so forcefully that her two red braids, which protruded from her Braves cap, flew like wings over her shoulders. In her own freckle-faced way, Red Wing—was it the flying braids or the big knife she kept in her boot that had earned her such an Army nickname?—was kind of cute. Not a goddess like Rebecca, but . . . cute. Definitely good enough to pass.

At thirty, Gwen was also the youngest person on the crew, and there was yet a touch of the girl about her. McGee would have bet his last dollar she was still a virgin. Unfortunately, the only things she seemed interested in were machinery, baseball, and the King James Bible. Sure, she was of humble origins, a coal-miner's daughter whose daddy had died of black lung. Nothing wrong with all that, he reminded himself, but it was too bad she had to wear it on her sleeve.

Townsend, Gwen, and Rebecca were an ill-assorted trio, but individually they were all superb at what they did; the basis for their selection on the mission had been obvious. And while rather cool toward McGee, they were at least civil.

But Luke Johnson was another matter. The geologist seemed to hold some kind of grudge against McGee. As astronauts went, Luke was only average, but behind-the-scenes Texas political pull had played a role in getting him chosen for the mission. While the other crew members might not know that, McGee, as a political insider, did. And Luke must know that he did. That had to be it.

McGee's thoughts about Luke were pleasantly interrupted by the return of Rebecca.

"Okay, Kevin," she said brightly. "Life support systems are secure. Now let's have a real look at that arm."

*   *   *

Dr. Rebecca Sherman was glad to be free of further responsibility in the post-landing ship systems checkout. As a doctor, her proper place was with the injured. Despite his bumps and bruises, Luke wasn't too bad off and would do fine with ice and a local anesthetic. He still had thirty teeth left.

McGee was another story, though. She leaned over her patient, probing around his arm and shoulder. As she worked, she noticed an oddly satisfied expression on his face. *I'll bet this really sends you, Kevin. Whatever turns you on.*

She stepped back. "Well, Kevin, you're a lucky boy. Lots of contusions and sprains, but no broken bones or dislocations."

"The luck of the Irish, to have my wounds place me in your arms."

Rebecca shook her head without comment. The writer wasn't a bad sort . . . in fact, he was not unlike the kind of men she dated back home. Funny, intelligent, and sensitive—for a man, anyway—and he clearly respected her for her mind. So what if he wasn't a trained scientist? Most of the so-called scientists she knew weren't really scientists either. They were just members of a profession that "did science," churning out meaningless papers in an endless pursuit of the next grant. Or they were research technicians with advanced degrees, like that jerk Luke Johnson, who'd been inserted on the mission by a bunch of idiots at NASA HQ.

Kato was like that too, although Rebecca would have preferred the chemist's company to the Texan's; the fact that Kevin McGee had replaced Kato on the mission was really no great loss for science, though it hadn't been fair. Kato had trained for six years, only to be replaced by McGee at the last minute.

Actually, it made sense to have a man of letters on the mission. And McGee's literate bent and poetic imagination made him much more interesting to talk to than the other members of the crew. The problem was, the writer was obviously infatuated with her, and if she gave him the slightest encouragement he'd fall madly in love with her.

Rebecca couldn't have that. She'd worked almost twenty years to make this mission happen, and there was far too much at stake to let anything interfere.

Maybe later, when it was all over and they were back on Earth, but not now.

She held an ice pack to his shoulder where the sprains were worst. "How does that feel?"

"Much better, thanks."

Rebecca noticed Gwen advancing toward them from across the cabin. Back during training, she'd been overjoyed when she heard about Gwen's assignment to her team; otherwise the rest of the crew would have been all male, and she didn't relish spending a total of two and half years in a locker room. While Gwen's career wasn't a path she would have chosen for herself, any woman who could make major in the U.S. Army and win a Silver Star in combat was clearly a plus. Rebecca had been sure they'd hit it off like sisters.

Unfortunately, that hadn't happened. Gwen might be a feminist of a sort, but it was strictly the Annie Oakley sort. Despite having overcome the disadvantages of poverty and gender discrimination to make herself a place in a man's world, Gwen was resolutely against any progressive reforms that would have made it easier for other women to do likewise. Beyond that, Gwen was a diehard conservative, a militarist and religious fanatic who seemed opposed to everything that Rebecca believed in. The more the two women had talked, the clearer it became that the major resented not only Rebecca's liberal views, but her modern lifestyle, her privileged childhood, her freedom from organized religion, her good looks, her education—everything.

Rebecca wished the two women were friends. It was too bad that Gwen hated her guts.

"You did real good today, Professor," Gwen said to McGee. "I didn't think you had it in you." She gave him a little salute and slapped him on the shoulder, causing him to grimace; then she strode off.

McGee looked sheepish, and Rebecca suppressed a giggle. "So, Kevin, looks like you really scored with Red Wing today."

"Yeah." McGee rubbed his shoulder. "Ouch."

Their attention was suddenly drawn to Townsend, who stood and stretched in his bomber jacket and peaked hat, the apparent lord of all he surveyed. Something about the colonel's macho appearance made Rebecca laugh. She nudged Kevin. "Can you believe that guy? 'The *Beagle* has landed.' Now, really!"

OCT. 26, 2011 15:50 CST
LAFAYETTE PARK, WASHINGTON DC

On all four corners around the White House, a huge celebratory demonstration filled the streets and sidewalks. People waved flags and held up newspapers with quarter-page banner headlines.

Behind the stone and wrought-iron fences of the White House grounds, a distinguished-looking man in his early fifties strode arm in arm with a stylishly dressed blond woman in her early forties. Eight secret service agents flanked them as they approached the gate, smiling.

As the President and First Lady emerged from the gate, the crowd greeted them with an enormous cheer, which they returned with hands raised, forefingers pointing to the sky in an "Onward!" salute that had come to symbolize the Mars program.

The crowd increased its cheering, and the President and First Lady smiled and beamed, basking in their unearned applause.

CHAPTER 4

TOWNSEND LOOKED OUT THE CARGO BAY WINDOW AT THE dawn of a new day on Mars. The sky showed bright pink in the east, and the rising limb of the Sun cast long shadows on the rapidly brightening but dark-red ground.

The crew had spent a restless evening checking the *Beagle* for damage after the hard landing, following which the commander had ordered a full night's sleep before the first sortie on the planet's surface.

Now it was time: Soon the first human footsteps would be made on Mars.

Townsend turned to face the crew. They were all outfitted in Marsuits with their helmets off, looking uneasy. Strange, the way people reacted when they knew they'd be participating in a historic moment.

He rapped on a crate to attract their attention. "Everyone ready for a walk outside? Time to make a few footprints where no one has gone before."

No answer. They all shuffled nervously, looking at their feet.

"Excuse me, ladies and gentlemen, is there some kind of problem?"

He might as well have been talking to statues. Finally, Kevin McGee looked up and met Townsend's eyes. "Why don't I just slip out first, Colonel, to set up the camera and record your step onto the surface? You can be the official first man on Mars, I'll just be the anonymous cameraman there ahead of you. Nobody needs to mention it in the documentation."

Townsend couldn't believe his ears. But he had no time to react before Luke drawled, "I should really test for soil toxicity first, Colonel. We don't know for sure if superoxides on the surface are hazardous to the EVA suits. Those Viking landers indicated pretty exotic chemistry from all that solar ultraviolet zapping down on the regolith, and the products they found didn't exactly meet Environmental Protection Agency standards . . ."

As the geologist droned on, Dr. Sherman stepped forth, beaming. "How about ladies first?" she asked sweetly.

Major Llewellyn didn't miss a beat. "Ladies first? I guess that means me."

This was ridiculous. Townsend rapped the crate again to shut them up.

"Enough!" he said, in his most commanding tone. "The descent will be in order of rank. I will be first, followed by Major Llewellyn, then Dr. Sherman, Dr. Johnson, and Professor McGee."

"Now just a gosh-darned minute," said Luke. "Since when does Rebecca Sherman outrank me?"

More bruising for a delicate ego. Too bad. Rank had its privileges, and the geologist would have to get that straight. "She's ship's doctor, which makes her essential. You're just a researcher. In my book, that means she outranks you."

Luke started to talk back, but apparently thought better of it and glared instead at Rebecca, who further silenced him with a devastating smile of superiority.

"Okay," Townsend concluded with a knowing smile, "let's go."

The crew put on their transparent helmets and tightened them. They stood in silence for a minute while the humming pumpdown units did their work. Then the outer air-lock door opened, revealing a spectacular sunrise over the red desert landscape. The *Beagle*'s ramp lowered and Townsend descended, the rest of the crew following one at a time.

At the bottom of the ramp, Townsend felt a thrill run up his spine as his boot crunched down in its first step on the dry Martian soil. *The first human footprint on Mars, and it's mine. Am I supposed to say something historic now? "One giant leap" or something like that? No, I'll wait until we raise the flag.* He scanned the horizon. Red sky, red cliffs. Impressive. The wind caused a faint low-pitched whistling sound in his helmet. *The sound of Mars*, Townsend thought. *Not unpleasant*. Then he heard metallic sounds, crunching sounds: the rest of the crew coming down the ramp.

McGee moved out and set up his video camera on an autotracking tripod, then ran back to join the rest of the crew flanking him on either side. "Okay, everyone," the professor said, "face the camera and smile."

This would be the photograph for the books, Townsend knew. Not the first man on Mars, but the first team. His team. Townsend felt a surge of pride. He turned and faced the camera, giving it a cocky fighter pilot's thumbs up, knowing as he did so that he had just created an image as immortal as Washington crossing the Delaware. He thought briefly of his wife and kids. *Hey, Karen, how'm I doin'? Hey, Mike, Petey, look at your daddy now!*

Now for the flag. He indicated a hillock thirty yards off to the right. That would do nicely. Gwen climbed the slope carrying an aluminum cylinder, which she opened to reveal a telescoping flagpole that bore a wire-stretched American flag.

With a glance at the mission commander for permission, Gwen planted the pole, throwing Luke one of the stays while she spiked down the other two herself. Townsend frowned as Dr. Sherman ignored the ceremony preparations, instead stooping to examine a rock. *There'll be time enough for that, Doctor. First things first.*

Finally the flagpole was ready; Gwen grasped the hoist. "Crew, attention!" barked Townsend.

All stood, although not really in the military pose of attention. Townsend signaled with a chop of his hand, and Gwen slowly raised the flag. As she did, Townsend switched on a recording of "The Star-Spangled Banner," which played inside everyone's helmets. As the long anthem played out, Townsend and Gwen stood with respect, overcome with the moment, but the attention of the rest of the crew began to wander. Rebecca surreptitiously resumed her examination of the rock in her hand, while Luke started scanning distant cliff faces with binoculars.

We'll be here for a year and a half, Townsend thought, wanting to scold them. *There'll be time for all that later.*

McGee kept his camcorder focused on the ceremony, but his eyes wandered to the other members of the crew. He muttered into his personal recorder: "The Stars and Stripes now wave over Mars. For our officers, this moment is the climax of the mission. For the scientists, it is an irrelevant delay that must be endured before the real mission can begin. Which of them is right? Let history judge."

When the music ended, Townsend began his prepared speech. "Four hundred years ago, the first pioneer settlers arrived on the eastern shores of North America. Together with those who came later, they turned a wilderness into the greatest nation on Earth, a beacon of hope and a temple of liberty for all mankind. Today we have brought the flag representing everything they fought for, hoped for, and died for to a distant place, so that this planet, when peopled, will also be a land of the free. And so, with both humility and pride, in being the bearers of so great a symbol, carried by our ancestors over the fields of revolution, 1812, Mexico, and the South, carried by our grandfathers through the bloody trenches of World War One, carried by our fathers to the cruel beaches of Normandy and Tarawa, carried by our brothers through the jungles of Vietnam and the deserts of Iraq, we . . ."

Something was wrong, or missing. The speech was dull, rambling. Townsend paused, letting his eyes flicker over the vast windswept landscape, the distant cliffs and towering mountains. He was finally hit by the spectacular reality of it all. "My God, this is a whole new world we're on now!"

Rebecca murmured sotto voce to McGee, "About time he noticed."

Embarrassed by his outburst, Townsend said, "Oh well, there goes my chance for rhetorical immortality. Why don't each of you go before the camera and make your own speech? Major, you first."

Gwen took a step forward and then turned to face McGee's camera.

"This is Major Guenevere Llewellyn, the first woman to set foot on another planet. God created the planets and the Earth, and has now seen fit to show us, His chosen creatures, some of His handiwork. The heavens tell the glory of God, says the Good Book, and this place shows the wonder of His work. Let us give thanks to God for bringing us safely here and pray that we prove ourselves worthy to be the instruments of His divine plan, whatever that may be."

As Gwen concluded her speech, she glanced momentarily at Rebecca. Townsend noticed the gesture. Was she trying to get a rise out of the secular biologist? "Dr. Sherman," he intervened, "your turn."

Rebecca took a deep breath. "We came here from an ecosphere teeming with ten million species of life. We have journeyed to our seemingly barren sister planet in hopes of discovering life that once was, or perhaps life that never quite began. If Mars has life, either in fossil form or still existing, this will strongly suggest that life must abound in the universe, and that the billions of stars we see on a clear night may mark the home systems of lush worlds too numerous to count, which harbor species and civilizations too diverse even to catalog. Knowing they exist, the human race can find its place among them, as true citizens of our galaxy.

"But if we find no clue of life here, then we ourselves must become the first Martians. Here, we shall replicate the terrestrial biosphere and help Mother Gaia herself give birth to a second living world."

Townsend smiled, but felt inwardly annoyed at the deliberate mention of a pagan goddess, sure to irk Major Llewellyn. Sherman's scientific rationalist pose had already caused enough friction with the other woman. The doctor might be a famous genius, but apparently lacked something in the common-sense department. *Why doesn't anyone on this mission besides me ever think about maintaining group cohesiveness?* "Well said," he pronounced thinly.

Inside her helmet Gwen whispered, "For a flake."

Luke Johnson scooped a soil sample into a screw-cap vial and then advanced to take his turn before the camera. "From the surface, a geologist can find truth. From orbit, this planet resembled our Moon, but from this perspective, Mars is clearly different. There are obvious water erosion features, yet it's totally dry now. With no hydrological cycle, the whole surface is fossilized as it was three billion years ago." The geologist paused for a moment, then startled everyone with his shout. "I've never seen anything like this in Texas. Yeeeehah!"

"Ride 'em cowboy," Rebecca commented to herself. "Apparently not only Mars is fossilized."

Townsend turned to the professor. "Any words from our historian?"

McGee walked a few paces, and then turned to face the tripod-mounted camera. "We who are here today are fulfilling what has been a dream of humankind since before the dawn of history. The drive to explore has always been fundamental to the human psyche. It has taken us out of Africa, across rivers, mountains, deserts, and oceans. New lands have always given rise to new cultures, and human civilization has grown and become enriched. But always, before the reality, must come the dream.

"It is the dreamers, not the explorers, who are the greatest heroes of progress, because they can see with their minds what the rest of us can only see with our eyes. A century ago one dreamer who led us to Mars was Percival Lowell, a scientist who thought he saw canals spanning this planet, bringing water from its poles to a thirsty civilization.

"Our cameras looking down from orbit showed no canals, no civilization. But standing here today, I think I can dimly see what Lowell saw—there will be canals here someday. Cities will rise, proud towering cities, perhaps with names like those Edgar Rice Burroughs coined in his wonderful, imaginative novels: Helium, Ptarth, Manator.

"Perhaps in the future some John Carter from Earth will come here to find love in the eyes of a Dejah Thoris, his beautiful Martian princess, and sing her praises under the hurtling moons of Mars. Stranger things have come to pass. For ourselves, who have yet to face the rigors of mankind's first five hundred days on this still cold and desert planet, I can only hope that we do as well as Lowell's explorers did: 'We were not frostbitten for life, nor did we have to be rescued by a search party. We lived not unlike civilized beings during it all, and we actually brought back some of the information we went out to acquire.'

"Thank you Lowell, and Burroughs, for bringing us here; thanks to all the dreamers. Humanity owes its new world to you."

Luke touched his helmet to Gwen's and whispered, "And thank your partner on the White House staff for sticking us with you." He rolled his eyes. "To think we gave up our chemist for this blabbermouth."

Gwen didn't respond. Sure, the professor might be a bit loose around the edges, but there were worse sorts.

"Since that concludes the landing ceremony," Townsend declared crisply, "I suggest we all return to the ship. We have much to prepare before exploration operations can commence."

As they trooped back to the Hab module, Rebecca commented to McGee, "The American flag on Mars. What an anachronism."

Gwen overheard. That got her mad. "Now there's a fine example of modern liberal thinking," she fumed. "Sometimes I wonder where they find people like you."

Townsend observed the interchange, but said nothing. He would definitely have to keep his eyes on those two.

The hard work went on for hours as the crew unpacked the exploration gear from the *Beagle*. First they brought the pressurized rover out of the lower deck cargo compartment. Powered by a methane-oxygen combustion engine, the vehicle was designed to range as far as three hundred miles from the base at travel speeds of up to twenty-five miles per hour over the rough Martian terrain.

Then came the reserve-power solar panels and the inflatable experimental greenhouse. The unloading job wasn't easy. At three-eighths of normal gravity, each person was able to carry significantly heavier loads, but the inertia of each object was the same as on Earth. Most of the real work was done by Townsend, Luke, and Gwen. McGee's injured shoulder slowed him down considerably, and Rebecca was not a heavy lifter. But all five pitched in as best they could, and by evening the job was done.

Townsend surveyed the scene with some satisfaction. Boldly emblazoned with its flag-waving Snoopy mascot symbol, the *Beagle* would now serve as their base of operations, and as their home for the next five hundred days. Indeed, with the module's flying career over, the crew had already stopped referring to her as a "ship" and instead called her the Hab, a 38-ton living-module that resembled a huge drum twenty-seven feet in diameter and ceiling sixteen feet high. With two decks and a total floor area of 1,100 square feet, the Hab was large enough to comfortably accommodate the crew of five.

During the outbound flight, the lower deck had been crammed with cargo, and only the upper floor, divided into staterooms and function rooms, had been available as living space. Now that the unloading was complete, a significant part of the lower deck space would become available for human activity, providing the crew with a small workshop.

The added space also provided easy maintenance access to all systems necessary for surface operations. The Hab's closed-loop life-support system was capable of recycling oxygen and water, but successful, fully autonomous operation of such complex units for a year and a half was doubtful. However, with hands-on support to fix problems as they developed—especially with a mechanic as able as Gwen—the system could be considered nearly bulletproof.

The lower deck also featured an enclosure surrounded by the bulk of their food reserves. This pantry, which contained whole food for three years, also did double-duty by serving as the crew's shelter in the event of solar flares.

The work done, Townsend radioed a general recall and watched as his suited crew trooped back to the Hab, tired but in high spirits. Soon they would all be celebrating, perhaps passing around a tiny airline bottle of cognac and making mawkish toasts. For the moment, at least, their differences had been forgotten. The five shared the bonded friendship of climbers at the peak of Mount Everest or veterans of the same combat unit. Physical labor, done as a team, had brought them back together. That was a relief. But how long would the good morale last?

Morale was everything. As a former combat officer, Townsend knew that with high morale, everything was possible; without it, nothing was possible. Napoleon had put it well. "In war, morale is to materiel as ten is to one."

The NASA mission planners had shown a poor appreciation of that fact when they'd chosen an awkward Opposition-class trajectory for the outbound leg of the mission. As a result of that decision, the crew had been cooped up for ten months as the ship looped into the inner solar system on a Venus flyby in order to reach Mars the long way. That had been done so they could get to Mars in time for the November mission-abort launch window back to Earth.

But they would not need to abort, and if the mission hadn't been designed around that excessive safety option, the *Beagle* could have taken a direct trajectory that would have launched in December 2011 and gotten them to Mars the following June. That would have subjected the crew to only six months outbound in the can, and still given them fourteen months to explore Mars before the July 2013 return launch window.

As things stood, the crew was already a bit frayed with cabin fever. Personality clashes they had all easily concealed from the NASA shrinks during the selection process were now coming to the fore, and under the stress of the mission, would almost certainly grow worse. Townsend knew his most critical job was to hold the team together. But could he? Barring an abort before the end of November, they would be here for another twenty months.

A very long time.

CHAPTER 5

THE CREW GATHERED IN THE GALLEY OF THE HAB, bent over a map spread out on the table as they studied the surrounding regions of Mars. Rebecca had spent years poring over such maps back on Earth, studying orbital photographs. Now she pondered the significance of color changes, fluvial features, apparent layers of sediment. Soon she would know what it all meant.

Townsend began the meeting. "Ladies and gentlemen, now that our initial base preparations and local survey are complete, we can begin to explore. The question is, where?"

Rebecca glanced at Luke Johnson. The geologist had no idea what the real questions were, and his priorities would be all wrong. She decided to take charge immediately. "The key places to search are these biologically interesting dry riverbeds and paleolakes. It's virtually certain that they date back to the age when Mars had liquid water sculpting its' terrain and providing the medium for prebiotic chemistry."

Townsend regarded her curiously. "Prebiotic chemistry here, Dr. Sherman?"

"Yes, certainly," she answered quickly. It was clear Townsend didn't understand. To him Mars was obviously too barren to support life. *Without a scientific background, he looks around and only sees the present. The past is invisible to him.* She decided to take the time to explain. "You see, sir, Mars is cold and dry *now*—but it was once a warm and wet planet, a place friendly to life. It remained that way for a period of time, considerably longer than it took for life to evolve on Earth. Current theories hold that the evolution of life from nonliving matter is a natural process that occurs with high probability whenever and wherever conditions are favorable. What could be more favorable than a river or a lake? I say we start poking in riverbeds and the remnants of the nearest local lakes."

Townsend nodded, considering, but the Texan geologist was finally up to speed. "Ah'll have to disagree." He smiled unpleasantly. "That simply can't be our initial priority. With all due respect to our beautiful ship's surgeon, it's plain as day that there is no life here and never was. As far as ah'm concerned, the unmanned Viking landers proved that over thirty years ago. If this mission is going to accomplish any serious science, right from the outset, we need to thoroughly examine the geologically significant igneous and metamorphic rock deposits in the areas of uplifted terrain. The rocks in those highlands come from the interior. They'll tell us what makes this planet tick."

Rebecca groaned inwardly. It was bad enough that Luke was a chauvinistic jackass, but did he have to be an idiot too?

"That's ridiculous. We didn't come this far just to go rock collecting," she retorted. "The central scientific question concerning Mars is and has always been the possibility of life here, past or present. The place to look for life is where there is or was water, and that means those low-lying sedimentary beds."

"I beg your pardon." Luke's look was so patronizing it made her sick. "But at the scientific meetings that I have attended regularly for the past decade, the question of life on Mars has been rarely, if ever, discussed."

Rebecca's temper rose. "Well, I'm sure the scientific meetings you've attended for the past decade have rarely, if ever, included real scientists." Luke Johnson had never published a single refereed paper in any authentic journals. As far as she could see, what he called "scientific meetings" were probably little more than stag parties for the oil exploration industry.

"Excuse me, Dr. Sherman, but my Ph.D. is as good as yours."

That was laughable. "Right," she giggled, "from Texas A&M."

Rebecca had gone to Radcliffe and Cornell, places where the state universities are held in modest esteem. Actually, she had found the graduates of the state universities to be no worse scientists than those from the Ivy League, but she knew Luke had a bit of an inferiority complex on that score, so she decided to rub it in. The giggling was a good touch too. *Gets to you, doesn't it, Luke?*

Gwen broke into the brawl. "There never was life on Mars." Everyone turned to look at her.

Don't get involved in this Gwen, Rebecca thought. *I don't really want to crush you. Why do you have to shove your nose into business of which you have no understanding? If you can't be on my side, why can't you just stick to your machines?* The flight engineer stared at her hostilely. *Oh, well, since you insist . . .*

"Oh," said Rebecca, "and how would you know that?" This was going to be wild. Gwen had almost no scientific background at all.

"The Earth is the only planet with life on it," said Gwen. "It says so in the Bible—or didn't you read that at Radcliffe?"

The Bible! It's been four centuries since Kepler; we're on Mars, for crying out loud, and they're still throwing that crap at us! "That does it!" Rebecca exploded. "That's the limit! Colonel Townsend, I am the chief science officer on this expedition, and I insist that our science agenda be dictated by me and not by some redneck oilfield prospector or a Bible-thumping hillbilly mechanic. I—"

Townsend made a chopping motion with his right arm. "Dr. Sherman, that will be all. Since you scientists cannot agree on an agenda, I have decided that the first rover sortie will be a photo reconnaissance conducted by Major Llewellyn and Professor McGee. Major, you'll be in command." He ran his finger along the map. "Take the rover along this ridge. That'll bring you above the cliff faces and within sight of the big canyon. Try to get some nice pictures for the folks back home, McGee."

"You can count on it, Colonel," said McGee.

Rebecca was enraged. The first rover sortie, and she wouldn't be on it. But at least Luke wouldn't be either.

Trying to be conciliatory, the mission commander said, "We have a year and a half here, people. You will all have an opportunity to pursue your pet projects. Very well, you two hop to it."

As Townsend returned to the control console, Gwen and McGee eagerly exited the galley to prepare for the trip. Rebecca looked across the table and noticed that Luke was staring icicles at her. *Same to you, pal,* she thought.

Gwen eased up on the throttle, and upon reaching the top of the hill, shifted the rover into neutral. She set the parking brake and scanned the breathtaking horizon. Stretching out below her was a vast network of deep red-rock canyons extending in every direction. The spectacular panorama boggled her mind. She tried to compare it to the canyons she had visited during crew training in the American Southwest—but those were slit trenches in comparison.

Beside her, McGee picked up his camera and chattered wildly into his minicorder. With half an ear Gwen listened to his narrative while continuing to admire the view. It was obvious that the professor was awestruck as well; too bad he couldn't drop his academic baggage and simply take it all in.

"We've just reached the crest of a hill looking down the

north flank of the Coprates Chasma," McGee said. "We can see a vast system of interconnected canyons and dry valleys that appear to have been formed by a combination of faulting and water erosion. The scale, the sharpness, the extreme nature of all the features is like nothing I've seen on Earth. It's like somebody took the craggy peaks of the upper Cascade Range, turned them upside down and inside out, then stretched them out along the ground like an enormous region of spaghetti-like ditches. Most canyons are over three kilometers deep and some could be over a hundred kilometers across. In the central section, I can see three parallel canyons merge to form a depression that must be over five kilometers deep." He drew a quick breath. "That's deeper than Mount Rainier is tall! The sight of these cliffs is just incredible. They're dizzying. Someday, someone will rappel down them—the very thought sends shivers up my spine."

Gwen turned away from the canyon to look at him. "You've done some rappelling, Professor? I thought you weren't the military type."

He interrupted his monologue. "No, I'm not. My father was in the Army in World War Two, saw some combat, and advised me to steer clear of it. He said it was a very disappointing experience, not at all like the movies."

He smiled sheepishly at her. *Not a bad smile,* she thought. *You should try it more often, Professor. You might make some friends.* She decided to return it. "Oh, your daddy was right about that. I had my fill in the Desert War."

"So I hear. I saw the newscast when you brought that damaged copter filled with wounded GIs through the lines."

Gwen's mind raced back to that day: the dead pilot beside her, the burning copter filled with screaming soldiers. Iraqi bullets shattering the windshield, ripping through the fuselage. Blood everywhere. The noise, the smell, the terror. She shivered.

"It's not something I'd like to try again." How old had she been? Early twenties—barely out of her teens. It seemed like a million years ago. It seemed like yesterday.

McGee looked at her as if he understood. How little he knew.

"Anyway, my rappelling experience is strictly recreational. I used to do a lot of climbing in the Cascades. That's where I taught school."

Gwen smiled. "Ah, the mountains. I grew up in the mountains you know, in North Carolina. My daddy mined coal, just like his daddy did, and his granddaddy did back in Wales. I loved the mountains, but I couldn't stay and become a coal-miner's wife, watching my husband cough out his lungs, and when he's gone watch my kids go without shoes."

"So . . . you joined the Army?"

"Yep. And only regretted it that one day during my entire life. Still, I'd sure like to see those mountains again, smell that clean frosty air in the morning, and listen to the crickets chirp at night." She couldn't stop herself from asking, "Do you think we'll make it home, Professor?"

"Sure, how can we miss? We've got the ERV at the base, and if we really need it, we've got the backup return vehicle already landed on the floor of Valles Marineris, not sixty kilometers from here. The whole mission is checking out fine, isn't it? We'll get home, no sweat."

How can we miss? McGee clearly didn't know a damn thing about quirky machines. "I sure hope so. This place is incredibly beautiful in its way, but . . ."

"There's no place like home?"

"Yeah, that's it." Was she like Dorothy in *The Wizard of Oz,* both ready and lost? She noticed the light dimming in the canyon. "Professor, it's getting dark. We better be heading back to base."

She shifted the rover into gear and began driving downhill. McGee put down his camera. "The light is too dim for filming." He paused. "Gwen, I've got a question for you."

"Shoot."

"This morning, when Rebecca and Luke were arguing, you jumped in with a remark that there couldn't be life on

Mars, because the Bible says so. Now I've read the Bible . . ."

Gwen raised an eyebrow. "Good for you."

"And it doesn't say anything about the issue one way or the other." He looked at her hard.

Gwen blushed, but managed a bashful grin. "Okay, so I was bluffing a little."

McGee smiled his nice smile again. "Bluffing?"

"Yeah, McGee, you know, I'm just a country girl, and where I come from, a lot of folks think like that. I'm not sure if I do; there's a lot of ways to read the Scriptures, and maybe by searching here we'll find out the truth. So I guess I was out of line. It's just that that lady rubs me the wrong way. She always seems so sure of herself, and so ungrateful for everything that God and a world full of hard-working people have given her."

Again McGee nodded his sympathetic nod. But of course he could never really understand. He would never know what it meant to grow up being laughed at by the rich girls from town because you didn't have proper clothes, and then to struggle up from nothing, and at the end of it all still be looked down on by someone who had it all given to her on a silver platter. Someone who laughed at the beliefs that gave strength to those who grew the food she ate, mined the coal that powered her city, or fought for the flag that protected her rights to life, wealth, freedom, and ingratitude. Someone who scorned a God who had blessed her with the looks of an angel.

Someone who had once owned horses.

When Gwen had been a girl, the one thing she had wanted more than anything else was a horse. Of course, her family's poverty had made the dream impossible. As a teenager, though, Rebecca had owned two fine Tennessee Walking horses, kept for her occasional use in a stable outside the city. Shortly after they had all been selected, Gwen had read about it in one of the magazine articles about the crew. She had asked Rebecca about the horses, but the doctor said she couldn't even remember their names, or what had become of them.

A tear formed in Gwen's eye. If she ever had a horse of her own, she would know its name until the day she died.

Her thoughts were interrupted by McGee, who had pulled a diminutive guitar out of his rucksack.

"Do you mind if I strum a little?"

"Go ahead." She had heard McGee play plenty of times on the outbound journey; he wasn't too bad. Besides, it would be a long drive. McGee began strumming a vaguely Celtic tune, not too different from the Appalachian fiddle music she had often heard as a girl. Somehow it warmed her to hear it. She looked at McGee and smiled.

"You're a man of unexpected talents, Professor."

CHAPTER 6

TOWNSEND, MCGEE, AND REBECCA SAT IN THE GALLEY of the Hab and watched the NASA broadcast. Luke and Gwen were away on a rover excursion. *Lucky them,* thought Rebecca. *If I have to hear much more of Mason, I'm going to vomit. Too bad about the signal transmission delay. There's a lot I'd love to tell this bozo real-time. Instead I just have to sit here and take it.* She tapped her right foot on the Hab floor as Mason's televised lecture droned on.

"Look gang, due to reduced budget here in Houston, and the fact that you have some onboard artificial intelligence capability to provide advice, we've let you do your own minute-by-minute mission planning, within broad guidance parameters from us. As you know, your early mission abort window closed last week."

Thank Reason, Rebecca thought. *At least that opportunity to wreck the mission is out of your hands.*

"You're on Mars for the duration, and that means from here on you have to stay strictly within NASA-prescribed safety guidelines. The initial photo reconnaissance led by Major Llewellyn was by the book, but that first science sortie by Sherman and McGee was way out of line. They had no business going so far over the horizon from the base. We lost all contact with them for over seventeen hours, and let me tell you, I had the NASA Administrator himself all over my tail on that."

Rebecca looked at Townsend. Did the mission commander buy any of this? "Gee, sorry we worried his pretty little head. How were we supposed to reach the lake bed without going over the horizon?"

The buffoon droned on, impeccably dressed, wearing another subtle silk tie. "Furthermore, Dr. Sherman should have known that distant lake bed was a low-priority site, as determined by the site selection board of the Mars Science Working Group."

Rebecca shook her head. "Right. A committee of old farts making compromises with each other so that everybody can get something to publish in the *Journal of Geophysical Research*. Well, I'm here doing the hands-on work, they're not."

Townsend gave her an indulgent smile. Surely as a combat veteran, he understood that the people on the ground needed the freedom to make their own decisions.

Mason continued. "And, precisely as foreseen by the board, nothing of interest was found there. Unauthorized risk was taken, a week was wasted, and no results were achieved."

This was absurd. Rebecca slapped her hand down on the table to get Townsend's full attention. "Colonel, this is *post hoc, ergo propter hoc* reasoning."

He looked at her with a puzzled expression. "You mean like Monday morning quarterbacking?"

Now it was Rebecca's turn to be puzzled. *We're not speaking the same language. Monday morning quarts of what?* She turned to McGee; maybe he could translate English into Male.

"That's exactly what she means," the professor said, causing the colonel to nod. Separated by the long signal lag, Mason continued, oblivious. *It's not really a technical problem though,* Rebecca thought. *He'd still be oblivious if he were standing in this room.*

Now he spoke directly to Townsend. "Andy, after that unscripted landing of yours, some of the upper-level managers here at JSC started remembering the Skylab mutiny and suggested the need to tighten the leash on the Mars crew. Since then, it's been getting a lot worse. I know that if we take too heavy-handed an approach down here it's going to hurt the mission, but if your guys keep operating open loop, the pressure will be too much for me to stop it. Goddammit, Andy, you've got to get the situation under control. That's why you're there. I know you can do it, you old battle-ax. Enforce discipline. We're all rooting for you here. Keep up the good work. Mason, out."

The Chief of Operations disappeared from the TV and was replaced by a NASA logo.

Townsend turned to face her. "Well, there you have it, Doctor. Straight from the horse's mouth."

"Horse's ass is more like it."

McGee chuckled. "Rebecca, I'm surprised at you. Such language."

"I'm a scientist. I always use accurate language."

Next, the image of Mission Control's Al Rollins appeared on the monitor. "The Mars Society in Boulder is continuing the debate right now about the Martian life question. Thought you might be interested, so we're uplinking it to you live."

Rebecca grinned and winked at McGee. "Oh, this oughta be good."

The image switched to a panel of scientists on the podium of the Glenn Miller Ballroom at the University of Colorado. Lev Chelovkin, of the Russian Institute for Space Research, was talking. "Over the years we have devoted a great deal of discussion to problems of biological experiments. But the subject was sort of hung up in the air. Does the as-yet-fruitless search for life on Mars retain the same priority that it had at the time of Viking?"

Rebecca scanned the panel and predicted correctly that

Chuck Stein would answer this largely rhetorical question.

"Let me attempt to answer your inquiry, Dr. Chelovkin," Stein said. "In pursuing further life detection experiments on Mars, we should be looking at sites of greater potential interest than the ones that received cursory study during the Viking mission. Unfortunately, the *Beagle*'s landing site is far from the most optimal areas for a life search. In any case, I feel that the chances of finding extant life are very, very remote. While I think that biological experiments should still be done, given the large number of other important scientific questions that can be usefully addressed by the mission, the search for life should receive only a secondary priority."

"Thanks a lot, Chuck," Rebecca commented dryly. So much for old friends.

Now Magorsky of the USGS was talking. "It's too bad that the mission did not land near the North Pole's eroded areas, which extend down from the icecaps through the layered terrain. On Earth we have made remarkable finds by drilling through the Antarctic icecap, and there may well be living organisms at different levels of the icecap on Mars."

Even Townsend reacted to such absurdity. "They want me to land on the polar icecap? Right."

"Well, I guess you blew it there, Colonel," McGee joked. "What were you thinking as we were careening through the atmosphere?"

Rebecca regarded her crewmates. Perhaps they were beginning to understand what she'd always been up against.

Magorsky continued. "But since the *Beagle* is near the equator, the best place to look would be near lava flows, which release water. On Earth, we frequently see lichen established just a few weeks after a lava flow has cooled."

Rebecca hit her forehead in mock chagrin. "If only I had known. Colonel, could you please arrange for a small volcano to erupt, say fifty kilometers from here? It doesn't have to be very large, but please set it off in the early morning, so we can drive over there in daylight."

"I'll see what I can do, Doctor."

"Chuck, Harold, aren't you a little close to romantic wishful thinking here?" Rebecca recognized the condescending tone of Norm Harwitz, a cantankerous old pedant. "The Viking experiments were quite conclusive. Despite some people's wishful thinking, there is no life on Mars, and the expedition should not waste any time looking for it."

There was a comment from the floor, Carol Stoker from NASA Ames. *This should be fun,* Rebecca thought. "Now wait just a minute, Norm. You are interpreting the nondetection of life by the Viking biology experiments as the confirmation of nonlife on Mars—that does not follow at all. Viking found extremely oxidizing conditions in the surface. It indicated that peroxides were present. It showed that there was a metabolic-like activity going on in the Martian soils. The Viking team's experiments did not show life, but they may have had signal-to-noise problems. They may have failed to detect life because they were too impatient to incubate a spore long enough to wake it up. The point is, they did not prove that there was no life on Mars—far from it. And to claim that they did, constitutes an unfounded, unscientific assertion."

So there is intelligent life on Earth. Rebecca had to cheer. "That's the way to tell 'em, Carol."

Another panelist took the floor, Oleg Galenko from the Russian Institute of Medical/Biological Problems. Rebecca muttered, "I doubt he'll provide anything useful."

"Never, up until now," Galenko said, "have people had so rich an occasion to examine the essence of man as today, in connection with the conquest of outer space. Therefore, recognizing outer space as a part of the environment, in attempting to know Mars, to a great extent we begin to understand mankind, man's place in the universe, man's place in the world, man's origin and man's future, what man really is, and how in essence he has to live."

Yuck! Rebecca turned to McGee. "Why do I always have

to be right?" The historian shrugged sympathetically. She returned her attention to the TV.

Staritsa was next. An intelligent fellow, but irritating. "There are no secrets here, except for the secrets of nature itself, and to discover these we have set off to Mars. Finding life is not the issue. The most interesting things on Mars are the things that man does not yet know. Maybe men will see on Mars that which no human mind could possibly have imagined."

"In this day and age I have to listen to this chauvinist crap?" Rebecca vented. "They just don't get it. 'Understanding what *man* really is,' 'Maybe *men* will see that which no human mind could possibly have imagined.' " She shook her head in disgust.

Now Harwitz spoke again, his voice like fingernails on a chalkboard. "Getting back to the subject at hand, the fact of the matter is that Dr. Sherman and Professor McGee searched the dry lake bed and found no evidence of life—past or present. And, Dr. Stoker, I remind you that my evaluation of the Viking results is not idiosyncratic. The large majority of NASA's Mars Science Working Group agrees with my conclusions. The question of life on Mars is a dead issue."

Was there no one on the panel that would rebut this? Ah, Carl Shaeffer.

"Nevertheless," Shaeffer said, "although I recognize that my position is a minority one in the scientific community today, I must insist that the paramount question with regard to Mars is the search for life. We are morally obligated to give it our best shot."

McGee turned to Rebecca. "At least it seems like the grand old man of Mars agrees with you."

"I should hope so. I did my doctorate for him at Cornell."

There was a question from the floor. The TV showed a heavily pierced young man in the dark brown clothing of an ecogoth. "Dr. Shaeffer, to change the subject somewhat, how do you feel about the ethics of human colonization of Mars?"

"That's a very interesting question," Shaeffer responded. "In the short run, and speaking as a scientist, I believe that it is very important that we avoid the premature spread of terrestrial biota that might confuse the results of the search for native life. However, in the longer view, and speaking as an environmentalist, it seems to me that the action of converting the dead or nearly dead surface of the Red Planet to a new lush and diverse biosphere would be the most ethical thing humanity could possibly do. It would be an enormous positive act of environmental improvement on behalf of the whole community of life."

"Excuse me sir, but as an ecogoth I must disagree with your flagrant humanism. It is one of the central findings of ecogothic science that all human actions that affect the environment are intrinsically harmful. This must be so, because human motivations are by nature homocentric rather than cosmocentric. Therefore, your claim of a possible positive cosmic environmental role for the human species is a clear self-contradiction. Furthermore . . ."

Rebecca rolled her eyes in disgust. "Ecogoths. Noir-minded adolescents striking an ultra-environmentalist 'cosmocentric' pose. Antihumans would be a better term."

Just then, she heard the sound of the lower airlock outer door opening and closing.

"The rover team has returned." Townsend pushed a button that muted the TV, which continued to show images of scientists and the public debating.

Gwen entered the galley, followed by Luke Johnson hauling a bag of rock samples on his back, like Santa Claus carrying a sack of toys. "Ho, ho, ho! Merry Christmas!"

Rebecca confined herself to a single dry comment. "It's not Christmas," she observed. Luke just shrugged.

"Did you find anything?" Townsend asked.

He obviously had. Rebecca could see it by the triumphant expression on his face. This could spell trouble. A modest geologic find could divert the whole mission from what should be its true scientific purpose.

"Anything?" Luke dumped his samples onto the table.

"Why, just about every type of metamorphic rock money can buy. And even some that it can't."

The rocks on the table were an assortment of some of the finest crystals Rebecca had ever seen. McGee picked one up. "Some nice gemstones here." An understatement. Luke was clearly enjoying himself.

"That's right, partner. The little rock you're holding there is a three-ounce ruby. And that one's a topaz, and that's an emerald."

The find was incredible. For a moment Rebecca let her scientific curiosity get the better of her. She picked a very unusual crystal out of the group. It was translucent, violet, and a perfect tetrahedron. She had never seen anything like it. She held it up. "And this?"

"That, little lady, is a gem with no terrestrial equivalent. And guess what? It'll scratch diamond.

That got everyone's attention. There were several seconds of silence, finally broken by Townsend. "Let me get this straight. You've discovered a rock that is harder than diamond? That can be used to cut diamonds?"

"Yep."

"Well, this is excellent. Why, this could be of some practical importance!"

Townsend would fall for that. Industrial stones. Ready-made practical applications. As if discovering clues to the nature of life itself had no practical importance.

"Colonel, partner, you have a gift for understatement."

All right, enough was enough. *Is this a scientific expedition or an Easter egg hunt?* Rebecca turned to Luke. "Did you find anything that provides clues to the nature of the planet's tectonic activity? Rift-formation processes? Any evidence for recent volcanism, recent hydrologic activity of any kind?"

The geologist gave her his best condescending smile. Rebecca found it completely enraging. "Hold your horses, little lady. This was just our first geologic sortie. We'll get to all of that in good time."

"Did you get any good visuals?" McGee asked, apparently oblivious to the tension in the air.

"We got some beautiful views of the mountains," Gwen answered dreamily. "And coming back we passed the most gorgeous little box canyons you ever saw. Just like the old strip mine gully I used to swim in when I was a girl. We used to go at night sometimes, my sister and I, and swim by moonlight."

"I would've liked to have been there." Luke gave Gwen a salacious smile.

Instead of replying, Gwen kicked a leg of Luke's chair, causing it to fall over and sending the big geologist to the floor of the Hab in a low-gravity crash.

"Now mind your manners," Gwen admonished. Luke got up, grinning sheepishly.

Rebecca chuckled to herself. *Bravo, Gwen. There's hope for you yet.*

"Enough of that," said Townsend. "Luke, Gwen, good work. Now get some sleep. You can write up a full report in the morning."

As the rover team started to leave, Rebecca called after them. "Gwen, what's the rover's status?"

"Fully operational."

Rebecca thought quickly as the two explorers left the galley. The situation was critical, she realized. Timing was everything. "In that case, Colonel, I request that tomorrow I be allowed to take the rover over to the dry riverbeds near Maja Vallis to search for fossils."

"Well, Gwen will be needed here to help write the report."

"I'll take McGee." She smiled at the historian. His skills were not as useful as Gwen's, but he was a lot more fun to pass the time with on a long rover excursion.

"McGee's not a trained mechanic, and neither are you. If the rover should malfunction—"

"In the unlikely event of a rover malfunction, you can always send Gwen out in the reserve vehicle to help us. That was the procedure we followed last time. Why is

Gwen's nonavailability an issue all of a sudden?"

Townsend shook his head. "You heard what they said in Houston. Their safety concerns are a bigger issue than they were before. I can't let you go that far without Major Llewellyn."

Rebecca looked him in the eyes and made a conscious effort to control her voice for maximum effect. She had to change his mind. "Colonel, let me take the rover out tomorrow."

"I don't see why it can't wait a few days until their report is done."

Rebecca could see why. She had to make him see. "It can't wait because when Gwen is done, then Luke will be done, and he'll want to do another geology sortie himself. And with all the brouhaha he's going to cause with these trinkets he found, he's sure to be given priority by Mission Control. This might be my only decent chance."

"Dr. Sherman, these new gems are more than just trinkets. Possible applications for superhard materials could have major benefits for American industry. In any case, even if he's given control of the rover for the next few weeks, what of it? We're going to be here for a year and a half."

Rebecca shook her head. That was the problem. *Everyone thinks we have a year and a half.* "Not true, sir. In four weeks the dust storm season will begin. That could shut down rover sorties for up to six months, especially if this safety craze takes hold at Mission Control. Then, if the storms damage our equipment, we could lose the capability for long-range sorties afterward."

"That's a possibility, but . . ."

Rebecca saw her chance. *Add passion to reason, you can move him. But not too much—don't blow it.* She took a deep breath and focused. "Colonel, life on Mars is the real question we were sent here to answer. It's the key to whether life exists all over the universe. It's the mystery people have wondered about since time began. We've got to go look for it."

Townsend looked confused. "Those other scientists don't seem to think so."

"But you know that I'm right."

They sat in silence, Rebecca directing her eyes into his, pleading but morally certain. Finally, Townsend stood up and walked to the window, where he stared out at the night sky. He looked back at her.

This is my last chance, thought Rebecca. She allowed herself to give him a hint of a smile.

"Okay, Doctor, you can go."

She closed her eyes and sank into her chair. When her hands loosened their grip on the armrest, her fingernails had made little dents in the upholstery.

Townsend turned to McGee. "I don't know how I get talked into these things," he said apologetically, and left the galley.

McGee watched him go and then turned to Rebecca, who was now smiling like an angel. "Wow. Remind me to take you along next time I try to sell an idea for a new book to a publisher."

Rebecca just wrinkled her nose at him.

CHAPTER 7

OUT IN THE ROVER, MCGEE AND REBECCA RODE ALONG A ridge overlooking the dry riverbeds of Maja Vallis. In preparation for frequent EVA, they were dressed in Marsuits without helmets or backpacks. McGee drove while Rebecca surveyed the dry riverbeds with a pair of binoculars. He glanced over at her, admiring the curve of her elegant neck—definitely the best date on Mars. Earth too, possibly.

"Well, Dr. Sherman, exactly what should we be looking for?"

Rebecca answered without looking up from her survey. "I don't know, exactly. That's the hard part in all this. We're looking for macroscopic remains created by large numbers of microorganisms, probably calcified."

"Like coral reefs, or the chalk cliffs of Dover?"

"Could be, but probably not that obvious. I remember an expedition I took one time on Devon Island, looking for stromatolite fossils from the Ordovician, over four hundred million years old. We found them, but they looked like nothing you'd expect, kind of lumpy, bulging piles. Very strange."

"I see."

Rebecca gestured off to the right. "I wish we could get down into that dry riverbed. If anything was ever alive around here, that's where it would have been. Drive a little closer to the edge so I can get a better look."

McGee studied the ground. It was unconsolidated regolith, not the best place to be taking chances. "I'd rather not. We're pretty close to the edge already."

Rebecca smiled at him. "Come on, Kevin, we're driving at ten miles per hour. Don't be such a sissy."

Her smile made McGee feel both small and warm at the same time. There was no resisting. "Okay, have it your way. But I'm slowing down."

McGee cautiously steered the rover closer to the ridge edge. Rebecca peered into the valley, nodding her approval. "Ah, much better. See, no problem."

Suddenly the ground under the front right wheel gave way, causing the rover to tilt. McGee slammed on the brakes, but not quite in time. As he frantically shifted into reverse, the rover tipped slowly over the 40-degree slope of the gorge until its weight shifted completely, causing the scree to start sliding downhill, carrying the rover with it. Within seconds the whole slope began to tumble downhill in a roaring rush.

McGee shifted back into forward and accelerated, steering madly, trying to maintain some degree of control in the low-gravity ride. A huge rock standing firm in the midst of the avalanche loomed up in front of the rover, and he barely managed to avoid crashing into it.

He felt both terrified and enraged at having been goaded into reckless action. "Don't be a sissy, eh. No problem, eh!"

Smaller rocks, bouncing down the hill faster than the rest of the slide, pattered and ricocheted all around the vehicle. One stone the size of a softball slammed into the Plexiglas window on Rebecca's side. A network of cracks began to spread in the window. In seconds it would shatter and depressurize the rover. Rebecca stared at it, frozen.

"Rebecca! Quick-patch!" shouted McGee, snapping her out of it.

Rebecca tore off her seat belt and lurched to the back of the rover, reaching behind the seats to yank open a box in the cargo area. She withdrew a square-foot sheet of translucent plastic material with an adhesive back. In one swift motion, she peeled the cover off the adhesive and slammed the sticky plastic sheet into place on the window. She turned to McGee. "That was close—Oh no, watch out!"

McGee looked out his side window. An eight-foot boulder bounded down the hill on a collision course with the rover. He gripped the steering wheel, searching frantically for some way to avoid it. In desperation he tried flooring the accelerator, but the boulder kept pace.

"Kevin, hard right!"

McGee saw a steep depression in the terrain. She couldn't mean—

Rebecca's arms reached over his shoulder to jerk down the wheel; he cooperated, willingly tumbling the rover into the ditch. The monstrous boulder bounced harmlessly overhead, but the vehicle kept rolling. As McGee held himself in place, Rebecca was tossed into the rear, where she desperately tried to grab the back of the seat as the rover continued spinning, crashing, rolling, over and over.

Finally they landed miraculously upright at the bottom of the ravine. With a rushing, roaring sound, the rock slide came to a halt around them. As the dust settled, the two gaped out the windows, emotionally drained, speechless.

"Well, you wanted to get to the bottom of the gorge," he finally ventured. "McGee delivers."

Rebecca slowly raised her shaking hand and pointed. About twenty yards in front of the rover was a group of unusual-looking rocks. "McGee, look at that." Her voice was level with authority as she started to seal the fastenings on her Marsuit. "Let's go."

Still stunned by the very fact of their survival, McGee was mystified. "Go where? Rebecca, we better check out the rover for damage before—"

"That can wait."

Was she in shock? McGee had no time to investigate as Rebecca reached for her helmet, apparently preparing to depressurize the rover, whether he was ready or not. He fastened down his helmet just before Rebecca opened the valve to vent the rover cabin. Then the hatch was open, and she was off, running like a mountain goat across the rocky terrain. McGee watched her go. It was hard to believe someone so graceful could move so fast.

When he caught up to her he was panting, but Rebecca was already pouring nonstop geo-biological commentary into her recorder, snapping holograms of everything in sight.

"Slow down, Rebecca. Those things have been here for three billion years. They're not going to run away."

She turned to him. Her face was tear-streaked but never more beautiful. "Do you know what these are, Kevin? Bacterial stromatolites! See, look at this micrograph. Those rod-shaped pores in the material, that's where the organisms actually were. Classic coccoid bacterial structural form. Look, look at this chromatograph readout! There are even organic residues in the fossil structure."

McGee peered at the rocks. They certainly were odd—lumpy, porous—but had they been alive? He shrugged, uncertain.

"There was life here once!" Rebecca rejoiced. "That's all that counts." She hugged him in her Marsuit and started to cry, mumbling inside her helmet. "We found it, we found it!"

McGee held her, a little bewildered to be comforting a woman who had just made the greatest discovery of her career—and who had just caused the rover to crash down a steep ravine. Over her shoulder, he saw a blue-green discoloration among some rocks farther down in the gully. He stroked her back. "Rebecca?"

"Yes?" she sniffled, gradually emerging from her euphoria.

"I knew the Moon was made of green cheese, but Mars?"

Rebecca regarded him curiously. "What are you talking about?"

McGee pointed to the blue-green smear. When Rebecca saw it too, she stared at him in open-mouthed astonishment. She moved toward the rock slowly, almost as if stalking it. Finally she knelt, and McGee followed, leaning over her shoulder.

"What is it, Rebecca?"

She was very cool and deliberate now, completely composed. "I've never seen a mineral like this before."

She focused the holocamera on the mineral, scraped a little off into a sample bottle, photographed the rock again, and began a round of clinical description into the recorder. She went on for some time, sampling, photographing and recording, clambering all over the rock, paying no attention to McGee. Then she saw something and started to push madly at the boulder, trying unsuccessfully to tip it.

"Help me, Kevin! I've got to get under this rock."

"What? Whatever for?"

"This stuff up here is dead, but maybe only for a few hundred thousand years. What's underneath might be much better preserved. I've got to see."

McGee looked at the big boulder. He might be able to roll it under the low Martian gravity, but if it should slip it would have more than enough mass to crush Rebecca. "And you want me to lift this rock so you can crawl under it? Why not jack it up?"

She turned to him, her eyes bright with tears, her voice urgent. "There won't be time! If anything is alive, the current Martian environment will destroy it in seconds, minutes at most. You've got to lift the rock, and let me scramble under and grab a quick sample. That's the only way."

"Do you know how dangerous that could be? Houston would never allow it, Townsend would never allow it."

"They're not here, we are. We might never get another chance like this."

McGee looked up the treacherous scree slope. "This

whole hillside is nothing but avalanche debris. The neighboring rocks could give way in a second when I lift this boulder and you'd be crushed. I could never forgive myself if—"

"Please, Kevin, it's my life, and I'm willing to take the risk. For this." Again, the bright eyes, the pleading yet courageous voice.

McGee looked at her, then at the hillside. "Okay, but move fast. I'm not Superman."

"I'll be faster than light!" she cried happily.

McGee wedged his shoulder against the huge rock. "All right, then brace yourself here with me. I'll need your help to roll it up initially. When I think I've got its weight under control, I'll give you the signal—then you go like hell."

"Right."

"Okay, heave!"

"We can do it!" she cheered, then gasped with the effort. The rock began to rise, ponderously opening a gap about eighteen inches high at their knees. McGee straightened himself to form a rigid support where he could hold it himself, at least for a short while.

"All right, I've got it. Go."

Rebecca ducked under the rock, disappearing from the waist up. McGee strained to keep the boulder in place but the nearby pivot rocks restraining it from behind began to wobble.

"What's taking you, Rebecca! Get out of there now!"

"Just a minute." Rebecca's voice sounded husky in his suit radio.

McGee felt a stab of cold in his hands. The rock had pierced the insulation on his glove. "Rebecca! The cold's getting through. I can't hold it much longer."

"Just hold on a bit more." A bit. The cold seared his hands, penetrating his bones. Agony.

Finally, Rebecca backed out and McGee let go, the boulder collapsing back into place, missing her helmet by seconds. He stood with his fingers stretched out stiff and throbbing.

"Let's see those hands." She rubbed McGee's gloved fingers in hers. Then she slapped them together. He winced. "You feel that?"

"Ouch!"

"Good, then there's no frostbite." She smiled.

"Dr. Sherman, you really need some work on your bedside manner."

"Kevin, you and I have to get back to the *Beagle* at once, so I can examine these samples with the electron-scanning microscope and high-grade opticals."

She began marching back to the battered vehicle. McGee watched her for a moment, shaking his head in bewilderment, then finally followed.

When McGee examined the scraped and pummeled rover, he realized that getting back would not be easy.

In the first place, the vehicle obviously could not climb back up the loose and treacherous slope it had descended. "We'll have to drive for miles along the base of the ridge, after which we'll need to cross a hundred miles of bare planitia to get back to the base. If we can find it."

Ordinarily, that would not be a problem. However, in its tumble downhill, the rover had snapped off the antennas needed by both the over-the-horizon radios and the satellite navigation system. Without these, they could become fatally lost on the featureless plain.

McGee fiddled with his jury-rigged antenna, trying to make it work. From inside the rover came Rebecca's voice. "No luck. Nothing but static. Kevin, we've wasted precious hours trying to fix this thing. I've got to get these samples back to the lab for immediate analysis. Let's just bag the repair job and get going."

McGee groaned. Rebecca was so obsessed with her potential discovery that she was oblivious to their plight.

"Rebecca, I don't think you get it. Without the nav system, the odds of our finding our way back to the Hab are low, even in daylight. At night, it's going to be nearly impossible."

Rebecca exited the rover and joined McGee outside. She examined the repair job. It *seemed* like it should work. In all probability, a good mechanic could get the system functioning within minutes. Unfortunately, the nearest such person was over a hundred miles away, and without their radio, they had no way to call for help. Mars' weak magnetic field made compasses useless; they needed the satellite nav system to guide them home.

Rebecca stared bleakly at the wiring, then at the crumbly slope they had just descended. The avalanche had exposed bare and broken rock everywhere—Mars rocks free of deposited dust. They looked quite unusual. For a moment, the thought crossed her mind that she should photograph the slope for Luke. The fresh, raw image might have some geological value.

No, rocks could wait. She had to get back with her samples.

Rebecca looked to the west. It was a very clear evening, and the Sun was just going down. With no dust in the thin air, there was virtually no sunset, and no twilight. Instead, deep night fell like a thick curtain.

Suddenly McGee cried out. She turned, amazed at what she saw. The entire slope was glowing: soft pinks, greens, blues, violets, like an enormous mountain of iridescent jewels. It was eerie and beautiful—one of the most magnificent sights she had ever seen. For several seconds she couldn't breathe.

"Can you explain it, Rebecca?"

McGee's question broke her reverie, and her analytical mind switched into gear. "Phosphorescence, I think. The ridge is covered with calcite and fluorite, and other phosphorescent minerals. The avalanche exposed a lot of virgin surface, which is glowing due to excitation from solar UV. I don't think it will last long."

Sure enough, within less than a minute the glow faded, leaving the two explorers in a darkness lit only by a magnificent canopy of stars.

With the fall of night, the temperature, which had been

descending all afternoon, started to drop fast. The two spent a few moments admiring the constellations, then returned to the rover cabin for warmth. But McGee now had food for thought.

Inside the rover, he pulled off his helmet and waited for the doctor to remove hers. "Rebecca, I think I have an idea."

"What is it?" She asked with a trace of hope.

"The stars. We can navigate home by using the stars to provide direction, and the rover's odometer for dead reckoning against our maps."

Rebecca's expression brightened, then exploded into sunshine. "That's great! That means we can make it back tonight! Kevin, you're a wonder." She paused. "But we need to know the location of Mars' north celestial pole. It's not Polaris, I'm sure of that. Let's see: Mars' vernal equinox points toward Gemini, and tilts at twenty-four degrees. But to calculate the location of the pole we need to know—"

McGee cut short her calculations. "Rebecca, I know the answer."

"You do?"

"Yes. Mars' north celestial pole is located about halfway between Deneb and Alpha Cephei."

"How do you get that?"

"It says so right here."

Rebecca looked over at the text displayed on McGee's electropad. It had been many years since she'd first read it, but she recognized the passage instantly, from *The Case for Mars,* published in 1996.

Rebecca grinned. "Leave it to you, Kevin, to keep classics in your pad memory." She pointed out the window, "There's Deneb, Cygnus the Swan's tail, and there's Alpha Cephei. We'll lose them when we cross the equator, but if they mark north," she turned to look in the opposite direction, "that constellation will give us south."

Rebecca turned to McGee and smiled. "It's Vela, the sails of the Argo." She switched her penlite to illuminate her map. "So, to keep it simple, all you need to do is travel forty-four miles at bearing 090 and then head down at bearing 150 for another 115 miles—and we should hit it on the nose. It's all flat and level. At top speed, we can make it back in ten hours. Step on it."

McGee glanced out the window at the two stars. At bearing 090, all he would have to do is keep them directly to his left. Easy enough. "Aye, aye." He hit the starter.

And the two of them made it to the *Beagle* in eleven hours and forty-six minutes, guided by the light of the Martian stars.

CHAPTER 8

OPHIR PLANUM
DEC. 17, 2011 21:45 MLT

EVERYONE EXCEPT REBECCA WAS SEATED IN THE HAB'S galley. Colonel Townsend surveyed the assembled group. Immediately upon her return to the Beagle, the biologist had locked herself in the lab. She had been in there for the past sixteen hours, refusing to speak to anyone. It was time to resolve the situation.

Townsend turned to the historian. "Do you think it was a loss of judgment to abort the rover excursion, McGee? Those stromatolites were a real find, everything she was looking for. And now . . ." He gestured at the locked lab door.

"I think she's cracked," Luke interjected.

Well aware of the rivalry between the two scientists, Townsend said dryly, "Thank you for your insightful contribution, Dr. Johnson. Please allow me to proceed in getting the facts of the case." He continued to study McGee.

The professor appeared miserable. He was obviously soft on Dr. Sherman. Another problem to look out for. "I don't know. She examined the green-veined samples with the microscope in the rover, and they revealed no biological structure. But she said its magnification was too weak, and that she needed to use the more powerful microscopes in the Hab. She said she had to do it before the sample could die."

"Die? Rocks don't die. You mean she thinks the green stuff is *alive*?"

"That's what I think she believes."

Luke slapped the table. "Well, I'll tell you what I think— that little lady is off her little rocker."

Townsend winced. "I don't need to be lawyered on the subject, Luke." *And I don't need crew members trying to backstab each other.*

Gwen shrugged and looked at the sealed door. "Colonel, if you want, I can disable the lock so we can get her out."

Well, at least that was a positive suggestion. He could withhold judgment until he spoke to the doctor himself.

"Why don't we give her a little more time?" McGee pleaded. "Especially when we might have an answer one way or another any moment and end all this arguing."

"Your loyalty to your crewmate is commendable, Professor," Townsend said, "but I don't see the point. She's had enough time. Get your tools, Major."

Gwen got up, but before she could exit, the lab door opened and Rebecca appeared.

What a mess, Townsend thought. She looked completely exhausted, totally spent, played out. Hardly the composed scientist he knew from just three days ago.

Rebecca staggered into the room, clutching an optical disk. Townsend helped her to a chair, into which she collapsed. She handed the disk to McGee and motioned to the video player. McGee put the disk in the slot, and a blue-green background filled the TV screen.

"Okay, Doctor," Townsend said, his voice flat and deliberately neutral. "Let's see what you've found."

The whole crew watched as the TV showed the images, with a recording of the doctor's voice providing narration. "This is sample 12/16/11-9, series G, number 41, imaged optically under soft ultraviolet light at three hundred times magnification, with enhanced simulated color restoration. No biological structure is in evidence." Rebecca's recorded voice sounded ever more exhausted as the video proceeded. "This is the same sample imaged at one thousand times magnification. No biological structure is in evidence. I have now increased magnification to three thousand power. Again no biological structure is in evidence, however there is some indication of crystalline regularity to the substratum."

The video showed hints of tiny hexagonal patterns of shading within the blue-green background. *Looks like blue honeycomb,* Townsend thought.

"That's an inorganic mineralogical microstructure typical of cuprous silicates," Luke commented. "They're turquoise in color, too."

"But those shapes in the upper left of the screen seem rather odd." McGee offered.

Luke chuckled. "Those are fracture patterns, just like the ones that fooled people into thinking they were seeing fossils in Martian meteorites back in the 1990's. What you are looking at, Professor, is just a good old-fashioned rock."

Was that all it was? Townsend turned to Rebecca for her answer. The biologist said nothing. Instead, she just shook her head and stared tiredly at the table. Was that the look of defeat?

"This is the sample at eight thousand times magnification," her voice continued on the video. The TV image enlarged. Inside the hexagons, the liquid swirled.

It was apparent even to Townsend with his rudimentary background in biology that the motion was cytoplasmic in character. He turned to stare at Rebecca.

The doctor looked up from the table and spoke in a tired monotone with no hint of triumph, only certainty and completion. "It's alive."

Alive! The whole crew was speechless. Townsend turned to Luke, Gwen, McGee; all were transfixed watching the incredible swirling image on the screen. For a minute he, too, stared in fascination; then he looked back at Rebecca to congratulate her.

But the biologist was fast asleep in her chair and had begun to snore.

CHAPTER 9

BY LATE AFTERNOON OF THE NEXT DAY THE ATMOSPHERE in the Hab was relaxed, even happy. Sunlight streamed through the windows, and the door between the galley and the lab was open.

McGee looked up from his volume of *The Complete Shakespeare* and peered into the lab where Haydn's *Creation* was playing. While she bustled about taking measurements, peering through microscopes, and typing at lightning speed on her computer, Rebecca sang along with her prep school–trained classical voice. He thought she sang like an angel.

The biologist danced out of the lab and snatched a muffin off the galley table, flashed him a smile, then flitted back to her work. The smile made him feel warm inside.

The rest of the crew sat around the table eating, but apparently hadn't noticed. Townsend and Gwen were poring over maps while they ate, and Luke was examining some rocks with a magnifying glass.

"Now that is what you call one happy camper," McGee commented.

Townsend put his map aside. "I'll say. Well, I've delayed communication of the discovery long enough for her to get her ducks in a row. I think it's about time for a data dump." The colonel called out in the direction of the lab. "Excuse me. Excuse me! In the lab there."

Rebecca stuck her head out the door. "Yes?"

"If Miss Lily Pons would care to suspend her concert for a moment, the rest of the crew would be pleased to receive a briefing."

Lily Pons? Rebecca thought. Hardly a current star of the opera stage. She wondered how Townsend had even heard of her. Lily Pons had achieved popular fame singing the "Marseillaise" for the Free French during World War II. *Oh, that explains it.* She switched off the music and swept into the galley.

"Okay, here's the scoop. As I said yesterday, it's life." She smiled. "But it is not life exactly as we know it on Earth. Pre-cellular life, of course, more primitive than the living fossil blue-green algae back home. It has DNA and proteins, to be sure, and most of the amino acids and sugars are identical to those of terrestrial organisms, but I've found a few slightly different amino acids in the proteins. One of the four nucleotides in the DNA has a hydroxyl radical where DNA nucleotides on Earth just have a hydrogen ion. The DNA is organized into genes, which are dispersed in a redundant manner throughout the cell, rather than being centralized in well-ordered chromosomes. It's a simpler and less efficient arrangement than we see in terrestrial life, but much more robust against radiation damage during long periods of dormancy. There are also some novel proteins that act as a kind of antifreeze, greatly lowering the freezing point of the cytoplasm. It's a close cousin to terrestrial life, but not flesh of our flesh."

Gwen looked at her perplexed. " 'Not flesh of our flesh?' "

Townsend seemed equally puzzled. "But it's still fundamentally the same kind of thing as we might find on Earth?"

"Similar, but not the same. Actually, the basic chemistry is so similar that there may be a common ancestor."

"Or it could be that both were created by the same God," Gwen suggested.

Rebecca looked at the flight engineer. *Gwen, how can you believe such things? You're on Mars. Modern science has put you here. Why do you insist on rank superstition?* However, being in a good mood, she decided to be diplomatic. "That theory I'll leave for you to publish in your own article. All speculations aside, from the evidence here I'd bet the farm on two independent origins. You know, I'll probably get a special issue of *Scientific American,* with a foldout of me holding an ultracentrifuge tube up to the light and saying 'Eureka.' "

McGee tapped his camera. "I've already taken the shot."

"I'll bet you have, and I'll bet I looked a mess." She wrinkled her nose.

Townsend looked around the room, then out the window; sunset was upon them. "Well, I'd say that this is cause for a celebration. Two major discoveries in the same week."

"Right," Luke chimed in, as if wrestling with his pride. "Rebecca, I'm sorry I doubted you. I'll be eating some NASA prepackaged crow from the ship's stores." He pulled a bottle of champagne from under the table and began unwrapping the foil around its neck. "But if you'll forgive me, perhaps you'll do us all the honor?"

"Luke, I feel so good today I could forgive Hitler. Apology accepted."

She took the bottle from the geologist and pushed hard on the cork with her thumbs. The cork popped off and the champagne foamed hugely in the 5 psi cabin air as everyone cheered. Merrily, she poured out glasses for her crewmates.

Townsend held up his glass to make a toast. "To a successful mission and a safe voyage home."

"Hear, hear!" Gwen cheered.

Luke eyed the vigorous bubbling in his glass. "To some good drink for a change."

"To the Discoverers!" McGee said, saluting her with his drink.

Rebecca held up her glass and looked at it speculatively. What to say at a moment like this? Suddenly she remembered her grandfather's favorite toast. *How appropriate. Thanks, Grandpapa.* "To Life!" she shouted, and with a single dramatic motion tossed down the drink and hurled the empty glass to the galley floor.

To Life! To Life indeed, here and throughout the universe. It was great to be alive. Her very being glowed with the joy of it. McGee looked at her in wonder.

The party went on for hours. The professor entertained them with folk songs accompanied by his own guitar, Townsend and Luke told stories, and Gwen even performed a Celtic fling. One by one, everyone except McGee and Rebecca drifted off to their bunks. By midnight they were sitting alone by the window.

McGee strummed softly on his guitar. "The Streams of Mars" was a turn-of-the century Mars Society reworking of the ancient Irish ballad "The Minstrel Boy." Of all his repertoire, McGee knew this was the song that moved Rebecca most. He had saved it for this moment, and his tenor carried it well.

> *The streams of Mars are dry and cold,*
> *No current runs, no water fills them.*
> *Frozen still now since times long old,*
> *They wait for those who can revive them.*
> *Land now parched, but with hopeful art,*
> *Another world may someday be.*
> *One force with Reason thy life shall start.*
> *One spark of mind shall make alive thee.*

Rebecca smiled as she listened to the serenade. Outside the Hab window shone Phobos and Deimos, the two small bright Martian moons. Her luminous eyes reflected the faint globes. "Look at them, Kevin. How beautiful they shine tonight." Her voice was husky with transcendent thought.

McGee had never seen her look more lovely. "Not as beautiful as the light that is shining in your eyes, my princess."

" 'My princess'? Isn't that the term of endearment John Carter used for his darling Dejah Thoris?"

He was surprised she recognized the Burroughs reference so easily. "Yes, it's what a Martian man says to the woman he adores. The proper reply is 'my chieftain.' "

Rebecca laughed. "Well, you'll have to wait a long time if you expect me to call you that. Still . . . it's a sweet custom. Perhaps we should make it the law for our future Martian civilization."

"Yes, my princess, I think we should."

Rebecca drew back a little. "Oh, really. Stop being silly."

McGee felt a sinking feeling. "Who's being silly?"

"You are. You know the two of us can't get involved." Now she smiled at him in a sisterly way.

"Because I'm not a scientist? I share your passion for discovery, you know."

Rebecca shook her head, her tresses glinting in the soft double moonlight. "I know," she said sympathetically. "It's not that. It would just be wrong for the crew."

"Oh, I see. Bad for morale. Can't have that."

Rebecca put her hand on his cheek and looked into his eyes. "Please don't take it hard." She regarded him affectionately. "When we get back to Earth, things will be different."

McGee felt a surge of hope. "Really?"

"No promises—but, yes." Rebecca tousled his hair. "I really do think you're sweet, Kevin. It's just that now, with everything at stake, the mission has to come first. Just don't give up hope."

McGee sighed. "You sure have me where you want me."

She chuckled mischievously. "I suppose so, but that's the breaks. You know I'll always owe you for letting me get the live sample from under that boulder. And the idea of driving back at night using celestial navigation—what can

I say? You broke all the rules, and that's what made the difference. If anyone else but you had been there, it never would've happened."

McGee felt a glow of pride. He took Rebecca's hand and gazed out the window. "So, the stars. They've always spoken to explorers. The other night they showed us the way home. What do they say to you tonight, my beautiful Columbus?"

Rebecca looked out the window with him. Once again the moonlight glowed in her eyes. She was silent for a while, but when she finally spoke, her voice was moved with vision. "They're telling us that they're *alive*. That the universe is filled with life and civilizations. Those science fiction stories you like so much may be fiction, but they're not fantasy. There are star sailors out in all that vastness right now living such tales."

McGee gazed at the star-studded sky, then at Rebecca Sherman, deep in contemplation. His thoughts soared to poetry.

O brave new world, that has such creatures in it.

CHAPTER 10

GARY STETSON ACKNOWLEDGED THE WARM APPLAUSE OF the studio audience with a smile and a feigned gracious nod. Keeping his smile in place as the clapping faded, he turned to face his interviewer, a sleek and fashionable TV talk-show host.

"This is Leslie Nelson," she began, "with *Good Evening America*. Here in the studio to talk with us about the latest and most profound discoveries of science on Earth and throughout the universe is noted author, lecturer, and scientist, Dr. Gary Stetson. Welcome, Gary."

More applause. This time Stetson added a little wave of his hand to his nod and gracious smile. He let the host wait while he absorbed the cheers, then favored her with his most sincere smile. He had practiced it in the mirror. "Hi, Leslie. Glad to be here."

Nelson seemed gratified. "So, Gary, your new book *Enthalpy* is a bestseller of pop science. How does it feel to be the author of two in a row?

"Leslie, it feels great—not because of the money but because it proves that there's such a large intelligent reading public out there, who are willing to investigate important new ideas."

Again his fans applauded. This time Nelson joined them. Stetson glowed.

"Let's see. Your previous book was *The Illusion of Time,* in which you demonstrated the need for nonsequential thinking. You showed how important it is to view the world not just in the instinctive way that's been hard-wired by biology into the human psyche, but also to use the more holistic forms of apprehension practiced by insects and trees."

And which outsold its one-million-dollar advance to boot, thought Stetson. "Yes, Leslie. Not only was that book widely popular at its time of publication, but it has since become the basis for retraining programs for upper management of most of corporate America. It has introduced a paradigm shift in intelligent thinking."

"And now, you've published *Enthalpy.* What's that about?"

It's about a two-million-dollar advance, you dummy. "Well, 'enthalpy' itself is a fundamental concept in physics. Basically, it's the measure of the ability of a physical system to do useful work. You cannot create enthalpy, it can only be destroyed, and when it's all gone, then no more work can be done. The system and everything in it is dead. The Earth started out with a certain allocation of enthalpy, which we humans are using up today at an astounding rate. If we are going to prolong the life of this planet, we are going to have to drastically cut the rate at which we are consuming enthalpy."

Nelson responded with a smile that looked even more sincere than Stetson's best. This caused him a momentary pang of jealousy, but he managed to let it go. After all, the interviewer was a professional. Like himself.

"You certainly have done a lot of profound thinking about some of the most important issues facing humanity today. Tell me, Gary, how do you feel about this new discovery of life on Mars?"

The question took Stetson off guard. He had been expecting and hoping to keep plugging his book . . . but Mars? Who gave a damn about Mars? He looked at the audience. They clearly did, and awaited his judgment on the recent discovery. His mind racing, Stetson spoke slowly, giving himself time to develop his thoughts as he went along. "An interesting question, Leslie. I have to say that I agree entirely with all the leading medical experts. This is a very, uh, dangerous situation."

Nelson arched an eyebrow, surprised. Now she was genuinely interested, and so was the audience. "Dangerous to us here on Earth?"

Fear's the ticket. It always is. Stetson caught his stride. The line of attack was now clear. This issue could be played up for millions. "Yes, absolutely. The astronauts have been exposed to organisms against which no terrestrial plant or animal has any defense whatsoever. *Alien* organisms." Yes, that was the word to use. "If those reckless astronauts are allowed to return here, not only humanity but the entire terrestrial biosphere could very well be devastated by unstoppable epidemics. We have no way of guaranteeing the safety of the human race. None."

He spoke more forcefully now. "Under no circumstances must we allow that to happen. Unfortunately, our political leaders are so bound up with the macho American 'can-do' baloney that they're willing to bring five daredevils home and commit genocide, risking *billions of lives,* rather than allow their precious mission to fail by ordering the astronauts not to return."

Now it was Nelson's turn to be taken aback. The interviewer stared at Stetson for several seconds before responding. "So you feel that in the best interests of humanity, the astronauts should be . . . quarantined away from Earth? Forever?"

Stetson summoned his storehouse of inner rage, adding synthetic conviction to his argument. "Look, all five of those people on Mars willfully, knowingly, and maliciously violated the fundamental laws of cosmic bioethics." Nelson seemed puzzled. No matter, he could make it clear. "Ask yourself, who gave them the authority to contaminate Mars? How dare they trespass on another world after we've reduced our own Garden of Eden to an ecological cesspool?"

Nelson nodded in apparent or at least simulated understanding. "I'm starting to see your point, Gary."

Stetson continued with vigor. "And that awful Dr. Sherman actually suggests cross-linking Earth and Mars genetic material to create artificially engineered Frankenstein plants that will grow on the surface of Mars, or invade the few remaining pristine deserts on Earth. Read her report—she says it herself. Abomination! We need to keep Mars red, as much as we need to keep Earth green. We must not mix Earth life and Mars life, or the results will annihilate life on both worlds, mark my words."

The audience applauded, more for his performance than his rationale. He observed Nelson taking this in, gauging the audience's mood. Was she playing with the idea of a barbed counterpoint? *They're with me already, Leslie. Don't even think about posing opposition.*

"But what can the average American do about it?" Apparently she'd gotten the message.

Stetson faced the camera boldly, emphasizing his reply with a raised fist. "This is not the time to wait and let the bureaucrats muddle through. If ever there was a need for immediate grassroots action, it's now! Don't wait, or the human race will be sorry. People need to take to the streets and demand that the reckless astronauts not be allowed to contaminate our planet. They wanted Mars, let them stay there."

He leaned even closer to the camera. "We need to march on Washington, and on NASA Mission Control at the Johnson Space Center in Houston. Take whatever action is necessary. We need to tell our so-called leaders what we think. Keep Earth green! Keep Mars red! We must make our voices heard. The life of every living being on this planet could depend on it."

The audience cheered. Then someone began to chant, "Keep Earth green! Keep Mars red!" Quickly several others, then more, then all, joined in. "Keep Earth green! Keep Mars red! Keep Earth green! Keep Mars red!"

Stetson beamed. A new Movement had been launched.

WASHINGTON DC
JAN. 6, 2012 13:10 CST

On the sidewalk in front of the White House a mob of hostile demonstrators chanted: "Keep Earth green! Keep Mars red!" The crowd was mostly leftist-looking, including many young people wearing antiglobalist slit jeans, anarchist black, or ecogoth brown, but interspersed among them and marching alongside were older, more soberly dressed types carrying signs that read REPENT! SAVE OUR HOME! and PRIDE GOETH BEFORE THE FALL.

Standing on a makeshift platform at the eye of the storm, the charismatic Reverend Bobby Joe Stone and Gary Stetson harangued the demonstrators, increasing their zeal. A church choir stood behind these two men while TV camera crews filmed it all from the front.

Across the street in Lafayette Park a small pro-astronaut counterdemonstration proceeded more or less unnoticed. The group of space society types waved American flags and carried signs saying SAVE AMERICA'S HEROES and SAVE OUR CREW. TV evangelist Stone scoffed at their attempt at rebuttal.

"Brothers and sisters, those who mask their pride behind the imperatives of false science have led our people to the brink of destruction. Pride caused them to send a group of astronauts uninvited to Mars to find this deadly plague. They now say it would be immoral to abandon the astronauts to their fate on Mars. Immoral! Yet did not the Lord God himself sacrifice his only son Jesus Christ for all of us? Is it then too much for us to demand that five sinners pay the price for their own transgression to save all the creatures that God has placed upon this Earth? The astronauts cannot be saved. They have already been contaminated by the disease. Yet their souls can still be saved! Let us pray for their souls."

Stone stepped back from the microphone and the choir began to sing: "Shall we gather by the river . . ."

From the window in the John Quincy Adams meeting room, the President watched the stir outside and then turned to face his circle of advisors. Gathered in the oak-paneled room were the First Lady, chief White House political strategist Bill Wilson, Media Chief Sam Wexler, NASA Administrator Tom Ryan, White House Science and Security Advisor Dr. George Kowalski, Surgeon General Dr. Amber Wong, and General Bernard Winters, Chairman of the Joint Chiefs of Staff.

Wilson cleared his throat. "As you can see, Mr. President, we have a real problem on our hands. Virtually overnight, this Stetson character has created a nationwide radical organization—Redpeace—and they've joined forces with a big piece of the religious right. They're pulling together legions of fanatics who are going to campaign to help Fairchild beat you this fall. Every TV network in the country has been rerunning that old movie *The Andromeda Strain*. Demonstrations like this one are going on all over the country. . . ."

The President listened carefully to his political strategist. Bill Wilson was always politically tuned in. If he was worried, the situation had to be serious, not just a temporary squall of public opinion.

NASA chief Tom Ryan interrupted. "What do you want the President to do, Bill? Abandon the crew because a bunch of crackpots are causing a panic?"

That did not satisfy the President. *Crackpots and the people they panic can still vote.*

Now it was Science and Security Advisor Kowalski's turn. "That's oversimplifying the situation a bit, isn't it, Tom? Sure Stetson is a faker, and I for one have no use for TV evangelists, but there are plenty of well-credentialed scientists who believe that there is real danger here."

Real danger? The President remained silent, listening and considering. He hadn't paid much attention to the full seriousness of the situation.

Press Secretary Wexler cut in. "We've got some static now with crazy demonstrators on the streets and Bible thumpers screaming at us from their pulpits. But if anyone thinks this is bad, wait till you see what the press does to this Administration if we chicken out and stab the crew in the back."

That's true! They'll have my head!

Wilson raised his finger. "Wex, you're not being objective."

The press secretary slapped the table. "I deal with the media for this Administration, and I know what I'm talking about here."

"You're been a friend of Kevin McGee since you were boys." Wilson smiled genially. "You got him his slot on the mission. We all understand how you feel, but you can't let your personal emotions enter into a decision like this."

So Wexler has a personal stake in the matter, the President thought. *Gotta watch out for that.*

Dr. Amber Wong cleared her throat and waited until she had the room's attention. Then she intoned in her upper-class Hong Kong British accent, "And I, for one, will insist that the crew be ordered to stay put until I have proof positive that there is no danger to the health of the public."

Wilson nodded in vigorous agreement. "That's the only logical position."

Certainly.

"Don't give us your logic crap," the press secretary replied heatedly, "you're just capitulating to the pressure from our gutless friends on the Hill."

Wex's emotions are getting the better of his judgment.

"This is strictly a matter of public health," the Surgeon General pronounced with calm authority. "Pending certain proof that the Martian biota is completely harmless to all terrestrial life forms, Colonel Townsend and his crew must be ordered to remain on Mars."

The President felt both annoyed and relieved. Amber Wong could be a pain in the ass, but if he could pass the buck to her on this one . . . "Makes sense to me," he said.

General Winters looked upset. "I could give such an order, but I'm not sure that Townsend would follow it."

The President felt the beginning of alarm rise up inside. He turned to the blue-uniformed four-star officer. "What are you talking about, General?"

"Well, Mr. President, Andrew Townsend is a very individualistic officer." The usually confident Chairman of the Joint Chiefs now seemed timid. "I know this for certain. He served as a member of my squadron in the Gulf War of '91. He was a great pilot, but he used to like to write his own rules. Once, while we were returning from a raid, the Iraqis hit one of our planes. The pilot managed to bail. Instead of continuing home, Townsend turned back and flew through all kinds of flak for half an hour, engaging enemy ground forces long enough for our Kurdish friends to rescue the man. It was a complete violation of Pentagon policy. He risked himself and a fifty-million-dollar aircraft to save one guy."

Now both alarm and anger surged within the President. He looked the general squarely in the eye. "And yet you selected him to command our mission to Mars."

Winters tried to maintain eye contact, but failed, directing his gaze to the table instead. "Yes, sir. The situation being so novel, the Joint Chiefs felt that we needed an officer who possessed the maximum amount of creativity and initiative."

The President slapped his forehead. "This is great, just great. My military has decided to entrust the fate of this Administration to an anarchist."

Silence. Now everyone was looking at the table. Then a cheerful voice spoke up. "Now, let's not get overexcited. I'm sure this situation has a very simple solution."

The President turned to the First Lady with a trace of

hope. *Margaret, you've saved my skin before, but what can you do now?* As far as he could see, the situation was no-win and out of control.

"General," she asked, "if the astronauts refuse direct orders and come back without our permission, can't the Air Force shoot them down before they can land?"

"Certainly, but . . ." Winters appeared shocked.

"There you have it." She smiled brightly. "No problem at all. We'll leave it at that."

Wexler shot out of his chair like a rocket. "If we shoot down our own crew coming home from Mars, there'll be hell to pay with the press. Not to mention our own consciences."

"I'm sure you can handle it, Wex." Bill Wilson seemed confident.

"It certainly would be preferable to letting the astronauts spread an alien epidemic through our cities," added Science and Security Advisor Kowalski.

"Wait just one second!" NASA Administrator Ryan was more than a bit irritated. "Aren't we getting a little ahead of ourselves? There's absolutely no proof that the Martian organisms are dangerous."

Dr. Wong's response was firm. "But as Surgeon General, I require proof that they are *not* dangerous."

"But if we give you that proof?" Ryan asked desperately.

"If you can provide me with convincing scientific evidence that there is no epidemiological threat from the newly discovered microbes, then I'd certainly have no objection to the retrieval of the crew."

Ryan turned to the Science and Security Advisor. "And you, Dr. Kowalski?"

"I would also need proof that there is no threat to other terrestrial plants and animals. But, of course, if you could give me that," Kowalski smiled, "then I would be the first to insist that everything possible be done to assure the safe return of our astronaut team."

Ryan looked around the room like a tiger at bay. "All right, then, if that's how it is, we'll give you proof. Dr.

Sherman has been conducting a comprehensive set of tests using cultures of a wide variety of terrestrial life forms to see if any of them are vulnerable to infection from the Martian microbes. She says she'll have a complete data dump on her research ready to be downlinked to Earth in about eight days."

Doctor Wong seemed pleased. "Excellent. I will convene an examining board of the nation's foremost medical experts to review her work."

"We'll need nonmedical biologists as well," the Science and Security Advisor interjected. "Geneticists, ecologists, environmental scientists. I'll supply the names."

Ryan looked ready to raise another argument, but then apparently thought better of it. *With Kowalski choosing the experts, he doesn't have a prayer,* the President thought. But in the end all the NASA chief said was, "Fine."

Kowalski looked triumphant. "And it shall be we, and no one else—certainly not Dr. Sherman or any other NASA scientist—who will pass judgment on whether her tests have been sufficiently rigorous to demonstrate safety."

"Now hold on!" The press secretary was on fire. "I may not have a Ph.D., but I know a swindle when I see one. This setup isn't fair. There should be some NASA representation on the board of examiners, and in particular, Dr. Sherman needs to be given a chance to defend her own research, personally and face to face, against any criticism."

"You're trying to turn this into a circus, Wex," Kowalski said with professorial condescension. "This is a scientific review, not a campaign debate. We don't do things that way."

Dr. Wong arched her eyebrows. "I see no objection to a personal defense, Dr. Kowalski. In fact, under the circumstances, I think we owe it to Dr. Sherman to provide her with such an opportunity."

"See! It's the American way!" exclaimed Wexler, obviously delighted by Wong's unexpected support.

"It's not the sci—"

Kowalski's rebuttal was cut short by Dr. Wong. "I insist," she said decisively.

The Science and Security Advisor waved his hands to make light of his setback. "Oh, very well. Because of the signal time lag, we'll conduct our own debate here and uplink the video. She can review it and downlink a rebuttal the next day."

Ryan suddenly appeared upbeat. "I'll have the DSN make preparations."

Wilson turned to his boss. "Mr. President, are you really going to leave a decision of this importance up to a bunch of scientists?"

Ordinarily no, the President thought, *but under these conditions*—"Well actually, Bill, I kind of like the idea."

The political strategist was confused. "But . . ."

"That'll be all. The decision has been made," the First Lady scolded. "Let's not waste any more time on this."

The President assumed his command mode. "Right. The decision has been made. The examining board will judge. People, we all have a lot of work to do. I suggest we get moving."

CHAPTER 11

REBECCA TOSSED IN HER BUNK, IMMERSED IN HER WORST nightmare.

Young, frail, inexperienced, she stood in that old lecture hall at Cornell, nervously rattling out her Ph.D. presentation. It had been going well enough, until Professor Waldron raised his hand.

She could see him now, with that supercilious smirk on his face, asking her if she had read the JGR preprint by Osterman and Whitten. She hadn't. "If you had, then you would know that your assumed equality 3.1 is untrue. And without that equation, it appears evident that your entire thesis has no foundation."

She turned to the blackboard and watched as the terms in equation 3.1 seemed to lose their solidity and turn into meaningless spaghetti. Panicked, she looked to Carl Schaeffer for support, but he just sat there impassively with a look that said, "You're on your own, kid."

My thesis has no foundation. Five years of work down the drain . . .

It had been the worst moment of her life. She remembered the sadistic grin on Waldron's face as another old fart patted him on the back, the knowing smiles and snickers of the jealous post-docs in the rows behind them. Then a voice spoke inside her, *I can't let them do this to me. I won't let them do this to me.*

She started to walk back and forth in front of the blackboard, ignoring the vultures, forcing herself to focus. Equation 3.1 had made so much sense when she'd first written it into her thesis outline years ago. It had still seemed solid that morning when she'd reviewed her presentation for the final time. How could it suddenly be so weak?

Maybe it wasn't. She picked up the chalk and started to scribble. Now let's see—regroup terms, integrate both sides by parts, apply the chain rule . . . these terms cancel . . . regroup again, apply Leibniz's rule . . . Fourier transform. *Maybe I'm getting somewhere—No, I'm stuck.* Hold on, the right-hand side can be represented as a Maclaurin series . . . these terms can be integrated after a Riemann transformation in the complex plane. This other series reduces to a superposition of hyperbolic trigonometric functions, which can be shown through a set of standard identities to equal these other terms, and the rest of it is just a restatement of conservation of momentum and energy. Proof!

She drew a box around her final result and turned to face the crowd. She stared at Waldron like he was her dinner while she tossed the chalk carelessly over her shoulder. Then some of her fellow grad students in the back of the room started to clap their hands, and an instant later applause resounded throughout the hall. As Carl stepped up to shake her hand, she noticed out of the corner of her eye a red-faced Professor Waldron slipping out the door.

In her bunk on Mars, the sleeping scientist smiled. There was a knock on the door and she awoke.

"Rebecca?" Townsend's voice could be heard through the wall. "The DSN is waiting to receive your rebuttal to the examining board now."

She sat up in her cot, taking only a few seconds to

smooth her hair. It was a foolish, nonsensical argument, panic-driven, with no basis in science . . . but Rebecca knew that the fate of the entire crew rested on how convincing she could be now.

I beat Waldron, I can beat Kowalski. "Okay, I'm ready." She stepped outside of her cabin, entered the galley, and seated herself in front of the video screen.

McGee gave her a grin and an encouraging thumbs up. "Go get 'em, tiger."

Rebecca gave him a wink. "I'll do my best. Let's have that disk of their summation one more time."

McGee slipped the disk into the player, and the examining board appeared on the screen: Drs. Wong and Kowalski, Administrator Ryan, and eight other doctors and scientists. Kowalski's image began to speak.

"In summation, Dr. Sherman, the board commends you on your flawless and thorough laboratory technique. The set of tests you performed was quite comprehensive, I would hasten to add almost astonishing, involving as it did cultures of various organ tissues of literally hundreds of species of animals and plants, under both normal and a host of abnormal physical and chemical conditions. All of your infection findings were negative, and no member of the board disputes them.

"Nevertheless, it is my feeling that you have not adequately addressed the issue of delayed incubation. As we know full well from terrestrial diseases such as AIDS, an incubation period of as long as a decade is sometimes required before symptoms of infection appear. Until and unless your cultures are allowed to incubate for at least such a period, and still test negative, you have not demonstrated complete epidemiological safety. While the probability of such a danger is admittedly remote, the consequences of making this mistake would be so grave that, under such circumstances, I cannot recommend that we permit the return of the crew."

"That fork-tongued faker!" Luke grumbled. "He knows you can never perform such a survey."

"Bastard." Gwen made as if to spit at the video screen.

Drawing a deep breath, Rebecca motioned for silence and signaled McGee to turn on the *Beagle*'s transmission camera, which was mounted on top of the TV screen. Looking intently at the camera and speaking in a deliberate, authoritative manner, she began the most important presentation of her career. *This one is for keeps, Becky.*

"This is Rebecca Sherman, chief scientist and ship's doctor for the U.S.S. *Beagle,* presently located on the surface of Mars. Dr. Kowalski has alluded to a hypothetical, although in his words 'remote,' possibility that Martian autotrophic organisms with completely incompatible cellular chemistry could present a delayed incubation threat to some species of terrestrial life. He has recommended that a multiple tissue culture study be conducted for an indefinite duration to prove that such a threat does not exist. Obviously, his suggestion is not useful or feasible, as it is clear that such an experimental program could never be carried out, nor, if it were attempted even to his specifications, could it ever provide convincing proof to any mind that thought it necessary in the first place. Indeed, an empirical proof of the nonpathogenic nature of the Martian microorganisms does not and can never exist."

"What's she saying?" Gwen whispered to the others in alarm.

Luke flushed with anger. "She's saying that she'll sign our death warrant."

"Hold on, people," Townsend urged. "I'm sure Dr. Sherman knows what she's doing." Gwen looked at Townsend. He sure didn't sound sure.

Unperturbed, Rebecca continued her lecture. "However, the issue in science is never one of absolute empirical proof. No one can ever know anything on the basis of empirical proof. On the basis of the type of empirical proof Dr. Kowalski requests here, no one can 'know' that the sun will rise tomorrow. Actual predictive knowledge, as opposed to mere customary belief, requires a theoretical framework. We 'know' that the sun will rise tomorrow because we know celestial mechanics. The Earth rotates, and it will continue to rotate, because the laws of physics mandate that angular momentum be conserved. We know that the sun will rise tomorrow not because we have records that it rose many times in the past, but because we know *why* it must."

McGee nodded approvingly. "I think I see where she's going."

"Biology is not a branch of witchcraft," Rebecca went on. "It is a *science*. It has laws. Laws of evolution, adaptation, and system development. One of those laws is that disease organisms are specifically adapted to their hosts. The bacteria and viruses that infect humans have been co-evolving with our ancestors for the past four billion years. They have been engaged in a four-billion-year-long arms race to maintain their ability to breach the defenses that have continually been evolving in the bodies of our ancestors. No would-be pathogenic species that has failed to track us in this way has the remotest chance of infecting us. That is why human beings do not catch Dutch elm disease, and trees do not catch head colds. It's utterly impossible."

"Good point," Townsend noted.

"These Martian microorganisms have been separated from the terrestrial biosphere for their entire evolutionary history. All the laws of biological science tell us that the notion that they could be pre-adapted to represent a pathogenic threat to any Earth-based life is not only incorrect but intrinsically absurd—acausal reasoning.

"However, harmless as they are, the Martian microbes represent a genetic treasure, as they have developed means for survival in extremely arid and cold environments. If their genes could be appropriately spliced with terrestrial plants, it could lead to species with the ability to grow in the Arctic or in the harshest deserts, thereby alleviating world hunger. To forego such benefits on the basis of a superstitious and nonsensical argument that an endless program of laboratory research needs to be conducted to prove the absence of risk from such a source is not rational. It is mindless hysteria, and a complete abandonment of the scientific method."

Rebecca waved her hand to McGee to turn the transmitter off.

The historian slapped down the stop switch. "Well, you may not have stopped them from killing us, but at least you got in a few good insults."

HOUSTON
JAN. 28, 2012 16:20 CST

In the examiners' meeting room at the Johnson Space Center, Rebecca's broadcast was just concluding. Kowalski frowned in disgust. "That's all she had to say? I have never heard so much empty rhetoric masquerade as science in my entire life."

NASA Administrator Ryan smiled. "Actually, George, I think she just cut your balls off."

"I quite agree," said Dr. Wong flatly. "It is necessary, however, for the board to vote on the substance of the matter. All those who believe that the level of risk is low enough to allow the crew to return, please signify now by raising their right hand."

Ryan raised his hand immediately, followed by a few of the assembled scientists. *Not enough,* Ryan thought. Then Dr. Wong raised her own hand, and others followed, until all hands but Kowalski's were raised.

Agitated, the Science and Security Advisor looked around the room for support. Finding none, he reluctantly raised his own hand in agreement with the rest.

CHAPTER 12

TWILIGHT ILLUMINATED THE LAWN IN FRONT OF THE EX-
aminers' meeting-room building at the JSC. The gathered
security guards cast long shadows. Nearby, the usual group
of a few pro-crew demonstrators maintained their vigil, listening to a folksinger strum the chords to the final verses
of "The Beagle Has Landed."

Beyond the pro-crew demonstrators, a huge crowd
chanted "Keep Earth green! Keep Mars red!" As they
marched in front of a bandstand, the agitated people carried
signs decorated with green crosses. On the platform, Gary
Stetson and the Reverend Bobby Joe Stone stirred up the
crowd in anticipation as Administrator Ryan, Surgeon General Wong, and the JSC security chief approached a podium
in front of the main NASA building across the way.

Looking proud and satisfied, Ryan stepped up to the microphone. "Ladies and gentlemen, I am pleased to an-
nounce that the examining board has reached a decision. It
is the unanimous verdict of the board, based on sound scientific principles and investigation, that the Martian microorganisms represent *no threat,* and that the crew be allowed

to continue their mission and at the appointed time return safely to Earth."

An instant cheer went up from the pro-crew demonstrators, but a split-second later the anti-crew mob screamed in outrage.

Stetson could not believe it. "This is genocide! This is ecocide! You'll never get away with this." He turned to his followers. "They've signed all of our death warrants!"

From a distance, Ryan looked directly at Stetson. "The board's decision is final."

The NASA Administrator's aloofness was even more infuriating than his decision. Stetson's blood boiled, and his anger reflected in his crowd of supporters. "No it's not!" he yelled. "Let's get them!"

Stetson's supporters seemed confused, but he knew what to do. Grabbing a green cross, he charged off the stand and ran directly at the pro-crew demonstrators. Immediately he was flanked by his hired shills, carrying along several dozen of the most volatile members of his crowd.

By the time Stetson's vanguard crashed into the pro-astronaut picket line, the mass of Redpeace demonstrators had begun to surge forward. The scuffle began, the two groups striking at each other with signs and placards, kicks and fists. In most places along the skirmish line Stetson's mob prevailed, but in some instances they were driven back into the main Redpeace mass, knocking down some of the older Fundamentalist folks.

That ignited the main Redpeace contingent's rage, and they rushed forward, scattering the pro-spacers like chaff. It was a total rout. Some spacers fled toward the uneasy police line. The slower ones didn't make it that far.

As Stetson watched, the folksinger who had initially rallied the pro-spacers was caught in her flight and trampled to the ground. Her guitar was smashed. Now an army in full charge, the Redpeace mob hit the line of police and NASA security guards who tried to resist with billy clubs, but were quickly overwhelmed. A few cops farther back shot tear-gas canisters, which were promptly picked up by several of the bolder Redpeace members and hurled back.

But the whiff of tear gas had done its work: Within seconds, the Redpeace mob was completely out of control. When the secondary police line broke, the crowd began smashing windows and lighting fires.

From the balcony of the main building, Dr. Wong surveyed the advancing rioters and turned to the JSC security officer standing beside her. "Is there a back way out of this building?"

"Yes, right this way." As the dignitaries were shown to safety, the uniformed man picked up his cellular phone. "This is Captain Martino at JSC. Get me the governor's office."

HOUSTON
JAN. 28, 2012 19:55 CST

That night the Johnson Space Center burned.

Sirens howled as torched buildings exploded into flame. Firefighters attempting to reach the engulfed buildings were stopped by the screaming mob. NASA employees attempted to defend their offices and labs, but in most places were routed.

Even as the destruction raged, not all of NASA's opponents engaged in direct action. Some cut broader and deeper. Thus, outside the burning Public Information Office, a mobile television crew focused its lens on a live broadcast by a portly, expensively dressed man in a minister's collar.

"Mars has monsters, yes it does!" the Reverend Stone intoned. "Those monsters may be too small for the naked eye to see, but they can murder your mother, your father, your sweetheart, and your sons and daughters."

The camera zoomed in on Stone's face, illuminated with flickering yellow-orange firelight. "Those astronauts on Mars are contaminated with *red death,* the mother of all plagues. They went where human beings were not meant to go, and now they must pay the price. *Them,* not us!"

A fire engine screeched to a halt in front of the burning Public Information building, but before the firefighters could act, the mob pulled them out of the cab and beat them senseless. Then, grabbing the firemen's axes, enraged Redpeace adherents chopped through the hoses, and charged off to assault another fire truck that had just pulled up. Nearby, men in leather jackets systematically smashed in the windows of cars marked NASA—Government Use Only.

Televangelist Stone brushed from his shoulder a charred fragment of CADprint without taking his eyes off the camera. He raised his rich voice. "The safety of our entire world must come before that of a handful of overpaid daredevils. They knew the risks when they set forth, but let the lure of fame and fortune lead them on. Well, now it's time for them to pay the piper. The wages of sin are death. The astronauts must never, *never* come home."

The sermon continued until it was interrupted by the arrival of a helicopter, which hovered overhead, dropped down cables, and released a swarm of camouflaged SWAT-team security guards carrying automatic weapons. Hitting the ground running, the team deployed quickly to secure a perimeter under sporadic fire. That done, waves of additional helicopters carrying reinforcements rapidly swelled the numbers of the forces of order.

But they were too late to save Mission Control from the mob. Using a steel desk from the lobby as a battering ram, the rioters knocked down the locked doors, then brushed aside the makeshift force of security guards and NASA personnel who tried to stop them near the entrance. Seconds later, the nerve center of the American space program was in chaos. Glass shattered as a volley of stones hurled by several of the invaders crashed through the main viewscreen.

Phil Mason, head of Mission Control, clung to his post like a captain on a sinking ship. Ducking the glass fragments, he picked up his microphone. "Mason to Security! They've broken in! We need help fast!"

As the mob smashed their way inside, most of the Mission Control operators picked up chairs or fire extinguishers to try to mount a defense. As they did, Darrell Gibbs—Special Assistant to the White House Science and Security Advisor—ran to the far side of the room and pounded in numbers on his special cell phone.

Craig Holloway, Mission Control's cheek-pierced ecogoth, also dodged the intruders. Running from one console to the next, he typed on one station after another, ignoring the plight of the diminutive Alicia Castillo, who struggled desperately with a very large attacker.

Al Rollins tried to keep his post, but was hurled to the ground by a member of the mob. Rollins scrambled free, only to find another madman about to chop him with a fire ax.

Then a SWAT team entered the room. There was a hail of gunfire, and the ax-wielder was cut down.

"Everybody freeze!" the SWAT officer shouted. "All non-NASA personnel are under arrest."

As the protesters were rounded up and led out, Rollins surveyed the damage. Mission Control was a shambles. Finding himself at Craig Holloway's desk, he noticed with annoyance a copy of a book called *Enthalpy* sticking out of the ecogoth's briefcase.

Rollins limped over to his own station and sat down. Monitoring the readouts, he typed a few keystrokes, and threw a switch.

```
MISSION CONTROL, NASA, JSC
JAN. 29, 2012 09:30 CST
```

By the next morning Mission Control was still a mess, but had begun to function again. Al Rollins, his face bruised, sat at his console running status checks. He motioned Mason over. "Chief, I think we have a serious problem here."

Rollins showed Mason his indicator readings.

The Mission Control chief looked at the data in horror. "That can't be. Have you checked the secondary readouts?"

"There's no doubt about it. The propellant tanks in the ERV *Retriever* at Mars Base One are empty. Telemetry from the onboard vehicle health-maintenance recorder indicates that the *Retriever*'s computer ordered the propellant vent valves opened at 0219 GMT last night. By 0240 the tanks were empty."

Mason forced himself to be calm. "0219 GMT. That would be 8:19 PM here, just a few minutes after the fight. No wonder no one caught the malfunction. Well, at least the crew still has the backup ERV *Homeward Bound,* in Valles Marineris. Quick, check its tanks."

Rollins typed furiously and a new page of data appeared upon his console screen. He looked up, stunned. "Empty. I don't get it. An identical malfunction happened at the exact same time."

By this time a crowd of Mission Control operators had gathered around Rollins's console, listening in and peering at the data readouts.

"Chief, they're stranded!" Rollins finally cried in dismay.

"Dead is more likely," interjected Tex Logan.

Alicia Castillo looked at the others with astonishment. "Why? Why can't we just send out another ERV?"

"Laws of celestial mechanics," Craig Holloway answered. "The next launch window to Mars would get a new ERV there after next year's return launch window to Earth closes."

"And the next return launch window after that?" Alicia pressed.

"Not for another two years. The crew's consumables will run out long before."

Alicia drummed her fingers nervously, then banged her fist down on Rollins's console. "Well, then, we could send out another Hab filled with supplies."

Tex Logan regarded the diminutive Hispanic woman with sympathy. "We could, if Congress would come up with a two-billion-dollar add-on to the program to fund it. With public opinion running the way it is, there's not much chance of that happening."

Rollins interrupted. "Chief, we've got telemetry coming in from *Beagle*."

"Put it on your screen."

Townsend's image appeared on Rollins's TV monitor. "This is Colonel Townsend. Last night a signal was received here from the DSN that caused the ERV *Retriever* to completely vent its tanks. I demand an immediate explanation." The screen went blank.

"Now that is one pissed-off fella," Logan drawled.

Rollins faced Mason anxiously. "He's nuts. We didn't uplink any commands last night."

Alicia sat down at her station and began to check the log. She typed several sets of commands and then froze, staring at her screen. "No, he's right. DSN records show a data transmission out of Goldstone at 6:03 P.M. Pacific Standard Time last night."

Mason felt faint. "What? Authorized from where?"

"According to Goldstone records, it was authorized from here. By you."

Hostile eyes turned on the Mission Control Chief of Operations. "Wait a second! You don't think that I—wait, 6:03 Pacific, that's eight o'clock here. About the time of the riot. I wasn't the only person here at that time who knew the DSN command authorization. There was Rollins and Holloway and . . ."

"That's all," Tex Logan concluded.

"Hey, I didn't do it," Rollins said. "I couldn't have. I had my hands full fighting a maniac with an ax."

Alicia Castillo turned and faced the remaining suspect. "But Craig stayed out of the fight." Her voice was cold.

"No I didn't," Holloway protested. "I . . ."

Cold went to hot. "Yes you did, you coward!" Alicia exploded. "I saw you! I was being strangled on *this* desk, and you were sitting *there,* not four feet away. You didn't lift a finger to help me. You were too busy typing something."

"OK, I released the evening news data update and E-mail bin. That's all. I thought it important for the crew to get it before the mob shut us down."

Alicia persisted, "Then why all the typing? You could have sent that with a couple of keystrokes."

"I was safeguarding the controls." Holloway started backing away. "In the middle of that melee, if someone bumped them accidentally, it could've . . ."

Rollins walked slowly over to Holloway's desk and pulled a copy of *Enthalpy* from the ecogoth's briefcase. "Interesting reading, Craig. That Stetson guy is pretty thought provoking, isn't he?"

Now the predatory eyes turned to the ecogoth, who looked more and more like a cornered rat. "You guys want to scapegoat me! You're going to blame me for your own screw ups. Fine, go ahead and say I did it. Tell the world that I saved the Earth. Send me to prison if you like, I don't care. You technofreaks think you're so smart with all your gadgets, but you never think of the consequences of what you're doing. Doesn't it mean anything to you that if those astronauts come home, it could mean death to every living thing on this planet? Don't you even care?"

Mason exchanged a knowing look with Gibbs, then motioned to two security guards by the door. "Get this piece of garbage out of here."

As the guards handcuffed Holloway and led him out, Gibbs turned to Logan. "Well, Tex, there's your man."

Logan appeared thoughtful, as if he was not quite convinced. "Seems that way."

Mason picked up his phone. "This is Phil Mason in Mission Control. Get me Administrator Ryan."

WHITE HOUSE MEETING ROOM
FEB. 4, 2012 13:00 CST

Several hours later, a glum group consisting of the President and the First Lady, NASA Administrator Ryan, Surgeon General Wong, political strategist Wilson, Media Chief Wexler, Science and Security Advisor Kowalski, and General Winters met again in the Adams Room to consider the Administration's options.

"Mr. President," the political strategist began, "the situation has deteriorated considerably. The examining board's decision has provoked massive public opposition, regardless of the scientific considerations. Our mail right now is running three to one against mounting any kind of rescue effort. It's even worse on the Hill and among the European allies."

"That's because the public is still being stoked by the media in an anti-NASA direction," Media Chief Wexler interjected. "But let me tell you something, I was a journalist once, and I know how these people react. They don't care about rational arguments. They're like cannibals. Right now they're demanding that you abandon the astronauts, but the instant you *do it* they will turn on you and rip you to shreds for betraying America's heroes."

The President looked from his policy strategist to his press secretary and shook his head. "I know. I'm damned if I do and damned if I don't. If I maroon the crew, everyone in the country will call me a Judas, but if I try to bring them home, I'll alienate the allies, and I'll have to use so much muscle to get the congressional votes needed to fund a rescue that the Party will split, and we'll be doomed this November anyway. There's just no way out. We're ruined."

The First Lady almost offered her distraught husband a handkerchief, but refrained for appearance's sake. "Let's think about this, dear," she chided. "I'm sure this problem has a simple solution, and we can find it if we just focus and use a little elementary logic."

The great man turned his red eyes on his wife. "I've

learned by now that your thinking cap is always on, Margaret. What do you think our answer might be?"

The First Lady bridged her fingers thoughtfully. Her eyes became hard and calculating. "The press will annihilate us unless we at least put out the call to rescue the crew. So we formally request a rescue mission. But we know we'll lose all our friends in Congress if we *force* them to go along . . . so we don't force them. And if we don't pressure Congress to vote our way, they won't, and at the end of the day, a rescue expedition will never be funded, thus satisfying the Europeans. You see, everyone will be happy."

"Except for . . ." Wexler's interruption was cut short by the policy strategist.

"That's great. That'll work like a charm," Wilson shouted.

The President felt as if he were floating on air. He squeezed the First Lady's hand. "Honey, I don't know what I would do without you."

NASA Administrator Tom Ryan was not pleased. "Mr. President, these are human lives we're talking about here. Brave men and women, five of America's finest. We sent them there, and we can't just abandon them."

"Now, Tom, no one's being abandoned." The President was calm, authoritative, back in control. "Our position is that a rescue expedition should be funded. If Congress votes us the funds, we'll do it. Admittedly, the chances of that happening are remote, but we have to be practical. If I use the power of this office to lean on Congress, we'll lose the upcoming election, and next spring when time comes to launch, the political opposition will be right here in the White House, and the mission will be canceled anyway. But if we stay cool and all play the parts we need to play in order to win this fall, then next year, when all this fuss has calmed down, I will bring in the House and Senate leaders and do a little hard bargaining. We'll get the funds next year. Just be patient."

"But if we don't push for funds this year," Ryan persisted, "we won't be able to launch the resupply flight in

2013 or early 2014, and the next window isn't until two years later. The crew will starve by then."

"Not necessarily, Tom." Kowalski spoke in the tones of sweet reason. "The *Beagle* is carrying a demonstration greenhouse unit. If the crew makes good use of it, they could grow enough food to last until . . ."

Ryan was flustered. "The greenhouse is just a small experimental unit! It's doubtful that it could produce enough food to sustain one person, let alone five."

The President was not impressed. Ryan clearly needed to stop emoting and get with the program. "Well, if necessary, it will just have to do. This discussion is closed. It's a difficult situation, and I know that we all have very strong feelings about it, but our game plan is set and I expect all of you to be team players. Is that understood?"

There was a moment of silence. Wexler and Ryan shared glances, searching each other's face for some useful support, but found none. "Yes, Mr. President," they both said, in chorus with the rest.

The First Lady was radiant. "I'm sure everything will work out just fine."

CHAPTER 13

THE DEMORALIZED CREW GATHERED IN THE GALLEY OF THE *Beagle,* doing a great deal of nothing. Gwen looked up from her third re-reading of the transcript of the President's statement and the accompanying encouraging remarks from Mission Control.

"They're lying to us, they're all lying to us." She gritted her teeth in frustration. "They're going to let us die and not even look us in the eyes when they give the death sentence."

Luke ignored her, choosing instead to zonk out to the music of Hank Williams crooning about melting someone's cold, cold heart, until Rebecca abruptly slapped off the audio. In its place, the chords of a Bach toccata filled the cabin.

The Texan geologist looked up in irritation. "Can't a man give his soul a little peace without that organ-grinder nonsense?"

"Organ grinder! This happens to be a work of musical genius by Johann Sebastian Bach, you ignorant redneck."

Gwen snapped at the doctor, "None of this would have

happened if not for you and your damned germs."

Rebecca was taken aback, but only for a moment. "*My* damn germs? I thought it was your God who created life, or didn't you read Genesis at North Carolina Christian Tech?"

"Shut up, all of you. You're squabbling like a bunch of snot-nosed school kids." With all the authority he could muster, Townsend switched the audio to a John Philip Sousa march. "Patriotic music, that's the spirit we need now."

For a full minute no one spoke, then McGee began quietly. "Gwen's right about one thing, Colonel—they are lying to us. I got the straight story from my friend Wex at the White House. There will be no push for funding a relief expedition this year, which means no resupply launched in 2013 or early 2014. Maybe in 2016 at the soonest, but that means no possibility of return until 2018. We're here for the duration."

"Yes, I know. I got the same message through my back channel from the Joint Chiefs."

"Not until 2018!" Luke exclaimed. "That's six years from now. We only have supplies for two years at most."

McGee nodded in agreement with the geologist's facts, but continued with his own conclusion. "We've got to start thinking about how to stretch our resources for long-term survival."

The thought of positive action stiffened the colonel's spine. Somewhere in his soul a dormant faculty of his mind awoke. "Right. Dr. Sherman, how low can we cut our rations and still maintain strength?"

"For an extended period, no less than three-quarters of the NASA minimum standard. The meals we're used to have been about twenty percent larger than the NASA minimum."

Townsend felt his belly, which in recent years had pouched a bit heavier than desired. *Think of this as an opportunity to get back into shape, Andy.* He grinned inwardly. "Well, so much for high living. Effective immediately, the whole crew will be placed on rations, seventy-five percent of NASA minimum."

Luke shook his head. "That still won't get us there."

The colonel was unflappable. "I know, we still need more food. I want that greenhouse powered up ASAP. Dr. Sherman, you're the biologist. Effective immediately, you will suspend your exobiological investigations and devote yourself full-time to the management of the greenhouse unit."

Rebecca smoothed her hair in thought. "It's only an experiment. At maximum design capacity it could produce fifteen, maybe twenty percent of what we need."

"Then modify it, make it produce more than it was designed for."

"Increasing yields above design max won't be easy."

The conversation suddenly became interesting for Gwen. "What would you need?"

Rebecca looked at the resourceful flight mechanic and allowed herself a momentary surge of admiration. *Never say die, eh, Gwen? OK, I'm with you on this.* "In the first place, we'll need additional racks for more plants."

"I can make them."

"And, we'll need more power and light in there. The autonomous photovoltaic array that comes with the greenhouse is too small to support much in the way of crop yield."

That was harder, but after a moment's thought Gwen had a response. "I can run an auxiliary power cable to the greenhouse from the reactor. As for lights, I could pull the landing beacon lights off the ERV, but . . ."

Townsend was firm. "Do it, Major. We're not expecting visitors any time soon."

Rebecca went on. "But light and heat are not enough. We'll need fertilizer."

That caught Luke's attention. "Some of the sediments in the layered terrain to the east are rich in nitrates."

Rebecca nodded. "That's true, and they might do in a pinch. But we still need—"

"Water," McGee concluded, with the hint of a laugh.

"Imagine that. We're the first five Martians, and we'll either find water or die. Percival Lowell predicted it in 1895. He wrote, 'In the Martian mind, there would be one question perpetually paramount to all the local labor, women's suffrage, and Eastern questions put together—the water question. How to procure water enough to support life would be the great communal problem of the day.' "

"Thanks for the literary note, Professor," Townsend commented sourly. "Luke, are there any ice deposits near here?"

"No, surface ice can't last at this latitude. The nearest likely ice deposits are at least two thousand miles to the north."

The mission commander slapped his fist into his palm. "Dammit, that's too far. The rover's one-way range is only six hundred miles."

"When the Israelites were thirsting in the desert," Gwen mused, "the Almighty provided them with water when Moses struck a rock with his staff."

Rebecca felt her temporary admiration for Gwen ebb rapidly. "Too bad real life isn't like storybooks."

Luke, however, appeared inspired. "Hold on, Gwen's got a point. There is some water content in the soil here. Not much, only one percent on average, but two or even three percent in some places."

Three percent water sounded like a lot, but Rebecca knew that it wasn't. "Still too dry to support agriculture, and even if it could, cycling moist soil around the plants would disrupt their root structure to the point where growth would be impossible. We need liquid water."

"If there's some moisture in the soil, can't we bake it out, concentrate it somehow?" McGee suggested.

Townsend turned to the mechanic. "Major?"

"Microwaves might work. We'd need a powerful source."

"The lab autoclave?" Rebecca offered.

"Much too small." Gwen thought furiously. "Wait, the spare S-band TWTA transponder is rated at five kilowatts rf.

I could jury-rig a wave-guide out of some of the aluminum tanks from the *Beagle*'s landing stage, and use another tank as an oven. You'd have to shovel the dirt in manually, then close it except for a vent line that would be wound as a condenser tube. It wouldn't be portable, because we'll need the power of the reactor to drive it . . . but I think it could work."

Maybe, Townsend thought, *except for one thing.* "But if it's not portable, we'll need fuel for the rover to transport the high-grade dirt." *And we're out of gas. Death is in the details.*

The hope that had animated the room only moments before disappeared from all except McGee, who apparently had not understood the implications of the colonel's last remark. "Why are you all so down? You heard Gwen, we've got the answer."

Luke looked at the historian with disdain. "But we don't have the fuel."

"Yes, we do."

"Excuse me, Professor?" Townsend said.

"Sure, we've got it. Last week, I was having so much trouble piping propellant from the ERV's ascent stage fuel tanks to the rover, that I transferred five tonnes to its landing stage, where it would be easier to reach. The JSC saboteur only emptied the ascent stages. We still have enough fuel to drive around."

Townsend leaned back in his chair and slowly allowed a smile to fill his face. "What do you know? Even laziness has its points." Then he leaned forward and the smile was gone, replaced by the mask of command. "All right, then, we have work to do. Dr. Sherman, to the greenhouse. Major Llewellyn, I'll assist you in the fabrication work. Luke, McGee, you two rig the trailer cart to the rover and go fetch us a load of the wettest dirt you can find. Move!"

With grim determination, the crew went to work, fighting not for science or for glory, but for their own survival. Within hours of the meeting, Rebecca transformed from a

world-class exobiologist to a scientific gardener. While
Gwen and Townsend worked overtime to fashion additional
plant racks from scrap material, Luke and McGee under-
took sorties to gather soil samples, which Rebecca tested
meticulously for mineral and nutrient content. They found
nitrates, and all Martian soils were rich in iron and sulfur
by terrestrial standards. As for the rest of the required plant
nutrients, all the samples tested were overrich in some and
deficient in others, but Rebecca was able to synthesize a
satisfactory mix. To this growth medium, she added waste
from the ship's galley recycler and various strains of de-
composing bacteria. *It might not be a bestseller at the soil
section of a suburban plant nursery,* she thought, *but it
ought to do the trick.*

As the soil racks filled, Gwen and Townsend augmented
the greenhouse's power supply. While rated at 100 kW, the
base reactor was only required to put out that much power
when synthesizing propellant to fill the ERV. That phase
of its life had ended before the crew had ever launched
from Earth. Since then, the reactor had only to meet the
Beagle's life-support-system requirements, which rarely ex-
ceeded ten kilowatts, never more than twenty. This meant
eighty kilowatts of spare power was available, round-the-
clock. Cables were run out from the reactor, allowing up
to 50 kW of extra power to light and heat the greenhouse,
as necessary. Another 30 kW was made available for the
microwave oven to bake water out of the Martian soil. The
power allotments were more than ample. *Thank God for
that nuke,* Gwen thought.

Moving the landing beacons from the ERV to the greenhouse took less than a day, but the construction of the
microwave oven was considerably more complex. Nevertheless, Gwen was up to the job, and the spare S-band Traveling Wave Tube Antenna, or "tweeta," was pulled out of
the *Beagle*'s communication bus and reinstalled on a simple
platform within an aluminum pipe that Gwen pulled from
the ship's now-useless landing stage.

The S-band unit worked at a frequency of 2.5 GHz, very

close to the 2.45 GHz commonly used in kitchen microwave ovens on Earth, whose resonance allows for very efficient heating of water. At this frequency, its emitted radiation had a wavelength of 12 cm, or five inches, which allowed the five-inch-diameter landing-stage pipe to function as an excellent wave-guide. Since the fittings were already in place to attach this tube to an aluminum landing-stage propellant tank, setting that up as the oven was straightforward, with the tank's pressure vent ports providing a means to extract the water vapor produced from heating the soil. The hardest part was cutting a porthole in the tank to allow soil to be shoveled in, then fabricating a leakproof flange to close the hole while heating was underway. Gwen was able to do this with only the help of hand tools plus the miniature lathe, mill, drill press, and buzz saw on the *Beagle*'s lower deck—a testament to skill that few but an expert machinist could appreciate.

As the oven was completed, the search for water—or damp soil—began. Luke suggested the dry lake bed, so he and McGee went there first. The dirt at the surface proved to be as dry as any on Mars, but a foot beneath the surface they found spots where the soil water content approached three percent. The two men dug out a trailer load and returned to the base. Finally, about a hundred pounds of this (really not very wet) material was shoveled into the oven.

Gwen sealed the port and threw the switch. A humming sound throbbed through the suits of the anxiously watching crew, as stray S-band emissions interfered with their radios.

Other than the hum, nothing seemed to happen. Gwen put her glove on the exit pipe from the oven vent. Patiently she waited, feeling nothing. Then she felt it: first vibration, then heat. Steam in the pipe! She ran to the other end of the apparatus where the transparent condenser was rapidly clouding over; water droplets began to form.

Less than an hour later, Gwen held aloft a transparent plastic gallon container, more than half filled with water. As the crew cheered, Gwen lifted her eyes in a silent prayer of thanks to He who dwelt beyond the purple Martian skies.

Thank you Lord, for this bounty. May we prove worthy of it.

Rebecca ran off to test a water sample; it would be useless if it was excessively saline or contained toxic elements. It tested pure.

Not bad, she thought wryly. *On any planet, if you want a good still, find yourself a hillbilly.* She poured the contents of the plastic jug into a rack of seedlings in the greenhouse.

The next day she did the same, and over the following two months as the crew dug more soil and produced more water, the seedlings grew, until every rack was filled with leafy greens.

But as the plants grew more lush, on low rations the crew grew thinner and hungrier.

HOUSTON
MARCH 15, 2012 15:20 CST

Craig Holloway left the courtroom to the catcalls of disappointed multitudes. It was horrible to be the object of popular rage and scorn, but at least the pretrial hearing had turned out well. Put simply, the government didn't have enough evidence to hold him.

The citizens of Houston were rude, though—very rude. Holloway winced as he passed several holding a noose. "You'll hang, Holloway!" But despite their verbal ferocity, no one in the crowd made any attempt at physical assault. Against his expectations, Holloway made it to his electrocycle in one piece.

Negotiating the usual set of detours caused by downtown Houston's endless road construction, Holloway rode on to Interstate 45 and headed south toward his home in Clear Lake. Quiet and clean, the electrocycle was dwarfed in size, sound, and odor by the surrounding traffic, but its iron-ion battery could move it at sixty for ten hours. A devout ecogoth, Holloway would drive nothing else. It was his contribution to saving the Earth.

The situation was laughable. Half the people at Mission Control believed he had dumped the ERV propellant, but they couldn't prove a thing because they had no idea how he'd done it. When it came to computational literacy, NASA was a joke.

Holloway recalled the story of how in 1997, the space agency had finally upgraded the space-shuttle computers to IBM 386's, thereby making the organization only eight years behind the average technology available at Radio Shack. They were even further behind today.

The idiots had examined his transmission for fuel-dumping instructions. Of course they had found none. As if he'd be dumb enough to do it by attaching an executable code to E-mail.

In his younger days, Holloway had been a serious recreational hacker and he still liked to keep his hand in. Self-erasing nano-encryption was an elementary technique for transmitting hidden programs. Apparently the self-described "techno-wizards" at Mission Control had not even heard of it. *What a bunch of bozos!*

And those nitwits presumed to gamble with the fate of the Earth. Not one of them cared a whit about the fact that the success of their precious mission could cause a global pandemic. Not one of them bothered to think for a minute about the ecological devastation that would ensue if the biotech industry ever got its hands on Martian DNA and started playing some of the Frankenplant crop-engineering games that Rebecca Sherman was already talking about.

Rebecca Sherman—now there was a piece of work. She pretended to be so enlightened, and so concerned about the welfare of the planet. Years ago, during the Desert War, they had both briefly been members of the Houston Peace Coalition. Yet her ideas of people adopting the role of agents of environmental improvement by spreading life were clearly nothing other than unreconstructed humanism. He had once offered to show her the errors of her ways by asking her out on a private date, where their differences could be worked out in a comfortable and intimate setting. But she had just laughed at him.

So much for NASA's enlightened intellectual.

Mason, Rollins, and the rest could eat crow. And as for the delightful crew of Bombs-Away Townsend, Saint Guenevere, "Hoss Cartwright" Johnson, Manifest Destiny McGee, and Rebecca the Ice Princess, they could sign their advertising endorsement contracts from Mars.

The Earth would do just fine without them.

CHAPTER 14

DINNERTIME ON MARS. A TIRED-LOOKING CREW SAT down to eat, and as they stared at their meager rations, Rebecca entered the galley carrying a small tray of fresh greens with a few small radishes. "Here it is, folks. Our first harvest. Get ready for Thanksgiving dinner."

Luke regarded the tray with contempt. "Now that is what I call one pretty little salad bar. Pretty little, that is."

"Maybe you'd prefer one pretty little punch in the mouth," Rebecca retorted. "Do you have any idea how hard I worked to raise these things?"

Townsend gave the time-out signal. "That's enough. We're all working hard. Dr. Sherman, what's the projected greenhouse yield rate?"

Rebecca managed to calm herself. "Actually, much better than I ever expected. We've packed it to the gills with racks and maxed out the possible rates of nutrient, water, and power flows. I don't see how any further improvements are possible. But with the cycle we have going now, the greenhouse will soon be functioning at a level that would allow it to support three people indefinitely."

"Which three did you have in mind?" Gwen glared at the biologist.

There was a moment of shocked silence in the galley.

Townsend cleared his throat. "That remark was uncalled for, Major. If we can maintain these yields, then by combining the greenhouse output with short rationing of the *Beagle*'s supplies, we can last until a resupply ship makes it out in late 2016."

Gwen was unconvinced. "*If* a resupply ship is sent out in 2016."

Townsend slammed his fist down on the table. "It will be."

"You don't know that, Colonel," Luke stated in a matter-of-fact drawl.

"No, I don't, but I believe it. We've all got to believe it." The mission commander looked around the room, fighting hard to suppress his own feeling of inner hysteria. "We can't give up hope. We can make it if we don't give up hope, and if we don't start tearing each other up."

Observing how Townsend's insistence was having the opposite of the intended effect, McGee wisely changed the subject. "Those radishes look awfully good, Rebecca. Mind if I try one?"

Gratified to have at least one appreciative customer, she smiled. "One, Kevin. Just one. There's one for each of us, unless of course Dr. Johnson here doesn't care to partake of this humble fare."

The geologist had spent the last several minutes staring at Rebecca's greens, and as small as they were, their freshness had overcome his resistance. "No, no, I'll do my part." He hastily snatched his portion.

Though they ate slowly, it did not take long to consume the meager amounts. Still, Townsend realized that the first harvest on Mars needed to be regarded as an event of some significance. *This really is our Thanksgiving dinner,* he thought. *Let's treat it that way.*

Pretending to be full, he patted his belly, which two months of hard digging had transformed into a washboard that would have been applauded by any Air Force fitness instructor. "Well, that was excellent. Why don't we celebrate our first harvest a little? Professor, would you mind singing us one of your songs?"

McGee was surprised at such a request from Colonel Townsend, but felt that a celebration was in order, too. "Okay."

Gwen's eyes were suddenly filled with longing. "Make it something about home."

It took McGee only a moment to retrieve the undersized guitar from his berth. Seating himself, he strummed a few chords to tune his instrument. "All right, Gwen, here's to home." He began to sing softly:

> *Oh, Shenandoah, I long to hear you.*
> *Away, you rolling river.*
> *Oh, Shenandoah, I can't get near you.*
> *Away, away, I'm bound away*
> *Across the wide Missouri.*

As McGee strummed on, tears began to form in the corners of the major's eyes. Noting the effect the song was having on her, Luke decided to join in, leaning closer to the flight mechanic. "I'll take it from here.

> *Shenandoah, I love your daughter.*
> *Away, you rolling river.*
> *I'll take her across the yellow water.*
> *Away, away, I'm bound away*
> *Across the wide Missouri.*

The lusty way Luke sang made Gwen blush a bit. She rewarded the Texan geologist with her smile and attention, yet her eyes kept straying back to McGee, who softly continued his accompaniment on the guitar.

OPHIR PLANUM
MAY 26, 2012 18:15 MLT

The television screen showed thousands of people, hundreds of thousands, filling New York's Central Park with banners and green crosses. From the bandstand, opposition presidential candidate Senator Matt Fairchild raved to the cheering multitudes, saying exactly what they wanted to hear.

As Gwen watched in disgust, the pandering politician raised his hands with double V for victory signs to exult in the roaring approval of his supporters. Mercifully, the video clip ended and was followed by a newscaster at his desk addressing other events.

McGee turned from the newscast to pull the mission commander aside. "Colonel, I have bad news from my political friend in the White House. A secret poll conducted by the Administration shows things heading full-speed toward a loss in November. If that happens, our chance of a rescue flight drops to nil."

Townsend nodded. "Still, it's not over until—"

"Damnation!" Gwen shouted, suddenly interrupting them all.

Startled by the outburst, the colonel turned to her. "What happened?"

"The Braves lost again."

McGee exchanged a significant glance with Townsend. "Colonel, deep inside, every member of this crew knows no relief is coming, so they're all beginning to withdraw. I've seen this before, in the Arctic. Gwen's slipping into fantasy. Rebecca's gone silent, walling herself off from the rest of the crew."

Townsend frowned. "Doesn't sound too healthy."

Rebecca, who had just emerged from the lab, overheard the remark. "Healthy! I'll tell you what would be *healthy*. We should stop marking time and start thinking of a way to get ourselves out of this mess."

The colonel regarded her coolly. "And how would you recommend we do that, Doctor?"

Rebecca's eyes were filled with fire. "We're currently producing a lot more water than we need for the greenhouse. I say we electrolyze the excess and start making rocket fuel! Let's get home by ourselves."

Townsend shook his head. "I've looked into that. At our current rate of water extraction, if we used the excess as propellant feedstock, it would take a decade to produce enough fuel to drive the ERV home. Rescue is certainly more likely by then. We're better off keeping the water as a reserve for our consumable stock."

"No we're not. McGee may be playing amateur shrink, but his points are on the mark. This crew is cracking up. There's no way we'll last ten years, or even four. We've got to fight our way out of here, Colonel—this year, or it's all over."

"I admire your spirit, Doctor, but what you're suggesting is impossible. We'd have to up our water production rate by ten times."

"Five and a half times," Rebecca corrected. "Half of our current extraction is going to the greenhouse."

Townsend looked at her. In the past, Rebecca's appearance had always been immaculate, her manner calm, her logic impeccable. Now her hair was uncombed, her clothes unkempt. Perhaps her mind was even unbalanced. *Cracking up indeed.* He began to answer slowly. "Five and a half times, then. It's still imp—"

"No it's not!" She placed both of her fists on the table and leaned over to look the colonel in the eye. "Our current rate is based upon one two-man, six-hour digging shift per day. If we go to two two-person shifts, each twelve hours long, we'd have four times the soil throughput."

"Still not enough."

"It could be," Luke mused, coming into the discussion. "The deeper soil is likely to have greater moisture content than the stuff we've been shoveling."

"Precisely!" Rebecca welcomed this support from an unexpected quarter.

"But we still don't have the manpower to sustain even that level of effort."

Taking offense, Rebecca walked several steps from the table and then whirled around to face Townsend again. "Manpower? There are five of us here, Colonel. We can all dig."

Oh shit, Townsend thought, *here comes another feminist tirade.* He gave her a condescending smile. "Dr. Sherman, I'm sure you have your modern theories about the roles of men and women, but even in the face of death there are certain values worth defending."

"Screw your values, Colonel," Gwen interjected unexpectedly. "I don't want to die."

"Major, I'm just trying to make clear that . . ."

"You're a gentleman and a jackass." Gwen was unstoppable. "Look, you may be half a watermelon taller than me, sir, but I'm a miner's daughter, and I've done more hard work in my time than you or anyone in your family has done for the past hundred years. I can out-dig you any day of the week. The professor, too."

Townsend had to smile. "Okay, perhaps you can. But Dr. Sherman? I doubt she has ever used a pick and shovel in her entire life."

"I learn fast," Rebecca said firmly.

"Do you realize what you're talking about, Doctor? Long, grueling hours of hard physical labor, day after day, week after week."

"I can take it. I'm sitting here with the most important scientific discovery in human history, and I'm going to get back to Earth to present it, or I'll know the reason why."

The colonel turned to the muscular mission geologist. "Luke, where do you stand?"

"With the ladies, of course."

"Professor?"

McGee rubbed his chin. "I'm reminded of other expeditions that were stranded in remote locations, Shackleton's

1914 attempt on the South Pole, for example—"

Townsend cut him off. "Bottom line, McGee, your *vote*."

"I think Rebecca's right." McGee's voice was level. "We'll save ourselves or no one will. It may be futile, Colonel, but I'm game."

They've just volunteered to quadruple their workload, Townsend thought. Looking over his crew, he felt a warm glow of pride. *Maybe this bunch of prima donnas has the Right Stuff, after all.* He cleared his throat and summoned his command voice. "In that case, I'll make it unanimous. We start tomorrow, two duty shifts every day, each twelve hours, with one person, rotated daily, assigned to light duty around the greenhouse and Hab. That'll give each of us a day off from hard labor one day in five. . . ."

OPHIR PLANUM
MAY 27, 2012 07:00 MLT

The sun had been up barely an hour when Rebecca and Luke reached their digging site.

Rebecca gripped her shovel and tried to fight the sinking feeling inside her. She hated hard physical labor and had generally managed to avoid it all her life. There had been one exception: Devon Island in the summer of 2000. She had been there to be part of the initial crew of the Mars Society's Flashline Mars Arctic Research Station. However, when the crane sent in to build the station was destroyed in a failed paradrop, and the professional construction crew had deserted, the scientists were left to their own resources. They had rallied and, together with some Inuit youth who hired on, and some unsuspecting journalists who were pressed into service upon arrival, had managed to get the station built using brute-force ancient Roman construction techniques. It had been horrible, dangerous labor, involving fourteen-hour workdays in the high Arctic, but its success was critical for the cause, and Rebecca had pitched in as part of the team. The memory of that adventure gave her strength; it had given her the courage to become an astronaut.

But she had been twenty-eight then, and as tough as the Flashline construction work had been, it had only lasted a few weeks. Now, because of her own big mouth, here she was, at the bottom of an ancient Martian pond basin, preparing to dig—and do nothing but dig, all day, nearly every day, for the next year. The bleak prospect filled her with dread. Intellectually, she knew it had to be done, and she had managed to convince the others. But now the reality confronted her. She stared down at the barely moist dirt in dismay. Somehow, she couldn't move.

Luke Johnson held his gloved hands in front of his helmet and pretended to spit on each one. Then he thrust his shovel deep into the ground and heaved a huge lump of dirt into the trailer. Then another, and another. At last, he paused. "Well, little lady, care to get started?"

The redneck bastard, thought Rebecca. *He knows what I'm feeling. He thinks I'm not up to this.* She dug her shovel into the ground and lifted it. Her load was tiny compared to the geologist's, but it seemed heavy to her, even in the low gravity. She walked two steps to dump it into the trailer, losing most of it along the way. It was a pathetic first effort, and she knew it. Without looking, she could sense the malicious grin on Luke's face. She dug another scoop, larger than the first, and managed to get most of it in the cart. *There.* She looked at Luke in triumph.

The muscular geologist acknowledged her effort and started shoveling again, throwing load after load into the cart with the smooth flowing motion of a practiced ditch digger. Rebecca had no choice but to try to imitate him.

She shoveled for what seemed like an eternity. After a while her hip muscles started to ache. *When do we break? How long have we been doing this?* She looked at her chronometer. The answer came with a shock: forty-three minutes.

Another five hours, seventeen minutes, until lunch. Her body told her it was impossible. But cold Reason argued the contrary: *For the past five thousand years, most humans have labored this way. If they could do it, I can do it.*

Somehow she made it to lunch, though her every muscle was demanding that she stop. By the end of the day, she was numb beyond aching. But she kept moving, her limbs driven more by spirit than body.

Back at the Hab, she silently ate the briefest of dinners and collapsed into her bunk. Then, seemingly in seconds, her alarm rang.

It was dawn, and time to dig again.

OPHIR PLANUM
JUNE 3, 2012 16:20 MLT

Rebecca moved about the greenhouse, stiff limbs turning her previously graceful walk into a semi-stagger. All around her, plants bloomed, their odors filling the air; while not exactly fragrant, it still told the good news of the ex- uberance of life.

As she transferred seedlings from their beds to the inter- mediate growth bin, the doctor felt her spirits rise a little. Eight days since the full-scale digging effort had com- menced, this was her second greenhouse break-day. During her first day off, she'd been too numb to do more than stumble through the motions. While still dog-tired, her head had now cleared enough so she could begin to take stock of the situation.

The past week had been pure hell. By the fifth day of digging, she had fallen into a kind of exhausted trance, which had helped her make it through. But as useful as such a state might be in helping one sleep through a day of digging, she knew it could be a dangerous frame of mind. They were on *Mars,* after all, and the slightest mis- take could be fatal.

On the first day, she'd been too tired to eat much, but hunger had set in the following morning. The workload had increased everyone's appetite, and by the fourth day it was apparent that the previous short rations could not be maintained. Rebecca increased their allotments from seventy percent to one hundred percent NASA minimum . . . then to one hundred twenty percent, then to one hundred fifty percent.

No one seemed to notice. Even doubled, the meals were still modest, and the hungry crew gobbled them quickly. But Rebecca knew they had crossed a divide. By increasing the rations, she was throwing away all possibility that the five of them would last until the 2015 return window. If they continued to consume their larder at this rate, the crew would have to make it out in 2013, or else starve.

She felt her sore arm. The muscle had become a lot tougher. While she could never match the others' digging, she was becoming stronger and more productive with time. That was good. It wasn't just a matter of pride. She had done the math: Without her pitching in, they simply couldn't make it.

Rebecca watered the plants carefully. Thanks to the increased efforts, more water was available; barrels were now being carted over from the oven to the ERV for use in the propellant-making unit. She had been tempted to request more for the greenhouse and for the personal hygiene unit, but had resisted the impulse. Propellant was everything. If used with precision, the present greenhouse water allotment was enough.

Accumulated sweat and grime made the biologist itch. If only she could wash. She shuddered at how unkempt she'd appeared in the mirror that morning. What she would give for a shower, or even a sponge bath! But the logistics calculations were clear: Washing would just have to wait.

She hesitated; something seemed wrong. She stopped what she was doing. It was the sound. The greenhouse was too quiet. The ventilation fans had stopped working.

Stiff, she hobbled over to the control panel, which revealed the source of the problem clearly enough. Fuse 16 had burned out. *Easy enough to fix.* She opened the fuse box and looked inside. Sure enough, Fuse 16, a 1-amp unit, was fried. She pulled out a spare and replaced it, then opened the log to record the repair.

There, she spotted a notation written with a shaky stylus: "F16, replaced by GL, 6/2/12." So Gwen had replaced the fuse yesterday. *Curious that it should burn out so fast.*

Rebecca opened the unit manual and called up the specs for Fuse 16. That was strange: A 1.5-amp unit was specified. Yet Gwen had used a 1-amp fuse. It was certainly very unusual for the flight mechanic to make such a mistake.

Rebecca removed her 1-amp fuse again and inserted a properly specified 1.5-amp unit. When she threw the restart switch, she was gratified to hear the renewed hum of the greenhouse ventilators. Then she relaxed a bit.

She hadn't been in immediate danger, but it was a scary thought that if she hadn't noticed the ventilator failure promptly, she might have been overcome by a toxic overdose of carbon dioxide. It was already late afternoon, and without the ventilator, CO_2 would have built up within the greenhouse as the reduced solar light level caused photosynthesis rates to drop.

She checked the CO_2 monitor. It read yellow—outside of recommended limits, though not yet unsafe.

So why hadn't a warning sounded? She checked the alarm circuit, and discovered that it ran through Fuse 16. A chill ran down her spine. *I almost just bought the farm.*

Tiny mistakes like that could kill. She realized with a start that she was not the only one who was played out. Her companions might manage bigger shovel loads than she, but the rest of the crew—who had been tired enough before the intensified effort—were also transitioning into mental numbness.

She thought of how they would stagger into the Hab after a day's shift, lurching out of bed in the morning, becoming increasingly unkempt, punch-drunk, worn out. How long could they keep this up? As the crew wore itself out, so would their machines. And with increasing frequency, that would force repair jobs upon an ever-more exhausted Gwen. Formerly simple repairs would become hard, and formerly dependable work would become unreliable.

But they had no choice. It was launch in 2013, or nothing.

As the sun went down, Rebecca limped from the greenhouse to greet her returning crewmates.

HOUSTON
JUNE 15, 2012 12:30 CST

Dr. George Kowalski pushed his plate away and glanced impatiently around the private dining room in the Nassau Bay Hilton. The food had been acceptable, but Darrell Gibbs had already kept him waiting long enough. The Science and Security Advisor did not like to reveal his interest in certain delicate matters by forcing the conversation, but it was time to get down to business. "So, Darrell, have you completed your investigation into the events of January twenty-eighth?"

The Special Assistant faced his boss. "Yes, sir. I followed through, using our hand-picked people exclusively, just as you ordered. There's no doubt about it—the propellant dumping was done by Holloway."

Kowalski leaned back in his chair, surprised. "Are you sure? The NASA probe of his data transmission showed no appended instructions. FBI's keystroke-by-keystroke analysis of the internal video of Holloway's moves during the riot showed he did nothing more than transmit that harmless data file."

Gibbs smiled. "It wasn't harmless."

"No?"

"It included a self-erasing nano-encryption."

Kowalski raised his eyebrows. "He used a SENE? Really?"

Gibbs nodded.

"Clever boy," Kowalski said with genuine admiration. "So, does he have an intelligence background?"

"None. Not with us or anyone else."

"Then how? SENE technology is top secret."

"Apparently he picked up the trick in the M.I.T. Hacker's Club five years ago."

"You're kidding."

Gibbs spread his hands, palms outward, and shook his head.

Kowalski began to laugh, but managed to suppress his reaction. The scenario was hilarious. The government, under his direction, had spent $14 billion to develop SENE capabilities. Now it appeared that some M.I.T. brats had duplicated the feat in their spare time—at least three years before the Science and Security Advisor.

Gibbs waited for his boss to calm down, then he posed the obvious question. "So, do we pick him up?"

Kowalski steepled his fingers, thinking. This was a very interesting situation. Finally, he said, "No, I don't think so. That would be giving too much away. Don't you agree?"

Gibbs regarded his superior quietly. Keeping SENE from public view was a credible rationale for not arresting Holloway. However, Darrell Gibbs was anything but naive, and it was clear that more was involved here. This time the SSA was asking a great deal of him.

If Holloway remained free, it was quite conceivable that he could strike again, even from a distance, especially if it started to look like the crew had some chance of making it home. The Science and Security Advisor's views on the back-contamination issue were well known, but there was probably another hidden agenda beyond that.

Gibbs thought fast. Clearly, his future lay with Kowalski . . . but it would be best if all the cards were on the table. He framed his answer accordingly. "Certainly, sir. And I have to say, that while Holloway's illegal actions were reprehensible, it's clear to me that he acted only on the basis of the purist motives."

Kowalski glanced sharply at his assistant. "Pure motives" was SSA slang for fanaticism.

Gibbs didn't flinch. "I think it would be a shame for someone who has so much to offer the nation to spend the rest of his life in prison."

Kowalski smiled inwardly. He had chosen his protégé well. "So, you think Holloway may prove to be a national resource someday?"

"Quite possibly . . . if he feels called upon."

The SSA shared meaningful eye contact with his Special Assistant. "It's good to know that there are still young men willing to put themselves on the line for their convictions."

"I quite agree, sir," Gibbs replied.

CHAPTER 15

AFTER TWO MONTHS OF NONSTOP, BACK-BREAKING work, the crew took the day off. It was the anniversary of the Apollo 11 landing on the Moon and the Viking 1 landing on Mars. During the decades that had followed those events, space scientists, astronautical engineers, and activists used this date as a special time for conferences—technical and otherwise.

In 2012, for the first time, Space Day was observed on Mars. The celebration was simple: The crew slept in past noon and spent the afternoon in blissful idleness. In the evening they assembled in the galley to teleconference with Mission Control.

"You've got to stop this maniacal effort," flashed Chief of Operations Mason's video image. "It's no good. You're killing yourselves, and it's not working. Our calculations show that you're way behind on making enough fuel to launch by the time the 2013 Earth return window closes, and at this rate you'll all be dead long before the 2015 window opens. You've got to call it quits. Trust me, a resupply mission is in the works. Leave it to us."

Townsend looked at McGee, who just shook his head. In disgust, the colonel switched off the TV.

Gwen spoke up. "It's not over yet, Colonel. Maybe our present rate is too low, but the soil's getting wetter deeper down. We still might make it."

The commander turned to his geologist. "Luke, is it possible?"

The Texan didn't have the energy to argue. "No. We're too far behind for that to make a difference."

Rebecca slumped in her chair, feeling weak. "It's my fault. All my fault."

Townsend said, "We all agreed with the decision, Doctor. And we're no worse for trying." He stretched his aching back. "Not much, anyway."

"You don't understand." Rebecca shuddered, then appeared to gain control. "In order to maintain the crew's strength over the past several months, I increased the rations drawn from the *Beagle*'s reserve. Well before the 2015 return window opens, we'll have nothing left to eat but the greenhouse output, and that's only enough for three. Max."

McGee decided to lift their spirits with a joke. "Hmm. Just how did the folks at Donner Pass decide who got to be hors d'oeuvres?" It didn't work. Met with scowls from the others for his black humor, the professor retreated. "Okay, another stupid mistake. When will I ever stop putting my footnotes in my mouth?"

Townsend didn't like the way the conversation was going. "Let's get this straight. I'll be damned if I'm going to pick straws or flip coins to see who lives or dies. It's not the American way."

"It may soon become our only rational choice," Rebecca said icily.

Gwen fumed. "I don't care about what an atheist bitch calls 'rational choices.' "

"Major, please!"

Rebecca's face reddened, but otherwise she appeared to ignore Gwen's outburst. "Colonel, the greenhouse is filled to capacity, as is all available space on the Hab's lower deck. The only potential space we're not using is the interior of the pressurized rover." She shrugged. "If we decide to convert the rover into a stationary greenhouse, that might add enough output to allow one more person to survive. Maybe."

"Bad idea," Luke commented. "We need the rover."

The biologist was puzzled. "For what?"

"For prospecting." Now everyone gave him puzzled looks. "Look, we've been going about things the wrong way, processing large volumes of low-grade ore, when we should've been searching for the mother lode."

"What do you mean, mother lode?" Townsend asked.

"A concentrated source of liquid water."

Townsend looked quizzically at the geologist. "There can't be any liquid water on Mars. Even I know that. It's much too cold."

"On the surface, yes. But underground . . ."

Rebecca grasped the concept instantly. "So you believe in the existence of a subsurface Martian water table?"

Luke seemed almost apologetic. "I didn't used to, but the dating of some of my igneous samples shows volcanic action in Tharsis as recently as forty million years ago—in other words, back just one percent of the age of the planet. Might as well be yesterday."

"So . . . that means Mars has a hot core, like Earth?" McGee asked, trying to understand the implications.

"Right. And if the core is hot, then at some depth it must be warm enough for liquid water to exist. It's got to be there, somewhere, because the north polar cap is a low-elevation ice field that almost certainly continues underground as the terrain rises in the Borealis and Acidalia regions. Now, since subsurface ice is stable only above latitudes of about forty degrees—"

Sensing an incipient lecture, Townsend interrupted: "How deep would we have to drill?"

Luke rubbed his chin. "Around here, a kilometer, maybe two."

Dammit, another fantasy scheme. Townsend shook his

head pessimistically. "That's much too deep. Our drilling rig only has a reach of a hundred meters."

"I could double that by hooking the spares in series," Gwen offered.

"Still way too short."

Luke was undaunted. "True, but if we drive the rover down to the lower elevations in Xanthe Terra, the water might be much closer to the surface. We'd need to find a place that has a surface regolith layer of anomalously low thermal conductivity lying over a subsurface layer of high porosity."

Even with his limited knowledge of geology, McGee realized the Texan was describing a long shot. "But something like that has got to be a rare occurrence. We can't drill everywhere. How are we going to find it?"

"Electromagnetic sounding. Send low-frequency radar signals down into the ground. If there's water there, the bounce back will tell you."

Simple enough, Gwen mused, *provided we can produce the right type of signal.* "What frequency?"

"You can generally get down about ten wavelengths, so we'll need a twenty-meter signal."

"Twenty meters, that's fifteen megahertz, HF band," Gwen thought out loud. "Our over-the-horizon radios can access that frequency. I could rig up a quarter wavelength downward-pointing Yagi antenna and attach it to the rover, and put a pulsed modulator on the power amplifier. Then, as we drive along, we—"

"—do some honest prospecting," Luke concluded with a smile.

The colonel was far from convinced. "Now hold on, I've had a bit of experience with ground-penetrating radar in military applications. It's easy to get all kinds of false positives."

"True, we'll probably end up drilling ten dry wells before we hit the real McCoy. But with luck, sooner or later we'll find it. It's a gamble, sure, but I don't see how we have a whole lotta choice."

So now we're relying on luck, Townsend thought. "If we're going to make the launch window, it better be sooner."

Rebecca quickly parameterized the problem. "The probability of a quick find would rise in direct proportion to the intensity of the search."

McGee understood. "So we drive the rover fast and cover a lot of miles. But that means we burn a lot of fuel."

Luke was undeterred. "The ERV's tanks are over one-fifth full. We've got lots of fuel if we tap into that."

"Out of the question," the colonel said firmly. "That propellant is part of our ticket home. Think of all our hard work so far. We can't make the 2013 return window, but if we keep adding to it we can have enough to launch for Earth when the 2015 window opens."

"The three of us still alive, you mean," Gwen commented dryly.

Townsend began to feel confused. "It's a reckless gamble."

Sensing Townsend's weak spot, Gwen pressed the point. "All of us or none of us, Colonel. Isn't that what you said?"

"That was just betting greenhouse margin and wasted labor," he explained. "We knew there was moisture in the soil, and that bet paid off. We now have a way to get home."

"Some of us," Gwen said flatly.

This is so irrational, Townsend thought. "You're asking me to throw away all the work we've done, the only chance we have, on wild speculation." He turned to Rebecca. "Dr. Sherman, you're a scientist. Using your logic and not your emotions, do you really believe in this near-surface water-table theory?"

"No, I don't believe in it," she replied simply, to the horror of most of the crew.

Townsend, however, was gratified. "There! That settles it."

"But I think it is a reasonable hypothesis that should be put to the test."

Rebecca's reversal sent the commander mentally reeling. He turned to the historian. "McGee, where do you stand on all this?"

"Let me put it to you this way, Colonel. If you were deciding for yourself alone, and didn't have a crew to be responsible for, what would you decide?

Townsend paused for a moment and looked out the window, then returned to face the crew with a rueful grin on his face. "You got me there, Professor. If I were flying this solo, I'd go for the drill. But there's more at stake now."

McGee was puzzled. "I don't get what you mean."

"The mission." Townsend tried to appear decisive. "If even some of us get back, the mission will count as a success. We can now be sure of that outcome, simply by continuing our current digging effort, scaled back a bit so we can stand it. If we gamble on Luke's theory, we risk not only our own lives, but the success of the mission. NASA, Mission Control, will never agree."

His lack of inner conviction was apparent to McGee. "Do you really care?"

"Yes I do, Professor," Townsend huffed. "For your information, I happen to be a military man and I believe in following orders."

Gwen wasn't fooled. "Come on, Colonel, cut the crap."

"Major, that remark was—" Townsend looked at the skeptical faces surrounding him and gave up the pretense. "All right, so I don't give a damn what anybody on Earth thinks we should do. This is nuts. You people really want to try it?"

Incredibly, they all nodded in agreement.

He shook his head in wonder. "You're all out of your minds. I don't know what you're doing here. You should have been fighter pilots. Major Llewellyn, in the morning, I want you to start rigging the rover for radar sounding. I'll work on a report to explain our new course of action to Mission Control. And Dr. Sherman . . ."

"Yes?"

"Doctor, I want you to start compiling a psychological dossier on me proving insanity. I'll need it for legal defense at my court-martial."

"Don't worry, Colonel," Rebecca giggled. "If that's your plea, I'm sure I can provide you with an ironclad defense."

"A real sweetheart, isn't she?" the commander muttered to the others.

CHAPTER 16

NEXT DAY, INSTEAD OF RESUMING THEIR DIGGING ROU-
tine, Gwen, Townsend, and McGee set about assembling a
large Yagi antenna out of scrap aluminum stripped from
the ERV and Hab lander stages. The antenna resembled an
old-style TV rooftop antenna, but larger, designed to transmit "short-wave" radio signals that actually have a much
longer wavelength than VHF television. Five meters long,
the device was fitted crosswise across the rear of the rover
and hooked to an oscilloscope that Gwen mounted on the
right seat control panel.

Acting on the basis of a sense of humor unique to engineers, Gwen augmented the retro image of the gear by
wiring in an audio oscillator that pinged every time a radio
pulse was emitted, and sounded a slightly delayed answering ping if an echo signal was received. This gave the
whole setup an operating feel similar to World War II sub-
marine sonar.

Townsend looked at it and frowned. "Why is the audio
necessary, Major, when all relevant data from the radar
sounder is available in fully interpreted digitized form on
the rover's computer display?"

With a wink at McGee, Gwen insisted on the absolute necessity of maintaining a "direct channel analog backup" to the computerized data. The colonel walked away, shaking his head, but the oscilloscope and pinging system stayed in place. Stepping close, Gwen confided to the historian, "Besides, the pinger should make the radar rig a whole lot more fun."

As the construction of the radar set proceeded, Rebecca and Luke spent hours scrutinizing maps, attempting to deduce from available surface geological evidence the most promising locations for underground aquifers. Unfortunately, no locations showed any obvious hints of subsurface water. So where to search?

The rover's maximum speed during sounding would be ten miles per hour, and the sounding data could only be assumed relevant to a quarter mile in either direction from the ground track. This meant that in a ten-hour driving day, they could search fifty square miles. Since the rover's maximum sortie range was 300 miles, a total of about 280,000 square miles was available to be surveyed.

Even at fifty square miles a day, it would take more than fifteen years to scan it all. If the stranded crew were to find water in time to make propellant for the next launch window, they had time to probe only about five percent of the territory available.

While there were no obvious targets, some regions of low-lying topography looked more promising than others. With this in mind, the two scientists drew up a plan for a systematic search of the best five percent their landing zone had to offer.

The search sorties began on July 28, with Townsend driving and Luke at the radar console. Unfortunately, they heard no return echoes that day—or any day in the ensuing three weeks, as various combinations of the crew took turns at radar sounding, tried their luck, and failed.

The radar sounding was not as hard work as digging, though, and as the weeks went by, the crew began to recover from the sheer physical exhaustion of their previous efforts. Nonetheless, as the searches continued to produce only negative results, hope began to fade, and a demoralization even more thorough than before began to settle upon the crew.

Then, early on the afternoon of August 12, with a bored Gwen Llewellyn at the wheel and a daydreaming McGee on radar, an echo was finally returned. The unexpected ping woke the historian out of his stupor. "We got something! We got something! Take a look."

Before Gwen could react, both the amplitude and frequency of the return pulses increased dramatically. She stopped the rover and looked at the oscilloscope trace, then at McGee with wide eyes. "What do you have on digital?"

He punched through several screens of data. "It's great! According to this, the source of the echo is less than a hundred meters down."

The flight mechanic adjusted knobs, kicking in the frequency doubler to increase depth resolution. She stared at the data in amazement and, forcing herself to remain cool, picked up the microphone. "*Beagle,* this is rover, reporting from map coordinate Delta 62.2, Foxtrot 96.8. We may have found something. It's a fast echo, just seventy meters down. If it's water, it's within range."

There was a crackle of static and then Luke's voice came over the receiver. "Send me the data file from your EM soundings so I can have a look."

Gwen threw a switch, opening the radar log upload. "Sending."

For almost a full minute, they heard nothing but static from the receiver. Then the geologist's voice blared forth, loud and clear. "Hehaa! That's water all right."

Gwen reached out and joyously hugged McGee, taking him by surprise. Embarrassed, she pulled back and covered up by getting back to business, while the professor blinked rapidly. *Gwen, is there something going on in your mind that I should know about?*

"Water! We found it! Well, don't just sit there staring

like a silly old egghead, McGee—break out the drilling rig. We've got work to do."

McGee regarded her for a significant moment, then unbuckled his seat belt. "Aye, aye."

Moving quickly, they broke out the drilling rig, which consisted of sets of concentric tubing that could be extended by means of a rotating screw mechanism, a collapsible tripod to hold the upper end in place, an automole with a superhard drill bit to lead the descent, and an electric motor with a set of gears to turn the toothed exterior of the uppermost of the telescoping tubes. Then they ran a power line out to the motor from the auxiliary generator of the rover engine. The two set up the drill and started it running, then climbed back into the rover to pass the time.

Gwen put her feet up on the rover's dashboard and started thumbing through one of McGee's Edgar Rice Burroughs Mars novels, apparently subjecting the pulp adventure story to a systematic scan. McGee found this action curious, causing him to take out his electric notebook and enter a note in his private diary.

"It is strange," McGee wrote while looking thoughtfully at Gwen, "the kind of people you meet if you go to Mars. On the surface, Gwen seems ultra-tough, the ultimate tomboy. A decorated combat veteran, never far from that Bowie knife of hers. Yet something about her is so quiet, soft, peaceful. She's probably seen more of the rough side of the world than any other woman I've met, but somehow she still seems the most innocent. She's very intelligent, yet until now I've never seen her open a book other than the Bible or a technical work. I wonder what practical value she sees in Burroughs' novel. Surely she wouldn't touch it otherwise. She's certainly not my type; what a disaster she'd be at the faculty club! But, in her own way, she's a real gem."

The subject of his contemplation interrupted the historian's reverie.

"Hey, Professor, it says here in your book that there are underground caverns on Mars filled with flowing rivers."

He formed an embarrassed smile. "Gwen, that's a great novel, but it's just a work of fantasy."

Gwen was adamant. "Well, he's right about a lot of other things. Mars does have two moons."

"But no towering cities."

"Not yet, anyway. Right, McGee?" Gwen smiled. There was warmth in that smile.

McGee rushed to check some instruments. "Right. Looks like we're making progress."

The flight engineer returned to business. "Sixty-eight meters. Could hit the water any time now."

The radio crackled. "Rover, this is Luke. We have you approaching the discontinuity within sixty seconds. Keep an eye on the drill-bit temperature. As soon as you hit water, it should drop dramatically."

McGee checked the temperature readouts. "We're reading 560° centigrade now. How far should it drop?"

"Close to zero. Any water this near the surface is going to be icy. That drill bit is in for one heck of a cold bath."

"Sixty-nine meters," Gwen announced.

McGee watched excitedly as the thermal data began to shift. "The temperature's beginning to drop! 558. 555. 553."

Gwen gave a new depth measurement: "Sixty-nine point five meters."

"551. 549. 547. 546," McGee rapidly called out.

"Seventy meters."

"543. 542."

"Seventy point five."

Another burst of static came from the radio. "Luke here. I have you through the discontinuity now. The temperature should be dropping very fast."

"It's still going down," McGee cried. "541. 540. 539—"

"It's not dropping fast enough." All the exhilaration left Luke's voice. "Something's wrong."

"Seventy one meters," Gwen announced coolly.

"538. 537. 537. 538." McGee watched the thermal

data now with growing dismay. "It seems to be leveling off."

"Bad news, children." The geologist sounded as if he was offering condolences. "Looks like you've found a false positive."

McGee felt hollow inside as all hope died. "You mean it's a dry well?"

"More like a radar mirage." Luke's radio voice crackled with authority. "Probably never was anything but two regolith layers with different electrical conductivities."

Gwen's voice was as dry as the well. "Seventy-two meters."

"You might as well stop the drill," Luke advised. "You won't find anything there."

Gwen silenced the drill, then picked up the mike, dropping her professional cool. "Then why did you tell us to drill here, you know-it-all?"

"It looked good," Luke said sheepishly. "But there's no way to tell, for sure. When you get a radar return like that, you just have to drill and see for yourself."

McGee sagged in frustration. "We've searched for two weeks, and all we found was this one mirage. The colonel was right. This isn't going to work."

"I never said it would be easy." Luke sounded defensive. "I told you there'd be false positives. We just have to keep searching and keep drilling. Sooner or later, we're bound to find it."

The crackling static on the radio continued even after Luke disconnected at the other end.

Gwen slammed her fist down on the console. "Damnation!"

CHAPTER 17

NEAR JACKSON HOLE, WYOMING, THERE IS A SUPERLA-
tive golf course favored by the rich, powerful, and famous.
On August 21, 2012, the weather was splendid, and had
any reporters been allowed in, they would have seen cele-
brated personalities from Malibu, the Beltway, Central Park
West, and Silicon Valley. It would not have surprised them
to see a member of the President's inner circle traveling
about the golf course in the company of a well-dressed
young man equipped with a stylish set of clubs.

Darrell Gibbs, liaison to JSC Mission Control, golfed
with George Kowalski, Science and Security Advisor to the
White House. Gibbs was an excellent golfer, and a wise
one too. The game was close, but Kowalski was ahead.

The older man was clearly enjoying himself. "Darrell,
you're a very bright young man. You remind me a lot of
myself at your age. I'm sure you'll go far."

Gibbs grinned; he certainly hoped so. "Thank you, sir."

"Call me George."

"Thank you, George. I must say that I'm grateful for the
promotion to Senior SSA Staff."

"It's just the beginning for you. We need fresh young blood in policy-making positions in Washington."

Policy making, Gibbs thought. *Has a nice ring to it.*

A golf cart approached, and Gibbs was dumbstruck to see its passenger: Senator Fairchild, the opposition's candidate for President. In the cart with him sat a very overweight suit with a laptop, obviously one of the senator's campaign flacks.

Fairchild leaned out of his cart to shake Kowalski's hand. "Hello, George. Fancy meeting you here. How's life as White House Science and Security Advisor treating you?"

Kowalski shrugged. "A bit frustrating . . ."

Fairchild nodded sympathetically. "I know how it must be, stuck in an advisory role when you should be making policy from a Cabinet position."

"Indeed. So how goes the campaign?"

"Rather well," Fairchild chuckled. "Your boss seems to have painted himself into a corner by putting all his political capital into this Mars adventure. His only chance appears to be for a miracle to happen that gets the crew home."

Gibbs had watched this Olympian exchange in awe, but now that the conversation shifted to his own area of expertise, he seized his chance to join in. "I hardly think that's likely," he remarked.

The senator favored Gibbs with a pleased look. "George, you haven't introduced me to your young friend here."

Kowalski put a paternal hand on Gibbs' shoulder. "This is Darrell Gibbs. He's my Special Assistant at JSC Mission Control."

Fairchild gave the younger man a wink and a firm handshake. "Oh, yes, Gibbs. George has been telling me a lot of fine things about you."

The Special Assistant was stunned by the attention, and he responded with his best Ivy League smile. "You've got my vote, Senator."

"Thanks, son, I'm depending on you. Come November,

we'll straighten this country out. Well, I've got to be off. Good meeting you two."

Fairchild flashed the two of them a victory sign, then snapped his fingers and pointed ahead. The fat man in the suit set the golf cart in motion. As the two drove off, Gibbs observed that they carried no golf clubs.

Gibbs looked at his boss in open admiration and gratitude. The Old Man had just introduced him to the next President of the United States. They were onboard the winning team, and unlike most of the senior staff of the doomed Administration, they would not only survive the transition but rise with it.

Kowalski turned to his protégé. "So you see, Darrell, there is a great deal at stake in all this."

Gibbs nodded in solemn agreement. "You can count on me, sir."

While it was morning at Jackson Hole, it was evening on the Planitia. At the same time Gibbs and Kowalski were enjoying the superb lunch buffet offered by the golf club, the tired and hungry crew of the *Beagle* gathered in the Hab's wardroom for a meager dinner. As they watched with a combination of anticipation and resignation, Rebecca emerged from the galley carrying a very small plate of greens with one piece of Spam on it. She divided it five ways.

Suppressing the indignant cries from his stomach, Townsend took advantage of the moment to consult with his geologist. "It's been four weeks now, with nothing but three false positives to show. I think we need to move the search much deeper into Xanthe."

Staring at the minute portion placed before him, Luke replied in a monotone, "Okay by me."

McGee was more direct. "That's not much food, Rebecca."

His remark was spoken in irritation, not malice, but its obvious truth made it sound like an indictment. Rebecca tried to defend herself with a shrug. "That's our daily greenhouse output, plus one half meat ration. I'm afraid it doesn't go very far cut five ways."

Gwen glared at her, and Rebecca recoiled from the eye contact as if stunned. "Well, it doesn't!"

Gwen took out her sheath knife, causing Rebecca to take two nervous steps backward. The flight engineer then used the knife to stab her morsel of Spam and pop it into her mouth. "Damn Yankee atheist bitch," she muttered. Then, scowling at the doctor, she stalked out of the room.

McGee and Townsend exchanged worried glances. A new threat had emerged. Historian and officer both knew how much crew morale mattered. And it was disintegrating before their eyes.

CHAPTER 18

TWO MORE MONTHS WENT BY, FILLED WITH EVER DEEPER frustration as the search for ground water proved fruitless. Despite everything, the crew somehow managed to battle on, but more and more they seemed split into two groups: Gwen and Luke on one side, and Rebecca and McGee on the other. *Rednecks versus eggheads.*

Townsend tried to maintain cohesion among the crew, but his job was becoming increasingly impossible. In September, a dispute over whether the Hab audio should play Bach or Hank Williams almost came to blows. Unable to keep the crew working together, the mission commander chose to work them separately. With greater frequency, the rover sorties devolved upon the rednecks, while the others strove to keep things going back at the base.

On October 15, Luke and Gwen went out on yet another rover excursion, and as usual failed to produce any positive results. By the time they turned back toward home on their unproductive mission, Gwen was in a bad mood. "You can rack up another failure for your water-table theory, Dr. Luke. What's your score now, zero for thirty-six?"

He winced. "Come on, Gwen, cut me some slack."

As he continued to drive, Gwen turned away from him to stare out her window. "Sure. I don't mind. Who cares?"

Luke felt hurt by her attitude. Outwardly still confident, inwardly he was terrified that everyone on the crew blamed him for the failure of the water-prospecting campaign. He needed some support. "Please, Gwen."

As if sensing his need, she sighed and gave him the best remnant of her smile. "All right, what the heck? We may be hunting wild geese, but at least we get to see a bit of the country."

At this, Luke felt relieved, but only momentarily. A huge dust cloud had begun gathering to the west. "Looks like we're about to see some foul weather," he commented.

The sky grew dark as the rover rattled in the thin wind. Gwen stared in amazement at the storm shadow racing toward them. "Better step on it, Luke," she said, an edge of fear in her voice. "This is going to be a bad one."

But it was far too late. Within seconds, the storm was all around them. Visibility dropped to zero. Luke, who had briefly accelerated the rover at Gwen's suggestion, was forced to slow to a crawl. But it only took a few moments of driving in the dust blizzard before the engine stalled out.

"Come on, start. Come on. Come on!" Luke pushed the starter lever again and again, without success. The starter wouldn't even crank. Then the lights in the rover went out.

Gwen threw a switch, and dim orange lights came back on, glowing with battery power. In the fading emergency lights, the two explorers looked at each other. Neither had any doubt of their peril. Night was coming, and with it temperatures below minus 90° centigrade.

"Now what do we do?" An edge of hopelessness crept into Luke's voice.

The co-pilot gritted her teeth. "Now we try to restart the engine." She hit some buttons and projected circuit and plumbing diagrams and data readouts on the rover's dashboard computer screen.

Luke tried to interpret the tech readouts, but the schematics were completely incomprehensible. He frowned. "Better make it fast, Gwen. It's getting cold in here. I'll see if I can call Triple A." He picked up the radio and began to recite: "*Beagle,* this is rover, *Beagle* this is rover, do you read?"

The only answer was loud static.

"Damn! Electrical disturbances in this storm must be blacking out the radio. Find anything?"

Gwen looked up from her miniscreen. "Yeah. The CO_2 intake for the engine coolant loop is jammed with dust. The engine shut off automatically as soon as the line was blocked."

"Can you hot-wire it to run anyway?"

Gwen thought for a moment and then shook her head. "Doubt it. Wouldn't do much good anyhow. Without that coolant, the engine would overheat and seize up in minutes. The real question is why the filter jammed. There's a motorized fan that's supposed to keep it clean."

"Is the fan motor broken?"

"No, it's reading green. I don't get it . . ." Gwen looked at her miniscreen, then typed commands to bring up backup screens. Suddenly her expression changed. "Would you look at this! The autocontroller has it shut off."

Gwen typed quickly on the keyboard, then stared in disbelief at the dashboard computer screen. With each finger stroke her expression grew increasingly flustered. Finally she stopped and turned to Luke. There was a dark fire in her eyes.

"Well?" Luke inquired.

"The damn computer won't *let* me turn the fan on!"

That was supposed to be impossible. Luke was mystified. "It won't . . . What?"

Gwen exploded. "Somebody's been screwing with the rover software, that's what! And I think I know who it is, too."

Suppressing her anger, Gwen ducked down and crawled under the dashboard. On her back, she edged under the engine, which was forward of the driver's compartment, and examined the mechanisms with her flashlight. Then she squirmed out and faced Luke as he tugged on a sweater. "I think I can fix this. If we can move the lower cooler casing, I can get at the motor leads and short them around the control relay. It'll make the fan run nonstop . . . but so what?"

Adrenaline could take the co-pilot only so far. The temperature in the rover was already well below freezing. Even before she finished her report, Gwen started to shiver.

Luke handed her a sweater. "Here, you better put this on."

Gwen pulled the thick woolen garment rapidly over her head; it wasn't adequate, but better than nothing. "Thanks."

Luke glanced at the EVA stowage bin behind the front seats. "Maybe we should put on our Marsuits."

Still shivering, Gwen was tempted, but knew she had to reject the idea. "No. We can't fit under the console wearing them, and if we don't get that engine started, the suits aren't warm enough to keep us alive overnight. I'll need your help. Come on."

With that, Gwen put a flashlight headband on, grabbed a screwdriver and wrench, and slid under the engine again. Luke followed and lay down on his back next to her, squirming close.

With finesse, Gwen rapidly unscrewed the first three nuts from the cold machine casing, but the fourth one stuck. "I can't move it!"

"Let me help." The muscular geologist pressed closer to her, his warm breath next to her face. He added his strength to hers on the wrench, and the nut finally came loose. Their brief sense of triumph was muted by the increasingly frigid atmosphere inside the rover. Despite their sweaters and exertions, they both shivered hard; their breath fogged and formed ice crystals on the nearby plumbing.

"B-better hurry," Luke said, his teeth chattering. "Jesus, it's freezing in here. I think the air is starting to foul too."

With shaking fingers, Gwen removed the last nut and placed her hands on the casing to move it. At first touch, her hands recoiled from the bitter cold, then she tried again and pushed hard . . . but remained unable to budge it. "Help, Luke!"

He put his hands on the metal casing to push, but instantly jerked away from the freezing shock. Clenching his fists, he tried again; ignoring the searing pain, he pushed with all his might. The casing moved off its bolts, rising up about eight inches. "That's as far as it goes! Go for it."

On her back, Gwen put her hands through the gap between the casing and the electrical board. By the light of her headlamp, she tried to unscrew wires from their attachments. Her hands recoiled repeatedly when they accidentally touched ice-cold metal. Grimy with engine soot, her headlamp glowing dimly, she looked just like a miner as she worked. An odd thought came to her. *If only Daddy and Grandpa could see me now.* They had been miners. Now she was one too.

But they had both died in the mines. Dying in the fight for life.

The touch of frigid metal brought her back to the present, and she yanked out her hands. "Too cold!" The job seemed hopeless. It was so cold. She just wanted to pull in her hands close to her body, to somehow huddle and hide from the cold closing in all around her.

But then, a whisper seared through her mind; it was her father's voice. *You can't give up Gwen. Never give up.*

Then she started hearing a song. At first she didn't recognize it; then she knew it. It was the old Welsh battle song Grandpa had sung to her when she was a little girl. Only it wasn't just Grandpa singing this time, but many voices, as if innumerable souls from the distant past had risen to speak to her. Beginning faintly, their song grew louder. She couldn't understand the words, but she knew what the song meant.

Never give up. Never, ever, ever, give up. No matter what, we never give up.

In the cold darkness of the rover's sub-engine area, something warm moved through her blood. Moving like a stranger in her own body, she separated her arm from her chest, dredged up the will to reach down and pull her sheath knife out of her boot. Reentering the gap with her blade, she attacked the wire, madly hacking away with her knife.

"I can't hold this much longer, Gwen!" Luke's voice was filled with agony.

She used her knife to cut through the wire and then strip its insulation. Moving fast, she spliced one wire, then another. Then, bringing together two sets of stripped leads, she twisted them together with thick, numb fingers. She grabbed the final set and muttered a quick, silent prayer. Then she brought the ends together.

The engine started with a roar.

The effect of the revived ventilator fan was immediate. Breathable air flushed through the rover like a wind from heaven.

Her adrenaline gone, Gwen suddenly shivered violently, sagging against the big geologist. "Oh, I'm cold . . ."

Shaking with the effort and his misery, Luke lowered the casing back onto its bolts. Flushed with relief, he looked at Gwen with a deeper sense of closeness than he had experienced with her before, the desperate camaraderie of two people who had survived a terrible ordeal. The no-nonsense flight mechanic seemed so helpless there shivering in the cold. Instinct told him to grab her, to hold her close, to warm her with his body heat, even as she warmed him with hers.

Impulsively, he put his arms around her, telling himself he would hold her only until they recovered, only until they were both warm again. She did not push him away, and in a moment of intense relief, Gwen let herself snuggle close, the bodily contact unleashing a need she had never let herself feel.

Then another instinct started to grow in Luke. After so many months in intense training on Earth, and on the long trip and habitation on Mars, it had been a long time since he'd felt the warmth of a woman. Far, far too long. Before he knew what he was doing, Luke kissed her.

And, moved by a natural force that suddenly broke

loose inside her, she kissed him back, deeper and closer, as the heater warmed the rover interior.

They did not speak to each other, did not discuss what they were doing. Gwen and Luke had both just been to the edge of death, and survived it together. Now there was an emotional bond between them, and it dissolved all barriers. He pulled her very close, and two sets of feverish hands worked at the fastenings of their clothing.

In and among the equipment on the vehicle, near the warm engine compartment, they found plenty of room to make love.

Shaken and silent, Gwen drove the now-functional vehicle home through the dust storm and into the Martian night.

Beside her, Luke snored, apparently exhausted by the near-disaster on the rover, their ensuing emotional response to the ordeal, and then the boredom of the dark drive back to base.

Gwen's thoughts were wild. She had sinned horribly, and she knew it. She also had no illusions about the Texan geologist. There was no commitment, nothing sacred for him. Just a woman in his time of need, and she had been there. He might have some affection for her, but it was mostly just lust—and she had given her virginity to him! There had been plenty of opportunities in Gwen's life, but she'd always protected herself, saving her first time for someone special. The right person.

But she didn't love Luke. How could she have let this happen? It just had. She herself was as much to blame as the geologist. No excuses.

Dark dust swirled around the vehicle, and her thoughts wandered back to another nightmare, nearly a decade before. The grinding gears of the rover transformed to the *whack-whack-whack* of helicopter blades slicing through steady desert wind. The Martian electrical storm sporadically illuminating the horizon now turned into the flashes of shells bursting all over the landscape.

She was no longer a thirty-one-year-old major, second in

command of the first mission to Mars. Instead, she was a terrified girl in her early twenties, with second lieutenant's bars on her shoulders, flying a chopper filled with screaming, wounded GIs through a desert sandstorm. The dead pilot occupied the seat next to her. She flew low to avoid enemy radar, dodging dunes that became visible at the last second. Something loomed up ahead, and she squinted into the opaque dust, her teeth clenched together and her eyes half shut. Suddenly she saw it—an Iraqi pillbox directly in front of her at point-blank range. A rush of terror surged through her, as she braced for a fatal gunshot—

Gwen hit the brakes and froze at the rover's controls, panting like a winded hound. The dust subsided, and her vision cleared. The pillbox became the *Beagle*. Tears ran down her face. She shook her companion. "Luke, get up. We're home."

The geologist awoke. Without a word, avoiding glances in each other's direction, the two donned their Marsuits, exited the rover, and entered the Hab.

The nighttime dust storm drive had seemed like an eternity, but it was actually only about ten P.M., local time. The rest of the crew was still up and about, and came down to the lower deck to greet them.

After Townsend helped her through the airlock door, Gwen detached her helmet, revealing a dark expression close to madness. Observing the look on her tear-stained face, McGee tried to lighten the mood. "You sure look happy to be home. Tears of joy at the prospect of more greens and Spam, perhaps?"

Gwen lost control and kicked at him, hard, barely missing his crotch. Astonished, the historian fell back. "What did I say? What did I *say,* dammit?"

Townsend stepped forward, adopting a blocking stance to suppress any further violence. "What has gotten into you, Major?"

Gwen glared in response. She peeled off her gloves and flung them down on the steel honeycomb floor of the Hab's lower deck. "You jerks have no idea what's really going on here, do you? The rover was *sabotaged!* Somebody intended for us to die out in the storm."

The wildness of the charge sent the colonel reeling. "Sabotaged? How? And by who?"

Whether by chance or design, the "how" question was just what was needed to return Gwen to sanity. For her, the world of machines was the world of reason. Her answer was lucid and precise. "How? By derailing the controller system software. Luke and I would have frozen if I hadn't figured out a quick-enough workaround."

Townsend noted how the technical question calmed the flight mechanic. "It could have been a single-point upset to the computer memory caused by cosmic ray impacts."

Gwen shook her head. "Not likely. And as far as *who* could have done this, let's just say it was probably done by someone who thinks what we have will go further around here if only three of us are eating." She looked daggers at Rebecca.

Shocked by the wild hatred blazing in the flight mechanic's eyes, Rebecca countered self-righteously, "You're out of your stupid hillbilly mind."

Gwen met her look without blinking. "Am I?"

Rebecca was taken aback, but not intimidated. "If you want to make an accusation like that, be prepared to prove it. You have no evidence whatsoever for your insane charge."

Townsend intervened. "That's enough, both of you. I'll hear no talk like this among my crew. Major, do you have any proof that implicates Dr. Sherman?" He waited. "I thought not. You will refrain from further outbursts."

Gwen turned to him. "Open your eyes, Colonel. She's evil!"

That could not be tolerated. The colonel mustered his command tone. "That will be all! Major, go to your quarters."

Gwen regarded her commander with insolence. "Sure. Why not? It stinks in here."

CHAPTER 19

As McGee and Rebecca played Scrabble on the galley table, Townsend nursed a cup of dreary instant coffee. In the doctor's lap sat her pet lab rabbit, Louise, who, along with her rabbit-spouse, Clark, had parented the animals now populating the greenhouse's sizable array of hutches. These provided the only fresh meat for the crew's diet, but Louise's long-standing association with the ship's doctor protected the mother rabbit from a similar fate.

Since Luke was not around, and McGee tended not to fight about such things, Rebecca had been free to choose the background music. It was Italian opera, and vaguely familiar. Townsend didn't care much for opera, and he couldn't understand a word of Italian, but somehow he found the voices of the current song deeply moving. "What music is that?"

Concentrating on her tiles, Rebecca barely looked up. "It's Verdi's opera *Nabucco*."

That meant nothing to Townsend, but fortunately, the professor provided some additional detail. "What you're hearing now is a chorus of Israelite slaves in exile in Babylon, bemoaning the fact that they can't return to their homeland."

Townsend nodded. No wonder it had struck home. Even across an incomprehensible language barrier, the powerful longing for home in the voices was readily apparent. "Slaves in exile. Appropriate." He regarded his drink with distaste. "This coffee is fit for slaves. I wonder what genius at NASA decided to supply us with *instant* coffee for a two-and-a-half-year mission."

That remark brought a sympathetic sigh from Rebecca. "Yes, I'd give a lot for a good cappuccino right now. Ah, Starbucks." She put down six tiles. "Read 'em and weep, Kevin. 'Bequeathal,' with a double letter score for the Q, and a double word score overall, plus a few extra for 'bid' on the horizontal. Eighty-six points. You're going to owe me chore duty for the next week, cutie." She wrinkled her nose mischievously at her hapless victim.

McGee stared at the board. "Hmm. Looks grim."

Townsend had little interest in the game. "Do either of you know where Luke and the major are?"

Her tiles down and the game virtually won, Rebecca shrugged. "Can't say I do. They've been acting pretty weird since that rover sortie two weeks ago, mysteriously disappearing all the time."

"I think they're hanging out in the ERV," McGee said. "They don't seem to like our company anymore."

Townsend rose from his chair and began pacing. "This paranoia has got to stop. We can't have the crew split in half."

McGee's attention, however, was back on his tiles. "Well, this looks promising."

Townsend was uncomprehending. "What does?"

McGee put down all seven tiles. " 'Ambidextrously.' That 'bid' of yours sure came in handy, Rebecca. Let's see, triple letter score for the X, triple word score overall, and of course the bonus for getting rid of all seven tiles at once: 204 points. You'll find my laundry in the red sack in my closet." He smiled triumphantly.

Rebecca was dismayed. "Unbelievable," she muttered. "Unbelievable!"

The rabbit began to act nervous, agitated.

Observing its behavior, the biologist had a bizarre thought: Could it be that the rabbit was upset with her defeat? That even simple creatures required order in their universe? Rebecca tried to calm her pet with baby talk. "Don't worry, Louise. Mommy will win next time."

This proved ineffective. The rabbit started clawing madly, squirming in her lap. Now Rebecca was alarmed. Was the rabbit sick? "Louise, what's wrong, baby?" Strange, her own voice sounded high.

McGee stood up from the table and screeched. "Does anyone think it's getting stuffy in here?"

The colonel looked at the historian in amazement. "What's wrong with your voice?" His own pitch rose in apparent comic imitation.

But before Rebecca could laugh at the colonel's uncharacteristic attempt at humor, Louise leapt from her lap and went into convulsions on the floor. Suddenly, Rebecca felt very short of breath. She looked at the others in alarm.

"Helium!" she gasped. "The air. Check the readouts."

Rebecca tried to stand but collapsed back into her seat, hyperventilating. McGee and Townsend stumbled out of the galley toward the pilot's control booth. Suddenly weak, the colonel crashed beside the door.

Totally out of breath, McGee fell halfway across the room. Somehow, though, he found the strength for one final surge forward, making it to the panel. He looked at the array of controls in alarmed incomprehension. "What do I do?"

"Emergency oxygen," Townsend gasped, his voice high and tiny. "Switch 4A."

McGee saw it, two feet from his hand. Two feet too far. The room was going dark, and he had no strength left at all. He stretched his arm toward the switch and touched it, but then his vision blurred and he fainted. . . .

When McGee awoke, Rebecca was standing over him,

holding a breathing mask to his mouth. Observing her concern and angelic countenance, he wondered if this might be heaven, but the sight of Colonel Townsend behind her brought him back to Mars. He opened his eyes to full awareness, and she removed the mask.

"What happened?"

"The cabin atmosphere cycler replaced all of our air with a helium/nitrogen mix. It's lucky you made it to the oxygen switch, Kevin, or we'd all be dead."

Townsend appeared confused. "I just don't see how a malfunction like this could happen."

Rebecca's eyes flashed. "Really? I think it's pretty easy to see who could make it happen."

The colonel shook his head. "Doctor, you're a sophisticated person. I expect you to be above such paranoia."

Even with an edge of anger in Rebecca's voice, her argument was coldly rational. "What's paranoid about my assessment? She's accused me of planning to kill her in the rover, then she disappears right before a convenient equipment failure occurs, something she could easily engineer. Gwen's got a motive for murder, and she's got the weapon for it. Q.E.D."

Just then Gwen entered the Hab, followed by Luke. They were greeted by looks of curiosity from Townsend and McGee, and icy suspicion from Rebecca. Gwen and Luke appeared puzzled.

"What's the matter, Gwen, have you just seen a ghost?" Rebecca challenged.

"Ghost?" Gwen scowled. "What are you talking about? What's going on here?"

"The cabin pumps just tried to replace our air with a mixture of helium and nitrogen." McGee's tone was level.

Rebecca's voice was sharp. "While you two were conveniently away. We all almost suffocated."

"You're accusing me?"

The doctor didn't blink. "Yes. Where were you, Major? And you, Luke?"

"We were in the ERV," the geologist replied simply.

"And what were you doing there?" Rebecca's voice was inquisitorial.

The flight mechanic put her hands on her hips. "That's none of your damn business!"

Townsend intervened with all the authority he could muster. "That's enough. There was no sabotage. Not here today, not two weeks ago in the rover. They were both machine malfunctions."

"Oh, is that the official story?" Rebecca asked dryly. "Convenient."

Her tone was so supercilious that the colonel got angry. "That is the story, the only story. And get this straight—" he removed his belt and held it menacingly in his hand, "I am prepared to *flog* anyone who says otherwise." With that, he whipped the belt down hard upon the table, making a loud and nasty sound. He looked threateningly around the room. "If I have to, I will enforce the strictest military discipline upon this crew. I don't want to do that, but, by God, I will if I have to. I don't care what you think of each other; we will function as a team, or we will all die. Starting right now, these social cliques are history. No more rednecks verses eggheads. Got that?"

Rebecca stared at the belt in disbelief. Flogging? As unbelievable as it sounded, something warned her the colonel was serious. None of the others had any doubts. As one they all responded: "Yes, sir."

Pleased, and slightly amazed at this response, Townsend continued: "Right. The rover sortie that begins tomorrow will include all four of you. It will do you good to be crammed together for a few days of exploration."

"That'll be a pretty tight fit," Luke commented.

"It'll be fine, if you just stop hating each other," the colonel responded.

The crew members looked uneasily at each other.

"If you don't, then do me a favor and don't come back."

CHAPTER 20

THE PRESSURIZED ROVER WAS COMFORTABLE FOR TWO, but awfully snug for four—especially under such tense circumstances.

During the long sortie, Gwen drove with Luke beside her, pretending to watch the radar readouts. In the uneasy silence, the two tried with limited success to forget about McGee and Dr. Sherman in the seats behind them. The terrain was novel, for they had never been so far from base along this particular runoff channel. For Rebecca, such new landscape sights offered only a modest diversion; the others showed little interest at all.

Suddenly, the radar began to receive echo pings. Luke snapped out of his woolgathering. "I think we might be getting something."

Gwen ventured a side glance at the digital readout. Nothing she hadn't seen before. "You *think*. Tell me when you *know*. I don't want to drill another dud."

Luke could only shrug. "It's impossible to know for sure."

That was hardly good enough. Gwen shook her head.

"Well, this time, we'll just keep driving until something really jumps out at us."

Again silence prevailed—if anything, made worse by the hopeless hope the weak echo pings offered.

Realizing how intolerable the situation was, McGee thought to begin a conversation. "I wonder how our man in the White House is doing. There's supposed to be a new poll out today."

In response, Gwen turned on the radio. "*Beagle* this is rover. Do you read?"

After an answering crackle of static, Townsend's voice said, "*Beagle* here. I read you clearly."

"Roger that, *Beagle*. Do you have the campaign scores?"

More crackles, then, "The President trails Fairchild, 39 to 55."

McGee shook his head. "And less than two weeks to go."

So much for that. Gwen picked up the mike again. "Got any baseball scores? How are the Braves doing?"

This time the time lag before a response was radioed seemed longer. "The season ended two weeks ago, Major."

Gwen was stunned. Was she losing it? "Yeah, I forgot," was all she could muster.

As if to rescue her from her embarrassment, a change of subject was offered by Townsend's radio voice. "How's the search going?" he crackled.

"We've had a couple of radar hits," she reported, "but nothing special, so I decided to keep driving."

There were more static and whistles, typical of late afternoon conditions when the thinning Martian ionosphere made the rover's over-the-horizon shortwave radio unreliable. Soon it would be nonoperable. Gwen adjusted the frequency, obtaining a clear channel only in time to get the last words of Townsend's reply.

"Rover, I repeat, it's getting late." Townsend's voice was briefly clear, then the crackles and whistles got stronger. "You might as well try the next hit you get, or there'll be no time for drilling today."

This made sense. There was no point pinging if you don't eventually drill.

"Roger. Rover out." Gwen terminated the radio connection.

"I've got something now." Luke seemed faintly excited, but noticing Gwen's cynical look, he added, "Nothing out of the ordinary, though."

Gwen stopped the rover and stretched. "Let's give it a try. Break out the gear, people. It's drilling time again."

With four crew members, it took little time to set up the lightweight drilling rig, but once it was operative they had nothing to do but wait as the bit hummed and chewed its way through the Martian regolith.

Late afternoon turned to twilight, and a magnificent sunset developed in the Martian west, made more brilliant by the bright presence of Earth, shining as a wonderful evening star. Sitting on a rock next to McGee, Rebecca was taken with the scene. "There's Earth. Look how beautiful she is. Yet so unreachable."

Despite it all, McGee couldn't resist an inward chuckle at the thought of Rebecca sighing for an unobtainable beauty. "Frustrating, isn't it?"

The biologist was alert. "Now, Kevin, don't start," she smiled.

You can take the girl out of Central Park West, he thought, *but you can't take Central Park West out of the girl.*

Any further flirtation was precluded, however, by an announcement from Gwen. "I'm getting vibration in the rig! I think we should shut down."

She reached for the power switch, but Luke put his gloved hand on hers. "Hold on. That's not rig vibration—it's seismic activity."

The ground began to tremble.

McGee had lived in the earthquake-prone Pacific Northwest. He had felt this before. "Mars quake!"

Luke saw alarm spread across the faces of his crewmates.

They didn't understand. "Bullshit! It's, it's—" The ground seemed about to split beneath them.

"Run for the hill!" Gwen commanded, pointing to a nearby rise.

They scrambled for safety, but before they could take five steps, a torrent of steam gushed out of the ground, firing the drilling rig high into the sky. After an instant of terror, the crew stopped in their tracks to stare in amazement. With a whistling roar, steam spouted out of the ground like the Old Faithful geyser. Up into the sky it went, shooting several hundred meters high. Then, mushrooming out at the top of its trajectory, it came down as snow. All four were awestruck at the sight. Snow. *Snow!* Snow was salvation.

"It's an honest-to-God gusher!" Luke screamed. "Ya-hoo!"

Gwen emitted a piercing rebel yell.

McGee stared at the drifts rapidly forming around his feet, then kicked a mound into the air. "Snow! It's snowing on Mars! We're saved."

Rebecca picked up a handful of the beautiful crystals. When she'd been a child, snow had sometimes meant freedom from school; somehow that sense of hope always accompanied the stuff. And this snow was life itself. She wanted to jump, she wanted to sing, she wanted to play. Well, why not? Packing the snow into a ball, she threw it at McGee, hitting him squarely on the side of his helmet.

He turned to face her, obviously surprised, then saw the light in her eyes. He returned it, along with a powdery snowball of his own. But Rebecca was nimble, and ducked, causing the projectile to overshoot her and hit Luke. Mistakenly believing that the ball was thrown by Gwen, the Texan grabbed her and gave her a country swing in the low gravity. Gwen accepted her partner, but then, breaking loose, grabbed McGee and swung him as well.

It was crazy, but in an instant all were dancing with each other. All feuds forgotten, all tiredness gone, the four danced in the twilight as the blessed crystals of water poured down around them. Copland's *Rodeo* would have provided a great sound track for their wild dance. But they didn't need music to accompany them: They had snow.

The next morning, Townsend puttered around the Hab checking instruments. He'd had no contact from the crew since the previous afternoon. In the mid-distance in the plain, the rover suddenly came over a rise and into view. *About time they checked in.*

Switching on the radio, he heard singing: "I'm dreaming of a white Christmas . . ."

What the heck is going on?

Then he saw it. Behind the rover was a trailer carrying a huge load of snow. Townsend dropped the mike and rushed into his Marsuit. In less than two minutes, he was out the lock to greet the crew.

The rush outside was worth the effort. Townsend could only gasp in awe at the mountain of frozen water.

From inside the rover, Gwen gave him a big thumbs up sign, which the colonel returned with both hands.

Earth, here we come!

CHAPTER 21

WATER IN A GLASS CAN COOL A PARCHED THROAT. WATER in a shower can revive a dried, tired body. Accompanied by shampoo, it can turn a wild rat's nest of hair covering a woman's head back into spectacular long, shiny locks and tresses. Together with shaving cream and a razor, water can make a man's face look civilized again. With soap, sponges, and a mop, water can make a dirty ship spotless, and fill vases on its wardroom table with happy flowers.

Water was now available to the crew in torrents. As it filled their return ship with propellant, it filled their minds and bodies with hope and life. Like the holy rain that reportedly washed sickness and sin from the world when Christ died, the flood of crystal fluid washed away all tiredness and despair from the crew of the *Beagle*.

Light filled the ship. Everyone showered. Townsend shaved. Rebecca combed, and as she did, she filled the ship with the sweet sound of her well-trained classical voice. Luke, who but a few days before would have disputed her right to do so, now enjoyed her musical background as he arranged and classified his rock collection. As if by a miracle, the dingy Hab became spick-and-span, brightly reflecting the crew's rejuvenated morale.

By the second day after the return, the trailer load of snow had been melted into water. Stored in the ERV landing-stage tanks, it was piped by automated systems into the propellant-manufacturing unit. The hard work over, the crew's assignments were shifted to those specific to the return flight.

The most important of these—flight preparation of the Earth Return Vehicle itself—fell to Gwen. Assisted by McGee, she began testing every valve and circuit. Many people might have found such a job tedious, but Gwen and McGee, now lighthearted, considered it fun. Reflecting their mood, the ERV's music player accompanied their work with the playful sounds of 1960's rock and roll. As one system after another checked out, the Beach Boys, the Eagles, the Beatles, the Grateful Dead, and Three Dog Night all blared their best. By the time the two astronauts reached the pilot control board, Simon and Garfunkel were up at bat with, fittingly, "Homeward Bound."

Gwen attached her meter to a set of terminals. "Primary pilot control circuit reads green."

"Check," McGee replied.

She moved the connectors. "Secondary pilot control circuit reads green."

"Check."

"Primary life-support-system control circuit reads green as grass."

"Check."

She moved her meter wires to the last set of connections. "Flight control central processing unit reads . . ."

Her sudden silence was deafening. A shudder of uncertainty ran down McGee's spine. *Could there by a problem? Don't do this to me, Gwen.*

"Well, how does it read?" he finally demanded.

Gwen turned to face him, consternation in her eyes. "It doesn't."

Without another word, she picked up a screwdriver and

disappeared under the control panel. McGee waited anxiously until a few moments later she emerged with a charred and blackened computer board.

"The flight control CPU," she said flatly.

McGee looked at the unit. It was obviously burnt beyond hope of repair. "I don't suppose there's a backup to that?"

The mechanic shook her head.

In the background, the lyrics of "Homeward Bound," which had sounded so joyful only seconds before, suddenly seemed mournful.

But there was still hope. Perhaps the ERV could be flown without the CPU. Townsend was game to try. It took a few hours to reprogram the ERV flight simulator to mimic the behavior of the vehicle with the central flight control CPU out of the loop. Shortly after dinner, the crew gathered in the control section of the *Beagle* to witness the attempt.

With some ceremony the colonel, complete with wing-adorned leather jacket and peaked hat, sat down at the controls. He gripped the stick, then looked to Gwen seated next to him in the co-pilot's chair. "Okay, let's go for it."

Gwen threw some switches and counted down to zero. "We have ignition."

As the rest of the crew watched on the auxiliary simulator external viewscreen, a computerized image of the ERV *Retriever* rose on a trail of simulated fire from the digitized landscape surrounding it. McGee's throat tightened. *He's doing it, he's doing it.*

Suddenly, the *Retriever*'s image listed slightly to the right. A jet of computerized plume showed that Townsend had compensated, but the sudden tilt of the vehicle to the left signaled that he'd compensated by too much. Another plume in the opposite direction sent the vehicle toward the upright position, but too hard, and the image rapidly flopped over and crashed into the landscape.

The colonel heard the collective sigh escape from those gathered behind him. "Okay, people, that was just the first try. Gwen, reset for another sim."

"Roger. Here we go."

Again the vehicle flew. Again it crashed. Again it flew. Again it crashed. Townsend's attempts went on for hours, but on every try the simulated ERV lifted off the landing stage, rose a few feet, and started to lean to one side. Each time, the colonel compensated with the joystick, but always too much or too little, so that within seconds the simulated flight came to an end in a fiery crash on the virtual Martian sands.

Finally, the pilot had to admit defeat. "It's no good. Without the CPU, the ERV is completely unflyable. We wouldn't get three hundred feet. Dammit!"

Rebecca stared out the window into the slightly moonlit Martian night. "We were home free. How could this have happened?"

The question was rhetorical, but Townsend took it literally.

"I spoke to Mission Control. They reexamined the vehicle onboard health monitoring records. That board has been out since January 28, 2012."

Gwen looked up sharply. "The night the propellant was drained!"

"That's right. It must have been Holloway. He didn't just drain the ERV's propellant, he burnt out its CPU as well."

But the analytical part of McGee's mind was intrigued. "Could he have pre-programmed those other equipment failures as well? The rover breakdown, the air-exchanger problem?"

Townsend shrugged. "Maybe."

"I doubt it," Rebecca said sourly, looking at Gwen, but fell quiet when the colonel gave her a warning look.

He drew a deep breath. "There's no use denying that this is a massive setback, but don't give up hope. I'm going to confer with the flight control systems experts at JSC tonight. Maybe there's some way we can patch the flight control CPU from the *Beagle* into the ERV, and make it halfway flyable."

Gwen was unconvinced. "I don't think that'll work, Colonel. It's a totally different type of system."

Stripped so quickly even of this forlorn hope, Townsend could only mumble. "Well, maybe something can be done."

Rebecca turned away to stare out the window again. "Still stranded."

The colonel looked at the rest of the devastated crew. As an astronaut, he didn't have a clue what to do, but as an officer, he did. *I can't let morale collapse again. I need to show some confidence.* He cleared his throat. "I think it's time the four of you turned in. I'll do the telecon with JSC alone. Maybe I'll have good news for you in the morning."

The crew looked bleakly at each other. Having nothing to say, they obeyed.

Rebecca, however, could not sleep. Through the middle of the night, thoughts kept running through her head. *We were so close. How could the burnt-out CPU have gone undetected for so long?* True, Mission Control had been otherwise occupied, and no one had bothered much with the ERV as long as it had no fuel . . . but still. Whoever had sabotaged that board could also have doctored the ERV health-monitoring records. An inside job. That meant the sabotage could have been performed much more recently, most likely in the several days since the snow had been obtained. It could have been done at Mission Control . . . or here. Why couldn't Townsend see that?

Then she heard it. In the compartment next to hers, someone was getting up. *Gwen.*

Rebecca put her ear to the wall and very distinctly heard the sound of a Marsuit being zipped on. *She's going EVA in the middle of the night. Another sabotage attempt! Should I tell the colonel? No. I'll follow her and catch her in the act.*

Rebecca waited for Gwen to exit her compartment and then quickly and silently slipped into her own Marsuit. The flight mechanic was moving quietly herself, but Rebecca could track the sounds of her motions into the central solar flare shelter that served as the corridor to the lower deck, and then down below to the airlock. As soon as she was certain Gwen had gone downstairs, Rebecca slipped out of her stateroom and headed toward the central shelter as well.

On the way, she passed the control room and was surprised to note that Colonel Townsend was still in his chair, apparently conferring with Mason and some JSC engineers via telescreen. She managed to get past the open door without his detecting her and climbed down the stairs, closing the flare-shelter door behind her. Once she reached the lower deck and saw that Gwen had already transited out the outer airlock, she opened the inner lock door, cycled the system herself, and followed the flight mechanic out into the Martian night.

As her eyes adjusted to the darkness, Rebecca could see by the dim light of Phobos Gwen's lithe figure heading toward the ERV. She smiled grimly to herself. *Gotcha, you little redneck saboteur. This time you don't get away with it.*

Keeping low to avoid being spotted, the doctor followed Gwen across the dark landscape, and managed to position herself not twenty meters away as her opponent cycled the *Retriever*'s airlock and entered the vehicle. She calculated her next move. *The lock is in the ERV's lower deck. She'll go for the upper deck. That's where all the controls are. That's where she'll do . . . whatever it is she is planning.* Rebecca counted to sixty, then followed Gwen into the return ship.

Entering the ERV's pressurized lower deck, Rebecca eased off her helmet. As she crept past one of the workbenches, she spotted a crowbar. The sight of this object, both tool and weapon, suddenly made her realize how dangerous her situation was. The saboteur had already proven murderous intent, more than once. *If it's Gwen, she could attack me right here, then make up some story. Townsend would believe anything.* Rebecca felt a flash of fear, but strengthened her resolve. She picked up the crowbar, took a deep breath to prepare herself for the confrontation, and boldly climbed the ladder to the control deck.

As she entered the upper deck, she saw Gwen slouching by the control panel. The major had already removed her helmet and was bent intently over the controls. Hearing a creak of metal, a whisper of footsteps, she turned to see Rebecca advancing toward her holding a crowbar.

"This time you're caught!" Rebecca's face was grim.

Gwen was startled, amazed. "You!" she shouted, and leapt at Rebecca. The mechanic moved fast; before the doctor could swing her crowbar in the close quarters, Gwen snatched the weapon out of her hand and tossed it to the far side of the room. Reacting quickly, however, Rebecca seized the instant to deliver a well-styled karate kick, catching the flight mechanic in the side.

Taken by surprise, Gwen stumbled back across the room, moving oddly in the low gravity. "Where'd you learn to kick like that—ballet school?"

Rebecca smiled proudly. "Five years of karate."

Gwen's eyes were dark with hate. "Really! Well now I'll show you what you can learn in eighteen years in the Smokies."

As Rebecca maintained her elaborate karate stance, the miner's daughter doubled her fists and advanced like a tomboy street fighter. When Gwen got close, Rebecca lashed out with another fancy kick, but Gwen took a quick step back, parried the kick after its force was gone, and then stepped in to punch the doctor straight in the face.

Rebecca recoiled in pain, putting her hands up to protect herself, to little effect. As the flight mechanic advanced, pummeling Rebecca with her fists, the doctor, with her veneer of karate training gone, could only offer feeble, disorganized resistance.

She still had her sharp tongue, though. "So, you don't mind killing people with your bare hands . . . instead of little staged accidents?" she taunted, but the answering blow from Gwen told her that words would be of little use.

Rebecca tried to retreat across the cabin, interposing chairs and other objects, but it was futile. Again Gwen hit her, and again. Then she stumbled against the ERV control panel. *Help, I need help! Where's the alarm button? There!* She hit the alarm, then another blow sent her stumbling across the cabin.

Again the fists came toward her. All Rebecca's technique was gone, but she still had a fierce will to live. Knowing only that she had to stop those fists, she launched herself at Gwen like a brawler and grappled the other woman's hands—but in seconds, Gwen wrestled her to the floor.

The flight mechanic's face was wild. "I've had all I'm gonna take from you!"

Rebecca struggled, but could not get loose. "You stupid animal! How can you just kill us all? Why are you doing this?"

Then she saw it on the floor next to her—the crowbar. Somehow, she wrenched a hand free and grabbed the tool, giving Gwen a solid whack on the side of her shoulder. Her opponent winced, but countered, slamming Rebecca's arm down so hard that she lost her grip. The crowbar skittered away across the floor, clanging down the hatch, and taking with it Rebecca's last hope.

"That does it!" Gwen shouted. Her eyes crazed with rage, the mechanic reached down for her knife.

Pinned to the deck, Rebecca watched with horror as Gwen ripped the weapon from her boot, then swung it down toward Rebecca's chest with lethal intent. At the last instant, Rebecca summoned adrenaline strength and caught Gwen's arm. She struggled, using both hands to hold off the blade.

Gwen was forced to use one hand to hold Rebecca down, while she strained to push the knife with the other. In the low Martian gravity she had to poise herself in a kind of push-up position in order to shift her full weight forward to keep Rebecca's shoulders pinned to the deck with her left hand while trying to force down the knife with her right. But even with only one hand, the tough flight mechanic was much stronger than the doctor. The knife relentlessly moved toward Rebecca's chest.

There were only inches left to go. Rebecca screamed. "Gwen, stop! Stop! Help! Help!"

Rebecca struggled desperately, but it was hopeless. The point touched her Marsuit, pressing into the fabric. In seconds, it would all be over. But still, the doctor wouldn't give up. She writhed this way and that, kicking wildly, to little effect. As her last gasp, she finally got her knee up, and using all the force she had, hit Gwen in the lower abdomen. She couldn't strike hard, but the effect was dramatic.

Suddenly, Gwen recoiled, looking gray and sick. She dropped the knife and scrambled backward, clutching her belly protectively, eyes wide with disbelief and fear. Her eyes rolled, and her mouth opened. Gwen paid no attention to the knife as Rebecca grabbed for it. Instead, she stumbled over to the other end of the ERV cabin and started to vomit uncontrollably. Then she sank to the deck and cradled her abdomen, eyes wide, protecting her . . . womb?

Rebecca stared at Gwen with shock and the dawning of understanding. The flight mechanic had been keeping to herself a great deal, had often looked drained, perhaps ill. Gwen heaved again, but no vomit came out.

Through a haze of adrenaline, the doctor's clinical training kicked in. "You have morning sickness! You're pregnant."

Gwen coughed. "That's right, bitch."

"Who? When?"

"Luke." Gwen coughed again. "That bastard. In the rover."

Just then Colonel Townsend charged into the ERV upper-deck cabin, finally responding to the alarm and the shouts through the intercom. He surveyed the two disheveled women and the wreckage strewing the cabin. "What's going on here?"

Rebecca brushed back her brunette hair with one hand in a vain effort to appear presentable. "I heard Gwen slip out of the Hab in the middle of the night. I thought she was planning sabotage, so I followed her. When I got here, she attacked me."

The colonel turned to the mechanic, his expression pale and stony. "Major, what's your explanation?"

Rebecca preempted Gwen's explanation. "Colonel, she's pregnant."

"She's *what*?"

"Pregnant," Rebecca repeated flatly. Gwen looked away, not denying the fact. "It explains a lot lately."

Luke and McGee arrived in the cabin, hastily suited after the alarm. Townsend regarded the new arrivals sardonically. "Welcome aboard, gentlemen. I've just been informed that my flight engineer is pregnant. Would the lucky father please be good enough to reveal his identity?"

Gwen huddled against the metal wall as Luke sheepishly held up his hand. McGee seemed astonished.

Townsend stared the geologist in the face. "I hope you're proud of yourself." His sarcasm was searing. "Was it fun?"

Rebecca interrupted the dressing-down. "Colonel, this is a very serious situation."

Townsend turned to face her. "You think I don't know that?" he said excitedly. "As if we don't have enough problems around here, now we have crew members brawling in the middle of the night, or banging each other—and a baby on the way, to boot."

Rebecca forced herself to be calm and authoritative. "You don't understand. A child born on Mars can never return to Earth. The difference in gravity would almost surely cause developmental differences in bone thickness, blood volume, heart rate, immune functioning."

Gwen took alarm. "The hell you say."

Rebecca's voice was clinical. "This fetus has to be aborted at once."

"Aborted!" Gwen made a halfhearted effort to launch herself at Rebecca, but was blocked by McGee. "Baby killer! I'll never let you do that to my child, you liberal trash, you godless murderer!"

Townsend slammed his fist down on the control panel.

"Cut it out!" Somehow, Gwen recovered enough composure to silence herself.

The colonel waited a few seconds for order. "I just found out from JSC that there's a spare computer card for the ERV right here on Mars, in the second ERV that was landed down in the Valles Marineris. Its CPU circuits check out green. Apparently, Holloway didn't bother to wreck it. We've got only one chance to get it before the dust storms return. We need to leave as soon as possible."

A mission into the Valles Marineris! The shaken and confused crew waited expectantly for Townsend's orders.

"I'm going. I'll take Professor McGee, since his personnel profile shows mountaineering experience. We'll be back within five days and settle this matter then, when you've all cooled off." He swept his gaze from Rebecca to Gwen, huddled on the floor, to the geologist standing stunned near the stairway to the lower deck. "I must say that I'm disappointed in all of you. *All of you.* In the meantime, Major Llewellyn will sleep here in the ERV, and reside here except for duty watches. Dr. Sherman will stay in the *Beagle.* Luke, I want you to make sure that these two stay far away from each other."

"Yes, sir," Luke replied.

"All right, then, let's break up and get some sleep. The professor and I have a long hard trip ahead of us, starting at 0600 tomorrow morning."

NASA JSC, HOUSTON
OCT 29, 2012 22:30 CST

Tex Logan stared at the Mission Control records, examining the files over and over.

Logically, the data made no sense. There had been too many critical failures to explain away as "accidents." There had to be a saboteur, someone who continued to act long after Craig Holloway had been booted out of the picture. The old NASA veteran knew that some of the crew members suspected a wrecker in their midst, but that couldn't be true, since every single person on Mars had been targeted in apparent acts of sabotage. And even if that were not the case, a saboteur among the crew was just impossible. Tex knew them personally, every one. They all had rough edges, it was true. But they were all great people, real troopers. None of them could possibly betray the team.

And now there was this new mystery, the burnt-out computer card in the *Retriever*. Mission Control logs said the card had been destroyed months ago, on the same night the propellant had been dumped. But Tex was sure he'd checked the ERV flight control CPU the following morning, and the health-monitoring system had shown green.

After the fuel loss, Colonel Townsend had deactivated the reportage system for the ERV flight systems health-monitoring unit, since that data was no longer of any interest. Here at JSC, Tex had had no opportunity to check it for the past nine months. But no matter what anyone said about his memory, the old NASA veteran was sure of it. On the morning of January 29, that subsystem had read green. But now, according to the data logs, it had shown red.

Something very fishy was going on around here.

It was 10:30 P.M., and given the late hour, the only other leading member of Mission Control still present was Rollins. The others had gone home or to the bars; to their families, their hobbies, their so-called lives. Tex and Rollins had been the butt of considerable ribbing about their workaholism. According to the others, they could be found at Mission Control at all hours, because they had no "lives." Well, Tex had a life, and it *was* Mission Control.

He had joined at the age of twenty-one in December 1968, one week before the Apollo 8 launch. He'd been here when that crew first rounded the Moon at Christmas and read Genesis aloud to a marveling world. He'd been here the following July and cheered madly with the rest when Armstrong and Aldrin had first walked on the Moon. He'd been part of the team that helped save Apollo 13. He'd been there for Skylab and Apollo-Soyuz, and the first launch of the shuttle *Columbia* in 1981. He was at Mission Control when Sally Ride flew in 1983; he'd been there to cry out in agony when *Challenger* exploded in 1986. He'd been there when Hubble was launched, and when it was fixed—all three times. He'd worked the Mir missions and the Space Station missions, and the launch of the *Retriever,* the backup ERV, and the *Beagle*.

And he would be there when the *Beagle*'s crew returned, dammit! Because they would. He would see to it. No matter what it took.

Al Rollins was a much younger man, who had been posted at Mission Control for only a decade. But despite his youth, Rollins was old-school too. He would have fit in during Apollo.

Let the rest of the bunch enjoy their so-called lives. Al Rollins and Tex Logan had more than lives: They had a mission.

He called Rollins over. "Al, somebody has been screwing with this computer."

"Why do you say that?" Rollins liked the old guy, loved his colorful stories of the early NASA. In a way, Tex Logan was his model; but Tex's proclivity for conspiracy theories was legendary.

"Look. Remember the morning after the riot here? When the news came in that the ERV propellant had been dumped, I checked through all its flight systems. I remember it clearly—the primary flight CPU indicator read green."

Rollins felt a surge of pity. Tex obviously felt guilty for having missed the indicator. Well, no one else had caught it either. "Are you sure? It could easily have been missed in the confusion—"

"It wasn't missed, because it wasn't *there*. I know what I saw. Both the JSC and ERV computer logs are lying." Tex stared at his partner with certainty.

The younger man decided to take the matter seriously. "Well, then, unless you're willing to believe that there are saboteurs both at Mission Control and on Mars, there's only one answer. Our system has been hacked."

"Hacked?"

"Broken into from the outside by computer wizards who are sending mission-wrecking commands through our system."

Tex didn't know much about computers, having been born too soon. But he had heard about such things. He had only one question. "What can we do about it?"

"We need to be very careful about what we uplink to Mars. Everything containing an executable code should be sent to the simulator first. And I can try setting some traps, to see who modems into the system at key moments."

"Traps, huh?" Tex liked the idea. "In that case, we better keep it a secret. Don't even tell Phil. You know how he is about stuff like this. He'd never believe it."

Rollins nodded. It was clear that Chief of Operations Mason viewed Tex Logan as eccentric and semi-senile, especially when he talked conspiracy.

"And besides," Tex said, "the fewer people who know about the traps, the better the odds are that word won't leak out. I want to catch that bastard."

CHAPTER 22

THE CREW AWOKE WHILE IT WAS STILL DARK AND BEGAN preparations for the sortie that would decide their fate. By dawn, it was time for the rover to depart. As the Sun's edge peeked above the horizon, bathing the entire landscape in an eerie red glow, Townsend and Gwen put the vehicle through its final checkout. Moving quickly, they spoke to each other only in clipped, businesslike phrases.

In the lower deck of the Hab, McGee worked with Rebecca to assemble a formidable array of mountaineering equipment into two large backpacks. Finally, he shouldered one of the packs, and Rebecca handed him the other for the colonel. "So it looks like you're finally going to get to do some mountaineering on Mars, Kevin."

Slightly embarrassed by the intimacy of her tone, he answered, "Maybe a bit more than I bargained for. The Valles Marineris is three miles deep. We'll have to rappel down in stages, and hope we can leave enough ropes in place to enable a climb out."

The doctor stepped closer to him. "Kevin, I . . ."

Her eyes were luminous, her gaze beautiful. McGee felt

choked for words. "Yes?" was all he could muster.

But the moment was interrupted by the crackle of Townsend's Marsuit radio. "Hey, what's taking so long? We've got to get going."

Rebecca smiled and put one hand behind McGee's neck. "Kevin, be careful," she said, and kissed him softly on the lips.

McGee was awed.

Her big brown eyes searched his. There was affection in those eyes. Warmth. "Besides, if you were to kill yourself . . ." She paused, leaving McGee speechless.

Then she grinned broadly. "I don't know what I'd do for a game of Scrabble around here."

Her sudden flippancy enabled him to talk. "Don't worry. We'll be back home as soon as—"

Rebecca kissed him again, a long kiss, but as soft as the first. It was the kind of kiss a man remembers for decades—a statement, a farewell kiss that is almost a vow, a woman's final approval of a man's worth, a warrior's sendoff.

Her eyes searched his once more. "Take care." Then, stepping back into the lock that led to the upper deck of the *Beagle,* she closed it softly behind her, giving McGee a parting smile in the process.

It took him a moment to swallow the lump in his throat; then he snapped down his helmet, switched on the Marsuit respirator system, activated the pumpdown, and opened the airlock outer door. As the door opened, his eyes were greeted by the red-lit landscape of a spectacular Martian dawn.

Townsend stood beside the rover parked twenty meters from the Hab, its engine already running. Gwen, her work done, had backed away from the vehicle in the direction of the ERV. In the dim morning light, the ruddy landscape of Mars was stark and strange, both more beautiful and more threatening than ever. Somehow the sight brought home to McGee the immensity of this planet, its weird novelty, and the formidable nature of the expedition he was about to begin. It was a scene to engrave upon memory, and his mind reached for poetry:

"As when dawn lifts her rosy hand above the horizon . . ." *Homer, would that you were here to chronicle this Odyssey.*

Townsend waved him forward. "Let's go, Professor."

McGee strode down the ramp and entered the rover, followed quickly by the colonel. Moments later, Townsend closed the hatch and shifted the engine into gear. As they trundled away, McGee looked back to see Rebecca peering out the *Beagle*'s upper-deck window, waving farewell. Then, as they approached the ERV, Gwen stood outside in a Marsuit. She gave the rover crew a thumbs up, which Townsend returned. Within minutes, the base receded into the distance, and they were alone.

As they drove out onto the plain in the direction of the vast canyon, McGee dropped a disk into his electronic book and started to read aloud: "Here's what Carr says in his old write-up. 'Valles Marineris. The canyons are mostly flat-floored with steep, gullied walls. Many contain thick, partly eroded, layered sediments . . .' "

Townsend cut the lecture short. "Bottom line, McGee. Does he recommend a route?"

McGee shook his head. "From what he says, I think our best shot is to drive about half a day along the edge of the canyon, park near map point G-22, and make a descent along the series of natural switchbacks that appear to lie below it."

The colonel set his jaw. "Very well. Make it so."

Now where have I heard that before? McGee smiled inwardly.

"Yes . . . Captain Picard."

The two exchanged a comradely grin.

Four hours later, the two men arrived at the edge of the largest canyon in the solar system. Exiting the rover, they advanced to the cliff, and looked down into its vast depths.

McGee's memory flashed to his first view of Earth's Grand Canyon. He had seen it before in pictures, movies, even on Imax the night before—but nothing had prepared him for the real thing. Now Mars' canyon made Arizona's look like a ditch. Though he had already seen a part of it on that first rover sortie with Gwen a lifetime ago, the Valles Marineris still sent his mind reeling.

Townsend motioned to McGee, and they started down together. At first the descent was easy. A ledge ran along the side of the slope, and though the path was steep, it offered no significant difficulty. Then, without warning, the ledge ended in a sheer cliff.

McGee was prepared. Uncoiling a thin nylon line, he fastened one end securely around a massive boulder, and threw the other into the yawning gulf below. It would be an impressive descent, almost two hundred meters.

He looked to the colonel and gestured to the rope. "After you, Alphonse."

Townsend smiled. "After you, Gaston."

McGee picked up the line, fastened it to his safety belt, and walked to the edge. "See you at the bottom," he said, and kicked off.

Over the edge he went, and then down. After so many months on Mars, McGee was accustomed to the low Martian gravity, but this was the first time he'd let himself fall in it. He noticed the obvious slowness of the acceleration during his drop. One-third g meant that he could fall three times the distance that he could on Earth before he reached an equivalent speed. Both going down and climbing back up, rappelling on Mars would be a lot easier than on Earth.

Thank God for small favors, he thought. After so much

adversity, they would take any advantages wherever they could find them.

Still, the two-hundred-meter drop was awesome—and it was just the beginning. They successfully rappelled several more times, alternating with bouts of walking, bouldering, scrambling, rock climbing, and scree sliding.

After several hours they paused for water and a brief rest. Townsend, clearly more worn by the constant effort, turned to the historian. "It seems that I'm not as young as I used to be."

McGee had noted Townsend's limited technique during the descent, but had said nothing, mindful of the commander's pride. The military man was tough and game, and appeared to have been taught the basics of mountaineering at some point, but his lack of real experience was painfully obvious.

"Take it easy, Colonel. The gravity here is only about a third of Earth's, but the weight and clumsiness of our spacesuits and breathing gear makes this at least as tricky as a climb down any terrestrial canyon."

Townsend rubbed his sore left shoulder and added ruefully, "With the plus that if you fall and crack your faceplate, you die a blood-coughing, vacuum-breathing, agonizing death."

"Even a broken ankle could doom us, Colonel. So be very careful."

Tired as they were, they had little choice but to immediately resume their advance. Again they had to rappel, scramble, scree, march, and boulder. The pair made it to another good traveling ledge, which turned into a miniature canyon contained within the larger canyon's wall. As they marched downward quite a distance along this route, all view of the greater world beyond was cut off. Then suddenly the path bent, and before them was a sheer canyon wall towering thirty meters above them.

Trudging back several miles to the head of the channel and trying an alternative route was a prospect too demoralizing to contemplate. There could be no turning back.

"We're going to have to make a frontal assault on this cliff face." McGee pulled a set of steel pitons from his pack, and turned to the mission commander. Sheer guts and grit wouldn't be sufficient here. For once his voice was authoritative. "I'll climb the face alone, Colonel; then you can use my safety rope to follow."

For an instant it seemed as if Townsend would argue, but then he thought the better of it and simply gestured for the professor to proceed. McGee had to admire the man's courage. *Good, he's brave enough to be realistic. We might make it yet.*

He stepped up to the wall and perceived a tiny handhold above, and the slightest sliver of a foothold at about chest height. Carefully, he surveyed the remainder of the wall, a bump here, a crack there, and the concept of a route upward jelled in his mind. It had been nearly three years since he'd gone rock climbing, but his eyes were still practiced. Yes, there was a way. Five pitons. He selected six and put them in his belt pouch.

This wouldn't be so hard . . . if this were Earth, and I weren't wearing this Marsuit. Oh, for a T-shirt, shorts, and an old pair of climbing shoes. His mind went back to the first time he had rock-climbed, in Boulder. He'd been taken to an impressive formation called the Maiden by Kelly, a lithe young female climber, on a first date. Though he was an experienced hiker and mountaineer, ascending that sheer rock face had seemed impossible. But up Kelly had gone, ascending easily by means of invisible handholds and footholds. Then she'd waved for him to follow, merrily trapping him into attempting to duplicate her feat of terrifying lunacy. What had she called out to him?

Make yourself one with the rock.

Boulder philosophy. The Zen of rock climbing. Oh well, as bizarre as it seemed, it had worked that day.

Make yourself one with the rock.

He pressed his body as close to the cliff face as the suit would allow, dug his fingers into the cracklike handhold above, put one foot sideways on the minute shelf of a ledge below, and pushed. The suit scraped across the rocky wall, but it did not tear, and he was up nearly a meter.

Townsend's voice crackled in his helmet radio: "Careful you don't cut that suit."

"Roger that." He found his next set of handholds and footholds, and pushed again. Up another meter. *At least the muscle part of this is easy,* he thought. *One-third g is very cool for rock climbing. Eat your heart out, Boulder.*

He pushed again, and again. Now he was halfway up. The next handhold did not exist . . . but there was a hairline crack. He took his first spike and inserted its tip, then pulled the hammer from his belt and tapped lightly. The rock was sandstone and the spike went in easily enough. He lowered a climbing line to the ground, attached part of it to the spike with a carabiner, and then another portion to himself. This was "protection." If he were to fall, he could now fall not much lower than the spike.

Then up another meter, and another piece of protection. Two more spikes, two more pieces of protection, up again, another spike, more protection, up again, then another spike, up again, one more, another protection, then up, and up—and he'd made it to the top.

He pulled himself onto the mini canyon rim, stood up, and surveyed the downward slope that would have to serve as their way forward. More boulders and cliffs, but it was all downhill. It should be passable enough.

McGee fastened his end of the line around a medium-sized boulder, walked back to the ledge and waved to Townsend. "Come on up!" he shouted.

The shout was unnecessary, since they were communicating by radio, and his loud voice echoed uncomfortably inside his helmet. *OK, so I guess my adrenaline is up a bit,* he admitted to himself.

The rope went taut, and a minute later a panting Townsend appeared at the top. He looked McGee in the eye. "A bit excited, are we now?" he ribbed.

McGee answered with a shrug and gestured toward the

waiting path that led downward again. Without a word, they were on their way once more.

More of the same for the next few hours. They had to rappel down one cliff face after another, and climb their way out of several more box canyons. As they made their descents, the dislodged pebbles that rattled down canyon walls turned into small avalanches. On more than one occasion, a hand slipped, and a body went swinging out on a cable, only to be hauled back in by a stalwart companion.

Finally they reached the bottom and began trudging along a dry riverbed, flanked by the towering walls of the Valles Marineris. McGee and Townsend scrambled down boulders into a deeper ravine, which turned to the right, suddenly opening into a valley filled with huge stromatolites. Gigantic formations lay scattered everywhere, far more impressive than the stromatolites Rebecca and McGee had discovered on their earlier mission.

The historian was awed. "If only Rebecca were here."

Townsend just shook his head. "She'll have to settle for photographs. We've no room in our packs for any of those."

McGee took out his video recorder and scanned the stromatolites. As they marched on, the formations became progressively more complex and bizarre. In many places he saw the same blue-green signature that had led to the discovery of extant life, but here it was much more apparent. Some stromatolites even exhibited alternative varieties of blue-green pigment. *There's more life here than we thought. There is much here that is left to discover.* His sense of wonder reawakened, McGee tried to zoom in on some of the more novel objects as he continued the trek without pausing.

Eventually the two men made their way out of the ravine and into an open canyon floor region that was devoid of stromatolites. They marched on, trudging, bouldering, scrambling. Finally they rounded a bend in the canyon— and in the distance they could see the second ERV.

Townsend and McGee stood gaping in amazement for a

few seconds, then set off for the vehicle in as close an approximation of a run as the rough terrain allowed. Upon arriving at the ERV, they were winded, exhausted, but charged with excitement. They climbed the access ladder, Townsend first.

The outer airlock door opened easily enough, and the two climbed into the lower cabin without difficulty. The disorienting sight gave them a bit of a shock: Here were the snug, completely immaculate quarters planned for the next returning crew, who now would never be launched.

McGee took a sidelong glance at the pantry loaded with edible rations. Unfortunately, the two would not be able to carry much with them on the way back out, but at least they would eat well tonight.

Still, dining was not their mission, and they left the lower deck and climbed into the control cabin. Townsend ducked under the control panel, emerging seconds later with a computer card that appeared to be in perfect shape. The colonel applied a small electrical meter to two of the card's terminals, and the meter's green light flashed on. He applied yet another set of connectors, and the green light went on again. As one test after another showed green, McGee's spirits rose. Finally the colonel gave him a big thumbs up.

"Salvation," McGee said in a hushed voice.

Townsend put the computer card down. At the control panel, he threw switches and checked readouts. Satisfied with what he saw, he removed his helmet. "The life support system is working fine, Professor. We'll shack up here for the night. It's much too late to try an ascent today."

McGee was grateful for the opportunity to get out of his helmet and shuck his suit. "Can we call the *Beagle* and let them know we made it?"

Townsend shook his head. "This ERV's only radio is X-band, with no over-the-horizon capability. Its voice channel needs programming, and we don't have time for that. But we can try sending a signal to the DSN, via the ERV's engineering telemetry link, which is now up and running.

That'll at least let them know we're here, and they can relay the good news to the *Beagle*."

But the thought of the untouched pantry downstairs and McGee's growling stomach made it clear to him that they should have other priorities. "Great idea, but can't it wait till after dinner?"

Townsend grinned. "You bet it can." The two of them raced down the ladder to loot the food supplies.

Then they ate, and ate, in the manner of men who had put in a very hard day's work. It was several hours before they finished.

CHAPTER 23

IT WAS LATE THAT NIGHT VALLES MARINERIS TIME, MID-afternoon Houston time, that some strange events began to unfold at the Johnson Space Center.

In Mission Control, Al Rollins got the initial readout that set things in motion. He waved Phil Mason over to get his attention. "Chief, I just got a report from the DSN station at Goldstone. They say that the propellant level monitor on the ERV *Homeward Bound* is flickering erratically."

"That's strange." The well-dressed Chief of Operations scowled. "There is no propellant in that ERV. It was emptied the same night as the *Retriever*."

Tex Logan called across the room. "Let me have a look at that telemetry."

Rollins threw a switch, and an oscilloscope trace appeared on Tex's monitor. The old veteran stared at it for a few moments, searching for some kind of pattern, and then it was obvious. Tex looked up and grinned. "It's Morse code. See, these long bumps are dashes, and the short ones are dots. It says:

'L,O,J,S,C,C,A,R,D,G,O,O,D,A,L,L,F,I,N,E,T,A,N,D,M, H,E,L,' and then repeats."

The other flight controllers scribbled down the letters as Tex read them off. Rollins was first to spot words. "Good all?"

Alicia Castillo went further. "I get 'Card good all fine.' "

Comprehending at last, Mason's eyes went wide with joy. "They made it!" he shouted.

The Mission Controllers cheered madly. Though they had remained comfortable and safe in Houston, they'd been nearly as psychologically drained by the ordeal of the past year as the crew on Mars. For months, they had been wound like springs, watching hope ebb, measuring growing disaster on their dials. Suddenly, the *Beagle* crew had a fighting chance again. The whooping and hollering lasted over a minute.

Finally, things settled down enough for Mason to continue. He straightened his tie and smiled. "And the rest of the message?"

Tex had more of the puzzle worked out. "This part is a wraparound of 'Hello JSC,' but I still don't get 'TANDM.' "

"TANDM," Mason mused. "T and M? Townsend and McGee."

Again the flight controllers cheered.

Special Assistant Darrell Gibbs wandered over, looking oddly nervous. "Why don't we send them a reply, Phil?"

Mason hesitated, "Do you think we should? We're not budgeted for DSN transmission time right now."

Gibbs smiled. "Now really, what's a few bucks at a time like this?"

Mason nodded. "You're right. Sure, go right ahead." He rubbed his hands together happily. "This is great. This is great."

As Alicia Castillo leaned over and typed rapidly at her keyboard, Gibbs looked up at the NASA Select TV monitor. *I hope you're watching this, Holloway,* he thought.

From his flat in Clear Lake, Craig Holloway gazed listlessly at his TV, feeling bored. Though he watched the channel,

NASA Select was so dull, just endless dead time depicting nothing happening at Mission Control. It was amazing that a heavily subsidized TV network with a $14 billion per year special effects budget would produce such low-quality programming, day after day, month after month, year after year. If anyone with brains were running NASA Select, the channel could serve as an enormous educational tool and a means of growing support for space exploration. Evidently the space agency's PR hacks either didn't care or were brain-dead.

In the nine months since he'd been fired, Holloway had become a first-class TV watcher. Though uninteresting, NASA Select gave him all the information he needed to keep tabs on every aspect of the mission. And it did so on an hour-by-hour basis. From February through July, there hadn't been much reason for him to do anything, since the crew was doing a good enough job of making their own situation worse. Their efforts to dig enough moist dirt to fuel the ERV were obviously hopeless.

Then they had changed tactics to searching for subsurface water with radar and drilling. That was another matter, as it had opened the possibility that a lucky strike might provide the means for them to return and contaminate the Earth with a horrible alien virus, or ruin its remaining desert wildernesses with designer Frankenplants. Thus Holloway had been forced into action.

He had tried to be subtle; the rover fan malfunction had been a tour-de-force. Who would have expected Major Llewellyn to be able to fix it real-time? And no one should have been able to catch the helium oxygen purge of the *Beagle* in time. Bad luck that Rebecca had been playing with her rabbit at that exact moment, which acted like a canary in a coal mine and warned the doctor in time.

Then, before he could try anything else, the crew had gone off and struck water, just like that. Incredible!

Once that happened, Holloway had no more room for subtlety. Even with a risk that he might be caught, he had to save the Earth. Drastic measures had been called for. So, as soon as Townsend had reactivated the flight control telemetry receiver on the ERV, Holloway had found a way to fry the card. Backdating the blowout to January 28 had been a really cute idea, though, since it threw the event into the same bag as his successful propellant-dumping action. Since he had covered his trail perfectly, NASA had already been forced to drop charges with regard to that, and no court would charge him twice. Provided nothing else was required of him, he was free and clear.

It was interesting, that business about NASA letting him off without a trial. At first he'd thought no one in the government had a clue as to what he'd done. It had come as a bit of a shock, then, when he'd hacked into Darrell Gibbs' computer and discovered that the Science and Security Advisor knew everything—but wouldn't tell NASA in order to keep the existence of self-erasing nano-encryption top-secret! Apparently, Holloway wasn't the only person who recognized that there were more important things than the lives of a few adventurers.

But now something was happening on the tube. While everyone at Mission Control cheered, Holloway sat at home and cursed. The colonel must have made it to the backup ERV *Homeward Bound*. So now the crew had gotten themselves another computer card. He clenched his fists in frustration. It seemed like whatever he did, those bastards always found an answer. If Townsend got that card back to the ERV *Retriever,* Holloway realized, the colonel might cut off its engineering telemetry receiver from the DSN. If he did that, he would be home free. That couldn't be allowed.

On NASA Select, he saw Darrell Gibbs step over to talk with Phil Mason. The Chief of Operations nodded, and little Alicia Castillo started to type. Then Gibbs looked into the camera, on purpose. In a strange way, Holloway felt that the SSA Special Assistant was looking directly at him. *What are you saying to me, Mr. Gibbs?* Then Holloway realized what was going on. *He's getting them to send a message to the ERV. This is my chance! Thank you, Mr. Gibbs!*

He had no time to create any new programming, so he pulled up one of his former tricks—activating the onboard fire-suppression oxygen purge. That attempt had failed in the Hab, but Townsend and McGee had no inconvenient rabbits in the ERV. For good measure, he added a time delay. This time the purge would occur while they were sleeping. It was a very humane way to kill. The two men would simply never wake up.

Holloway typed furiously and hit the Send key. In seconds his modem was activated, and with the help of the Trojan Horse program he had left behind at Mission Control, his computer found all the required passwords and was past the obsolete security gate of the JSC computer system.

"Good night, boys," he said. "Sleep well."

At Mission Control, Alicia Castillo had finished typing out a message of congratulations addressed to Townsend and McGee from all the folks at JSC. "That's excellent," Gibbs murmured. "Phil, shall we send our greeting to the conquering heroes?"

Mason nodded, and Alicia began to input the transmission codes.

Tex watched the proceedings with dismay. Why did they have to transmit anything? They could be giving the hacker access to the ERV! Why would Al Rollins go along, when the stakes were so high? *Was he only humoring me last night?* Or did he think that just because Alicia was writing a simple message in clear view, it couldn't be dangerous. Tex wasn't so sure.

"Ready to transmit, Phil," Alicia said.

"Very well, proceed."

Was that a smirk of satisfaction that crossed Gibbs' face? Why did the SSA man want to send Townsend a message so badly? What did it matter, unless—

As the diminutive Hispanic woman reached for the transmit switch, Tex yelled, "Alicia, stop!"

Her hand recoiled as if she had touched a hot oven. Confused, she looked to Mason, who glowered at the veteran. "Tex, what do you think you're doing?"

For a moment, the old Texan was at a loss, knowing Mason would discount any hunch or conspiracy theory he had to offer. Then suddenly he had an idea. "The simulator. We should send the message to the software simulator first."

The ERV simulator was a computer programmed identically to the one on the *Homeward Bound*. Standard procedure was to send any engineering software uploads to such a simulator before transmission to an actual spacecraft. Years ago, the Soviets had lost two spacecraft because they had not followed this sound practice.

Gibbs frowned and said quickly, "That's hardly necessary. It's just a text message."

For Tex, that clinched it. He looked Gibbs square in the eye. "Why are you in such a hurry to send the message?"

The SSA man did not condescend to answer him. Instead he turned to the Chief of Operations. "Phil, are you going to let Mission Control be directed by a senile old crank?"

"Certainly not," Mason answered. Gibbs had hit him in a sensitive spot.

Al Rollins spoke up. "Chief. The telemetry to the ERV will be received on an engineering channel. Technically speaking, procedures do require that it be sent to the simulator first." He winked at Tex.

Gibbs smiled, looking very reasonable. "Oh, come on! Since when do we mindlessly follow the book around here?"

That comment did not sit well with Mason. True, the *Beagle* crew had violated plenty of procedures; occasionally in the heat of action, Mission Control had taken a few shortcuts, too. But there was no reason to make a practice of it. "I see no need to bend the rules when we don't have to, Darrell. If the procedures dictate simulator testing prior to transmittal on this frequency, then that's what we'll do . . . even if it might seem pointless." He nodded to Rollins. "Send it to the sim."

Rollins punched buttons on his panel. "Re-routing to simulator . . . There, message sent."

Mason turned to the old-timer. "Tex, do you have the simulator up and running?"

"On the board." The screen above his desk displayed numerous systems diagrams: propulsion, life support, avionics, all glowing red, green, and blue.

To the manager's eye, it was incomprehensible. "What's happening?"

Tex ran his tongue over his teeth thoughtfully. "The clock was updated when the message was received. Other than that . . . not much."

Gibbs wore a knowing smile of vindication, clearly exasperated by the fuss. "Now can we go ahead and send?"

Once more, Mason signaled to proceed, but as Alicia reached for the Send switch, Rollins gently moved her hand aside. "Chief, this is a low-priority message, so if you don't mind, just as an exercise, I'd like to run it through the backup simulator at Lockheed Martin as well."

The suggestion surprised even Tex, but then he thought, *Of course. The hacker could have screwed up our simulator too. Good thinking, Al.*

Gibbs's reaction was less favorable. "That's ridiculous!" But before he could continue, his cell phone rang. He opened it. "Gibbs here."

The SSA Special Assistant was shocked when he heard Craig Holloway's voice on the other end. "Gibbs, I know you're on my side. Listen to me! Whatever you do, don't let them run that message through the Lockmart simulator. The fate of the Earth is at stake!"

Rattled, Gibbs instantly terminated the call. He looked around the room, thinking fast. How did Holloway know? *What should I do? No choice, now I've got to pull it off.*

After he folded his cell phone again, Rollins looked at him curiously. "What's so ridiculous about running a sim, Mr. Gibbs?"

Regaining his composure, the SSA Special Assistant faced Rollins with all the superiority he could muster. "It's ridiculous because this is a two-sentence text message that we all just wrote right here. It was idiotic to simulate it in the first place. Now you want to send it to the backup simulator, which we haven't used in three years, even for executables. You don't think that's absurd?"

"Message sent to Lockmart sim," Tex announced.

Gibbs exploded, drawing stares from the others in the room. "Hold it! No one gave you permission to do that!"

The open hostility alarmed Alicia. "Hey, hold the machismo, boys. It's just a sim."

"Yeah," Tex smiled broadly at Gibbs and gave an innocent shrug. "It's just a sim. What could you possibly be worried about?"

"Well, as long as we're running it, let's see what we've got," Mason said. "Al, put it on our board."

The operators eyed the displays; there was no change.

Gibbs looked around the room. "Okay, what a waste of time. We've run the backup sim. Now can we transmit?"

"Proceed," Mason said.

Alicia began to reach for the switch, but was again blocked by Rollins. "Alicia, wait," he said, staring at the simulator board intently.

"What is it?" she asked.

"I'm not sure." Rollins' voice was calm again. "I thought I saw a change in the power distribution in the life-support system, but if it was there, it was just a little shift, too small to matter."

Though edgy, the Chief of Operations was not so dismissive. Software was every mission manager's nightmare; the smallest error could mean disaster. Little shifts could grow in time. "Tex, try accelerating the time vector on the simulation."

Tex quickly typed a few keystrokes. "Okey-dokey. Taking her to warp one, an hour a minute." He stood up, wearing an expression that was a mixture of horror and vindication. "Now, this is mighty interesting."

Al Rollins leaned closer. "Wow!"

"What's interesting?" Mason asked nervously.

"It seems that our little letter of congratulations—you know, the simple two-sentence text message we all wrote right here—caused the ERV to replace the oxygen in its air with helium." The Texan grinned, showing impossibly bad teeth. "Funny thing about friendly letters, they can do the darnedest things."

Rollins shouted at Gibbs. "So it was you! You were the one who caused the malf in the *Beagle*'s air system. You tried to kill our people!"

Mason looked accusingly at Gibbs, whose skin paled a bit.

"Phil, be realistic. How could I do anything? I never touch any controls around here."

For a moment, Mason was stumped. Then Tex interjected. "Al, do you have anything?"

Rollins typed a few commands and then peered at his computer screen. "Yes, it seems our system here in Mission Control has just had a visitor. Phone number 281-406-3647."

Alicia looked up. "That's Craig Holloway's number!"

Mason blew his stack. "Holloway! That nut has been doing this to us! He should have been in jail months ago." He turned to Gibbs. "And your people said there was no evidence against him!"

"Hey, Gibbs," Tex called, "that phone call you just got. Who was that from?"

Mason stepped closer to the SSA Special Assistant. "Let's see that phone, Darrell."

Gibbs backed away. "You can't have it. This phone uses White House encryption technology. None of you are authorized to carry it."

As Mason closed in on Gibbs, Rollins and Tex approached him from either side. From her desk, Alicia Castillo pulled out a pair of scissors, and snapping them in a nonchalant manner, started walking in the SSA man's direction. He quickly handed Mason the phone.

Mason punched the instant recall button, and the same

incriminating number appeared. He turned the little screen so that Gibbs couldn't deny it.

"He called me. I never called him." *That's right,* Gibbs thought to himself. *They don't have anything on me.* Furthermore, in less than a week, the Administration would be a lame duck, and his own friends would be in power. *I've nothing to fear from this pack of nerds.* His courage restored, the SSA assistant faced the Mission Control boss with a superior smirk.

Mason looked him in the eye. "From the beginning wasn't it? The rover failure, even the pyro bolts for the tether separation? And the ERV propellant tanks' draining, and the burning of the computer card? You did those, too?"

As if enjoying the manager's hysteria, Gibbs just smirked.

His tie askew, the Chief of Operations fought down the urge to strangle the arrogant young man. "Why? You're not a Stetsonite."

Gibbs chuckled. "No, certainly not."

The preppie's attitude was maddening. Mason took another step forward. "Then why?" he demanded again.

"Let's just say that the laws of cause and effect in these matters are a bit above your head. And well above your labor grade."

Above my labor grade, eh? Mason thought. *Ah, politics! I should have known.* "Let me guess," he began. "It's no secret that you have powerful friends."

"You might say that."

The whole business was now becoming clear. Mason began to relax a bit. "And some of these so-called friends told you they would appreciate it if our astronauts did not return?"

Gibbs just smirked again. To Mason, that was as good as a confession.

There's just one question left, Mason thought. *Maybe the ass will blurt the answer.* "In the Administration or the opposition?"

This time Gibbs' smile was not merely condescending, but almost sadistic. "I don't see how that's any of your business, but rest assured that they have sufficient influence to make sure I don't end up like that poor lunatic Holloway."

As the others stared at him in outraged amazement, Gibbs turned to leave the room. "Well, so long," he said with amusement. "Work hard, little people. Just think, if you're successful and get the crew home, you'll make Colonel Townsend a very rich man. Who knows, he may even send each of you an autographed picture of his new yacht."

Gibbs started to stride out. While his back was turned, Mason motioned to Alicia, who picked up a telephone.

"Darrell," the Mission Control manager called out.

Gibbs condescended to turn back a final time. "Yes?"

"Do you really think those powerful friends will go to the mat for you?"

"Of course."

Mason looked the younger man in the eye. "And why is that?"

Gibbs answered with the confidence of a teacher explaining the facts of life to a dunce. "Because if they don't, I'll implicate them."

Tex interjected. "I'll bet that's exactly what Oswald thought."

"Oswald?" Gibbs appeared slightly confused.

"Lee Harvey Oswald," the Texan explained, showing his bad teeth again. "Before your time. I suggest you get yourself some life insurance, son."

Gibbs paled. He made for the door, but was stopped by two big security guards who appeared in the doorway.

Mason smiled. "I think, though, that you'll get a chance to do a little more talking than Oswald did."

As the guards handcuffed the Special Assistant, Mason picked up his console phone. He held Gibbs' cellular in front of Tex.

"Now we find the man on the grassy knoll," the manager said dryly.

CHAPTER 24

UNAWARE OF THEIR NEAR-RENDEZVOUS WITH DEATH, THE
pair in the *Homeward Bound* ERV soundly slept the night
away. Townsend's wristwatch alarm awakened them at the
edge of dawn the following morning. The two explorers
would need the maximum time for their difficult trek out
of the canyon.

After a quick breakfast, he and McGee made final preparations for the hike out of Valles Marineris. They subjected every piece of their gear to a final checkout. The
colonel wrapped the computer card in soft packing material,
after which he placed the wrapping in a plastic container
and stuffed it into McGee's pack. The two men then zipped
into their Marsuits.

Townsend turned to his companion. "Ready for the hard
part, Professor?"

"You realize, Colonel, that once we start climbing,
there's no turning back and there's no stopping. We can't
survive a night outside in our suits. We make it all the way
back to the rover, or we die."

Townsend snapped his helmet into position. "Roger, let's

go." Through his helmet, his words sounded oddly distorted, but his resolve was unmistakable. McGee donned his helmet as well; then they strapped on their packs and cycled out of the ERV airlock. Townsend reached up to secure the outer hatch before joining McGee at the foot of the ladder.

McGee gave the *Homeward Bound* one fond farewell glance, and they were off.

It was about seven A.M., local time, but they set out at a rapid clip, knowing the climb would take longer than the descent, and that being caught in cliff shadows at sunset meant certain death.

At a forced march, they managed to reach the base of the first major ascent before noon. Along the cliffside hung the last line they had rappelled down the day before. Both men stared up at the endlessly tall wall of rock. The thin wind blew fine dust, and the rope swayed gently.

We've made good time, McGee thought. *If the weather doesn't get any worse, we might make it out. A big "if."*

McGee tested the line with a strong tug. "Ready, Colonel? There's no turning back after this."

Townsend gave a grim nod behind his helmet, and they began to climb. The two men reached the top of the first rope, then started scrambling across a boulder field. As they climbed the second rope, a wind blew ever more fiercely. Without pausing, they continued the ascent, climbing, trudging, bouldering, scrambling.

Finally, in the late afternoon, they reached the last rope. The wind, which had been only troublesome at the start of the climb, now blew out of control, picking up scouring dust and howling in the vanishingly thin atmosphere. The sky darkened with dust, obscuring the sunset in the west. McGee noticed the air temperature growing colder by the minute, and despite the thinness of the air, the hurricane-speed winds were delivering a horrible chill. He looked up the rope at the sheer cliff that extended high above them until it disappeared into the murk.

Townsend seemed exhausted. "Not the best climbing

weather," he said. There was a distinct shiver in his voice.

McGee heard that shiver and knew what it meant. *The colonel's not going to make it.* Age and lack of proper technique had taken their toll. The older man was clearly played out. With a little rest he might have had a chance, but neither of them had any time to rest.

McGee made the offer anyway. "Want to try waiting it out?"

There was a momentary pause. "No. Only an hour of daylight left. We've got to go. Now."

The voice of courage, McGee thought. *If we wait, we both get to live a few hours, until the night gently takes us. If we go, I have a fighting chance—but he will fall.*

Do not go gently into that good night.

McGee mentally saluted the colonel and started up the rope. The wild motions of the swaying line made the climb a nightmare. More than once, he crashed into a rocky outcropping that revealed its existence too late as it loomed up unexpectedly. He hauled himself up the line like a madman; he knew he couldn't take this treatment for long.

Suddenly there was no cliff face above him, only a ledge at face level. He scrambled over it and lay panting on the ground. It had taken six minutes of sheer hell, but he'd reached the rim of the endless canyon.

Now, how to get Townsend up? McGee had hoped to be able to haul the man up on the rope. But on the climb up he'd noted that the line was badly frayed. It was now too likely that a moving cord would scrape itself to pieces on some rock, and the colonel would drop to his death. No, climbing was the commander's only chance. He stood up and turned his Marsuit radio to maximum. "Colonel, I'm at the top. It's not too far. Go for it."

At the base of the final cliff, Townsend shivered in the howling gale. While waiting for McGee to climb, he had taken a short but necessary rest, but every muscle in his body felt sprained. He heard the professor's encouraging summons to ascend, but was realistic enough to know that he just didn't have it left within him. But he knew he couldn't stay where he was, either. It was getting darker and colder by the minute. To remain here meant death. To ascend meant death. Retreat was impossible.

From his belt pouch Townsend took out a picture, to gaze one last time at his beautiful wife and two fine little boys. *I'm sorry, Karen, I thought I could make it. Mike, Petey, I wish I'd gotten to see you grow.* A tear welled in his eye. He glanced up the rappelling line, now flailing crazily in the growing darkness.

"Colonel, you can do it!" McGee called, the feigned optimism in his voice all too obvious.

Townsend grabbed the line. "Okay, I'm coming." He looked one more time at his sons. *Remember me, boys. Remember how I lived and how I died. A man never gives up.*

Townsend pulled on the line and began to haul himself upward, finding hidden reserves of strength somewhere inside. He had not thought himself capable of climbing at all, but he pulled his body upward more with strength of will than the strength of his arms. Incredibly, he ascended more than halfway, lifted by force of spirit—then his luck ran out.

Three-fourths of the way up, an enormous gust crashed him into a rocky outcrop on the cliff face. In the violence of the blow, he lost his grip on the line, which disappeared into the inky darkness, leaving him stranded with one smashed arm and the other clutching weakly to the outcrop itself.

Up at the canyon rim, McGee saw the line go slack and knew that something had gone dreadfully wrong. He yelled into his radio, "Colonel! Are you okay?"

For several seconds, he heard nothing but static. Then a faint answer came back. "I think my arm's broken. I'm on an outcrop."

McGee stared into the swirling maelstrom below. He couldn't see the frayed line, or the ledge, or the man. But the colonel had kept climbing for quite a while. He could be close.

"Can you see anything?" McGee shouted. "What's near you?"

"Only this outcrop." Townsend's answer was barely audible above the radio static caused by the swirling dust. "It looks like a bird's beak."

The beak. McGee had noticed it too. It was only fifty meters down. Fifty impossible meters through gale-blasted freezing darkness. A rescue attempt under these conditions would be insanely reckless. He couldn't possibly do it.

"Hold on, I think I can get you."

"McGee, no!" Townsend's voice carried a kind of panic. "You've got the computer card. Go back to the ship."

The salvaged card would make the ERV flyable, it could let them all get back to Earth. But who would fly the ship? Gwen? Maybe. *But can I leave him here?*

"I'm coming down," McGee said. He grabbed the rope and prepared to start his descent.

"No. Go back! That's an order!"

McGee hesitated. His mind flashed back to their recent departure from the *Beagle*. He saw Rebecca looking him in the eye, tenderly telling him to take care. McGee stopped at the edge of the dropoff, then peered down into the swirling dust, concentrating. As if in a vision, he thought he saw Townsend clinging to his outcropping.

"Screw your orders, Colonel," the historian muttered; he grabbed the line and went over the side.

McGee swung wildly in the wind as he slid down the line. He let himself fall a few meters at a time, securing himself after the twentieth drop. *He's got to be around here somewhere*. McGee peered through the dimness in all directions. He switched on his suit lamp to make himself visible. "Colonel, where are you?"

"Over here, below and to your left."

McGee swiveled his head and searched in the indicated direction. At first he saw nothing but swirling dust, but then the beam fell on his target. Townsend clung grimly to the rocky beak with one arm; the other hung limp. He was five meters below and ten to one side.

"I see you, Colonel! Hold on."

McGee kicked out against the cliff wall to make some horizontal progress, but the wind slammed him back against a different rock protrusion. Fortunately, he managed to swing around and let his legs take the blow, and used the energy of impact to kick out even harder in the correct direction. For several more swings McGee bounced back and forth among various outcroppings, when suddenly he landed on Townsend's rock.

He secured himself by wrapping his legs about it from above. Quickly he reached down and looped a line beneath the commander's armpits, then clamped its end fast to his belt.

Townsend's voice was groggy with pain. "McGee, you're a goddamn anarchist. Wouldn't last a day in the Air Force!"

"I know, sir. Now shut up while I rescue you."

He removed Townsend's pack and threw it into the howling abyss below. Then he fastened another cable through the harness on the back of Townsend's Marsuit and attached it to his own harness, thereby adding the colonel to the load of his own backpack.

"Well, here goes."

McGee grabbed the thrumming rope and began the ascent through the storm. The winds blew him every which way, banging him against nearby outcroppings. With Townsend's additional weight, the going was very hard. But they ascended, one meter at a time.

McGee's arms ached, already strained by overexertion and bruised by impacts. *This is impossible,* he thought. *No it isn't. I'm lifting triple my mass . . . but this is Mars. I'm just hauling my own weight. It's only hard because of fatigue.* His brain tried to exhort his body. *You can do it. You can do it. . . .*

Arm over arm he went, using his feet to fend off slamming blows as the riotous winds repeatedly attempted to smash him into the cliff. Suddenly the wind slammed him sideways into an outcrop, and he was caught off guard. The shock of the impact was so great that he lost his grip on the rope. He fell into the dark, and Townsend fell with him.

The wind slapped the rope sharply against his suit, like a whip. The line bounced off, but McGee reached out and made one last desperate grab. He caught the rope, but the shock of jerking his fall to a stop nearly pulled his arm out of its socket. He loosened his grip, and the line ran through his gloved palm. Then somehow he managed to close his hands again, enough to stop the fall. In four terrifying seconds the two men had fallen nearly twenty meters.

They hung together on the strained rope, swinging crazily in the blackness of the storm-darkened night. The colonel was limp and silent, not struggling, not moving at all. McGee was in intense pain; that last grab at the rope had ripped muscles in his left arm.

The temperature outside was minus 70° centigrade, and convection from the roaring winds delivered a brutal chilling signal that cut mercilessly through the high-grade insulation of the Marsuit. A veteran of McKinley and Everest, McGee had always considered himself tough against cold—but this was too much. He began to shiver uncontrollably.

With his strength ebbing and the outside cold increasing, McGee knew he had only minutes left. *Climb*. His arms were not strong enough, but he still had strength in his legs. If only he could use them. *Climb!*

Or else they would both die.

The wind swung him around toward the cliff face again, and he saw his chance. He brought his feet around, restraining his instincts to fend off the rock, and instead used the impact to try to run up the cliff. It almost worked.

For a second as his legs compressed to take the blow, then expanded again, the dominant acceleration vector on the two men was horizontal, with the downward pointing gravity of Mars creating a moderate apparent uphill slope. But as soon as the expansion was over, McGee lost all traction and he began to fall again. He stopped the fall by quickly hauling in the slack in the line.

They had made three meters.

The wind banged him sideways into the cliff, but some-how he held the line, repositioned his feet, and during impact made another several meters' progress in his bizarre run up the side of the cliff. He could not see the top, could not think about how far he had left to climb. He repeated the impact-and-scramble again and again, more times than he could count.

And suddenly found himself on the canyon rim.

Swiftly, McGee crawled over the ledge and dragged himself and the limp colonel into a wind-sheltered nook created by several large rocks. He unloaded Townsend off his back like a sack of potatoes, then collapsed beside him. The wind howled around the rocks, but not within them, and without its help, the cold mercifully lost some of its punch. The Marsuit's electrical heaters began to gain ground, and within a few minutes the returning warmth allowed McGee to become functional again.

Scraping a few more threads of energy from his body, he turned to examine the colonel. Though uncommunicative, at least he was still breathing. McGee propped up his companion, and rubbed the man vigorously.

Gradually, Townsend came to. He blinked at McGee. "You shouldn't have done that."

Feeling his sore arm and aching body, McGee could only nod in agreement. "I know."

Townsend smiled. "But I'm sure glad you did."

The two men looked at each other, exchanging complete recognition.

"Thanks, McGee. You're a real super guy."

The colonel extended his hand, and McGee clasped it. "This may be a little late, but I'm glad to have you aboard, Professor."

Peering upward, McGee saw a star. The sky was clearing; the winds were letting up. "Colonel, can you walk? The rover's not far, but we have to get there."

"I think so."

He helped Townsend to his feet. Steadying each other, the two hobbled up the slope, painstakingly trudging the remaining two hundred meters to the rover. Ahead, a blue-white light shone near the horizon. It was Earth.

The historian's body had taken a terrible beating. But, despite all the aches and sprains and bruises, as he trudged through the Martian night with the computer card in his pack and Townsend by his side, McGee felt about as good as a man could feel.

OPHIR PLANUM
NOV. 1, 2012 17:20 MLT

When the rover arrived back at the Hab the next afternoon, Gwen was working outside. She ran after the vehicle, taking large steps in the low gravity, but McGee and Townsend did not slow the vehicle. They pulled up near the *Beagle* before she reached them.

Full of questions, Gwen followed the two men into the airlock. She could see immediately that they were both exhausted to the point of numbness. Townsend fumbled with the ladder, having difficulty moving for even such a simple task. Lending a hand, she wordlessly guided the commander inside and helped him to remove his helmet.

Followed closely by Luke, Rebecca came rushing down from the upper deck. "What happened?"

McGee pulled the computer card from his pack and unwrapped it for all to see. The faces of Luke and Rebecca lit up, but Gwen felt a mixture of emotions. She examined the computer card closely. "Does it check out green?"

"A-OK." Townsend started to take off his Marsuit, but stopped in mid-motion, grimacing from the pain.

"Colonel, you're hurt," Rebecca said, pushing forward.

"Nothing much. Just a broken arm."

Gingerly, the doctor zipped off his suit and with professional fingers probed around his arm. "Let me have a look at that in the lab."

McGee managed to get out of his Marsuit, in the process making his own injuries apparent. Gwen noticed his bruises, the haggard look on his face. "Hey, the professor's hurt too."

Taking a quick glance at McGee before she ushered Townsend out of the room, Rebecca rapidly sized up his condition. She reached over and tousled his hair.

"Oh, Kevin's okay," she said with a smile. "Come on, Colonel. That arm needs treatment, stat."

After Luke had helped the doctor escort Townsend into the lab, Gwen pulled some ice from the refrigerator, wrapped it in a cloth, and handed it to McGee.

"Here's some ice for those bruises, McGee," she said softly.

He took the ice and applied it to his bruised arm. "Thanks, Gwen."

McGee looked up and saw Gwen regarding him with deep concern, and he noticed that she had almost begun to cry. Their eyes met and she quickly looked away.

What can that mean? McGee wondered.

CHAPTER 25

THE HOUR WAS GROWING LATE AT MADISON SQUARE Garden as the final presidential debate sponsored by the League of Women Voters neared its close. The night had not been a good one for the Administration. As he entered his summation, Senator Fairchild looked out over the vast audience with confidence.

"And to conclude," the opposition candidate thundered, "nothing proves the irresponsibility and ineptitude of the current Administration more than how they have seen fit to throw away the lives of five fine Americans on a grandiose but hopeless mission to Mars. When he launched the mission, the President knew there would not be funds for follow-on or resupply flights. He knew he was sending a crew out without the necessary backup . . . but he chose to do it anyway. And now, perhaps to create martyrs in the days before the election, he has sent the brave mission commander and a crew member on a suicide trek into the deepest canyon in the solar system."

The President paled visibly, but was forced to keep his response in check.

"My friends," Fairchild continued triumphantly, "I enjoy great national accomplishments as much as the next person, but we all must realize that our goals must be conditioned by our means. To foolishly expend the lives of five of our finest citizens in a desperate bid to revive the glory days of Apollo can only be characterized as an action so ill-conceived that . . ."

As these final nails were being driven into the coffin of the Administration's political hopes, Media Chief Sam Wexler slipped into the podium area from off-stage and handed the President a note. Fairchild continued to talk, focused on his own words, but the audience watched the subtle distraction, curious. The President's eyes went wide. He looked to his wife sitting in the front row of the audience, and something incandescent passed between them. The audience began to murmur.

Fairchild faltered for a moment, and the President picked up his microphone to interrupt his opponent. "Excuse me, but I have an important announcement. I have just received word from NASA that Colonel Andrew Townsend and Professor Kevin McGee have just returned from their heroic journey to the bottom of the Martian canyon. They have successfully retrieved the spare flight computer from the backup return vehicle. It works!" He raised his voice. "The crew is coming home!"

The audience broke into mad cheers.

The President grinned from ear to ear. He called to the crowd: "Do our boys have the right stuff or what!"

The cheering and applause became overwhelming.

"The crew is coming back," the President bellowed, "and let me say this, ladies and gentlemen, our America is coming back! We're back. Let the whole world see it. America is back!" He held up his hand, pointed forefinger above looped middle finger in the "Onward!" gesture that had come to symbolize the Martian mission. Keeping his victory sign in the air, the President waved joyously to the crowd. "God bless you, and God bless the United States of America."

Not missing a beat, the First Lady ran up on stage and gave the President a joyous hug, then turned to face the cheering crowd, joining her Onward sign to that of her husband. Seizing the moment, knowing no one would dare interrupt her, she began singing spontaneously: "Oh beautiful for spacious skies, For amber waves of grain . . ."

The President joined in, then more and more people added their voices to the chorus. As the patriotic reverie swept over the audience, Senator Fairchild stood in impotent rage at his podium. Peering down at the front row, Fairchild saw Science and Security Advisor Kowalski, who looked as if he'd just been shot. Then the full nature of the situation became apparent, and Fairchild's own expression involuntarily transformed to one of deep uneasiness, then terror.

The change in Fairchild's face did not escape the notice of Wexler, who exchanged a nod and a knowing glance with NASA Administrator Tom Ryan. Both men locked their eyes on the senator's.

Oh, my God, Fairchild thought, *they know. They know everything.*

In the back of the hall, Reverend Stone made a discreet exit, with Gary Stetson anxiously following him. "Where are you going?" Stetson called in a hoarse whisper. "We can still stop them."

Stone turned and put his arm around Stetson's shoulder in a fatherly way. "Son, there's been a little change of plan."

"Oh?" Stetson glowered, trying to cling to his position.

"Yes, I have had a revelation. Starting tomorrow, my focus will shift to ensuring the health and safe return of America's heroes, who are doing God's work by staking the claim of this great nation to our neighbor planet."

"What?" Stetson was floored by this betrayal. "What about the enthalpic impact? You can't just change our line like that."

"Son, my only line has always been the bottom line, and I think it's time for you to move on."

"But what about money for my legal defense for the damage to JSC?" Stetson whined as the implications began to sink in. He was out on a limb. Without the support and popular base of this powerful, charismatic ally, he would be lost.

A well-practiced smile crossed the evangelist's face. "Try some management seminars," he advised helpfully. "Think like a tree."

CHAPTER 26

OPHIR PLANUM
NOV. 14, 2012 17:12 MLT

THE MEETING IN THE *BEAGLE* HAD DRAGGED ON FOR SEV-
eral hours, toward evening. The discussion had not gone
well for Gwen, who stood with her back to the door, tearful
but defiant.

Townsend, his arm in a sling, continued to press the issue. "You know the medical necessity, Major. You know
the consequences. And you still won't agree to an abortion?"

Gwen backed up tighter against the door. "Never! How
many times do I need to say it? Never, never, never, never,
NEVER!"

Rebecca tried to reason with the flight mechanic. "But
you don't understand, Gwen. Your baby won't have the
bone and muscle structure it needs to live on Earth. It'll be
a helpless cripple its entire life. It probably won't even be
able to survive on Earth, since its whole body will be adapted
for the one-third gravity environment of Mars."

"Then it won't go to Earth," Gwen said hotly. "It'll grow
up here on Mars. I'll stay here and bring it up myself."

Townsend was shocked by his subordinate's irrationality.

"What are you saying? Major, you're sentencing yourself to lifelong exile."

Luke said, "I'm the father, you know—don't I have a say in this? You can't expect me to go along with a crazy idea like that."

Gwen sneered at him. "I don't expect you to." Then she looked around the room and continued in a somewhat more civil tone, "I don't expect anyone to. I'm the one who sinned, and I'm willing to pay the price. But abortion, *never*. That's murder, and eternal damnation. You'll have to kill me first."

Rebecca turned to Townsend. "Colonel, you're going to have to deal with this."

Townsend shook his head. "I can't order an involuntary abortion."

"You've got to!" Rebecca slapped her hand on the table. "You know there's no way NASA will agree to our leaving a member of the crew behind. We fought our way out of this mess. We found the water, we got the computer card. That news just saved the Administration in the election, so now the President owes us big time. But if we disgrace ourselves by abandoning a member of the crew, it . . . it will destroy the entire space program, forever."

Still the colonel remained indecisive. "Yes, I know that. But there is no legal basis for—"

"Yes there is!" The tone of authority in Rebecca's voice was absolute. "I've looked up the mission regulations. Volume 43, section 12, paragraphs 881 through 912. They're very clear. In case of an inadvertent pregnancy, the fetus is to be aborted."

"NASA foresaw such a contingency?" Townsend asked.

"Yes, and their reasoning is crystal-clear too. It's obvious that no member of the crew can perform her duties to the best of her ability if she's pregnant, and the presence of a baby would disrupt the entire mission, impair the performance of every crew member, thus enhancing the probability of mission failure."

Townsend began to relax. He wasn't sure whether it was

right, but at least the regs gave a solid basis for a decision. "I guess when you step back from the problem like that, the decision becomes pretty clear."

Rebecca pushed her point. "Yes, it does. I suppose that's why it's best that regulations are written away from the heat of battle, so that cool heads can prevail. Colonel, you know what you have to do. The mission is at stake."

Rebecca could see the man was still reluctant, but almost convinced. She had to give him the strength to act. She fastened on Townsend with her beautiful, morally certain eyes. When he sheepishly nodded, Rebecca rewarded him with a hint of a smile. *Good. We'll save this mission yet,* she thought.

Suddenly there was an interruption. "Rebecca, turn it off!" McGee snapped at her.

She was stunned. "What?"

"I said, 'turn it off,' the eyes, the charm, the sweet reasoning—all of it."

Rebecca hadn't expected opposition from this quarter. "Kevin, please!" she begged. *Surely McGee must know what is at stake.*

Townsend was irritated. "I don't know what you're getting at, Professor. Dr. Sherman and I were debating the logical options available in the situation, and while I didn't agree with her at first, it now seems pretty clear that . . ."

"Colonel," McGee smiled sardonically, "with all due respect, you are no more capable of debating with Rebecca than a mouse is with a cat."

Townsend blanched. "Professor, that remark is an intolerable insult."

"Call it what you like, it's the truth." McGee looked the commander in the eye. "Colonel, she's much smarter than you are, she understands completely how you think, and she has an enormous emotional edge over you."

Townsend was puzzled. "What do you mean, emotional edge?"

"I mean that you are a lonely man, in command of a difficult situation that's way above your head, and you desperately need the approval of her wise eyes and lovely smile. She knows that, and can use it to yank you around any way she wants. Haven't you noticed how she always gets her way about anything that really matters to her? Remember how easily she convinced you to break the rules and give her the rover for that Maja Vallis sortie?"

Now it was Rebecca's turn to be offended. "But I was right!"

"True," McGee acknowledged, "you were right—incredibly, totally *right* when nearly everybody else was wrong. In fact, you're almost always right, and this mission would have failed to achieve its primary science objective if you hadn't used your magic to get your way. But you can't use it now, because this time you're not right."

This is unbelievable, Rebecca thought. "Kevin!" she pleaded, "surely you can't agree with this primitive religious nonsense."

"No, of course I don't agree with Gwen for those reasons," McGee said, "but I think I understand her. You don't. With that brilliant mind of yours, you can see right through me, or Townsend, or Luke—but to you, Gwen Llewellyn is a complete blank. In fact, you think she's insane. Gwen's not insane, she just thinks differently than you do."

"The sanity of religious ideology can be measured scientifically by its appropriateness as a guide for action in real situations," Rebecca pronounced. "By that measure, she is insane."

McGee shook his head. "No, she's not. Get this through your head, Rebecca: There's room on the sea of thought for more than one sail. You're one of those people always yakking about cultural diversity, but when confronted with the real McCoy, you recoil in horror. Maybe you *should* have read the Bible at Radcliffe. At least it would've given you some insight into what's going on here."

Rebecca's face turned beet red, and she spoke in a low voice: "Kevin, you can forget about anything happening between us on Earth. We're through."

McGee looked at her sadly. "Yes, I know, and part of me is crushed to hear you say it. Rebecca, in so many ways you're all I've ever hoped for in a woman. But this is where I draw the line."

After a few seconds of uncomfortable silence in the cabin, Townsend cleared his throat. "Professor, how you and Dr. Sherman work out your personal problems is your business. But NASA mission regulations and the logic of those who wrote them are very clear."

McGee turned to face the colonel. "Screw the logical mission regulations. We've got something with us here on Mars that overrules them."

"And what might that be?" Townsend asked.

"That!" McGee pointed out the window. Everyone looked. The American flag raised on the day after the landing was visible, still hanging on its telescoping pole, vibrating in the dusty Martian wind. A shock of recognition grew on Townsend's face as the flag reflected in his eyes.

McGee saw comprehension dawn in the commander and pressed his point home. "That, that 'glorious banner carried by our fathers over the cruel beaches of Normandy' says that she has rights!"

As Townsend glanced down at the flag shoulder-patch that adorned his bomber jacket, Gwen started to sob.

"And as long as it flies here," McGee continued, "*that's* the law we are going to follow. Mars will be free!"

Luke, however, remained unconvinced. "But what she wants to do makes no sense."

"Yes it does," McGee answered. "She may not understand it consciously, but what she's doing makes perfect sense. In fact, it's the only thing in this whole stupid mission that makes any sense."

Townsend was puzzled. "What do you mean?"

"Look, Colonel," McGee explained, "we didn't come here to look for pretty rocks, or even to search for evidence of life. We may have fooled ourselves into thinking that's why we came, but it isn't really the reason. Gwen knows—unconsciously perhaps, but she knows."

Townsend leaned back in his chair in exasperation. "Well, since none of *us* knows, Professor, and the major is not conscious of what she knows, but you are, why don't you enlighten the rest of us?"

"Gwen knows instinctively what I know as a historian. She knows that we came here to conquer a frontier, and that no frontier was ever truly conquered until some woman had the courage to go there, and raise children there."

The commander shook his head. "One woman with a child does not make a colony."

"But one family, with father, mother, and child, does."

Luke exclaimed, "But I'm not staying!"

"But I am," McGee said flatly.

A shocked silence filled the room. Then Gwen burst out crying.

Rebecca was the first to regain her composure. "Kevin, are you mad?"

"No, Rebecca, I'm not mad." McGee's voice carried a new firmness. "It's just that there comes a time when a man has to stand up and put himself behind what he believes. I've spent my whole adult life lecturing people about the importance of opening up new frontiers. I can't go back. I couldn't live with myself if I did."

Gwen looked at him with amazement. "You're willing to spend the rest of your life here with me?" she sniffled.

"Yes," McGee said tenderly, "if you'll have me."

Gwen's eyes were wide. "You'll be my husband?"

"Yes . . ." McGee smiled. "My princess."

Gwen smiled tenderly in return. "My chieftain," she said softly.

McGee was astonished by the response, and his face showed it.

Seeing his astounded expression, Gwen had to laugh. "Don't look at me like that, you old egghead. You've been talking about those Burroughs' John Carter of Mars books for the past year. Don't you think I'd take the trouble to read them?"

With a new lightness in her step, Gwen skipped over to

McGee and landed in his lap. She kissed him warmly on the lips, and then pulled back to smile at him with love in her luminous eyes. McGee could only smile back.

Gwen gently tousled his hair. "My chieftain," she whispered, and kissed him again.

OPHIR PLANUM
DEC. 16, 2012 15:00 MLT

"Are you ready yet, Dr. Sherman?" Townsend called from the galley.

"Just a minute," Rebecca responded from inside the lab. "Okay, you can start now."

The commander looked to McGee, who was standing to his right. "Are you ready, Professor?"

"You bet. Let's do it." McGee seemed nervous. Townsend smiled and pointed to Luke, who stood behind the historian. "Begin."

Luke threw a switch, and music began to play, filling the cabin with the joyful strains of Mendelssohn's *Wedding March*.

McGee's eyes shifted to watch Gwen make her entrance. She appeared, wearing a white lab coat that had somehow been modified to resemble a wedding dress. Her face was lit up by happiness, and a garland of greenhouse flowers adorned her head. *She looks like spring itself,* McGee thought.

Rebecca followed her, holding a bouquet. As the two women made their ceremonious advance, McGee marveled at his bride-to-be. *What a gem you are, Gwen. Why did it take me so long to see you?*

Gwen took another tiny step forward. She could see that the slow timing of her approach to the altar had McGee on edge, so she shot him a mischievous look and answered his objections with a grin that spoke as clearly as telepathy. *This girl's only getting married once, and I intend to make the most of it. Relax. I'll get there soon enough.*

McGee smiled sheepishly. *What a nice smile,* Gwen thought. As a little girl, she had secretly hoped that she would meet her Prince Charming someday. Not finding him among the rough types that surrounded her, she'd preferred to make herself one of the boys rather than allow herself to be one of their objects. Then she had met Kevin McGee, so good, so fine, so smart, so light spirited and strong hearted. The more she'd gotten to know him, the more she liked him. It had seemed impossible that the distinguished historian might ever notice a simple country girl like her. Then he had, and showed himself when she'd needed him most.

Back on Earth, it was night in North Carolina. She thought of her family back home. Perhaps they were looking up right now, seeing Mars in the sky.

I'm getting married in the sky, she marveled. *This is a marriage made in heaven.* She reached the altar, and turned to face McGee.

Townsend began reading.

"Dearly beloved, we are gathered here today to . . ."

CHAPTER 27

IT WAS THE MIDDLE OF THE NIGHT AT MARS BASE 1, AND only one member of the crew was awake. Four months had passed since the wedding, allowing plenty of time for research and rethinking. In the solitude of her cabin, Rebecca stared at the medical records displayed on her laptop. Their message was dismal.

Two of Gwen's aunts, one cousin, and one of her grandmother's sisters had died in childbirth. Poor rural medical facilities were partly to blame, but that wasn't the whole story. Genetics had loaded the decks against them. The family had a history of large, late infants, which, when combined with the tight-hipped boyish build of most of its women, made for high-risk pregnancies. It was the first baby that was usually the killer. After that, the anatomical changes brought about by the first birth made things a lot easier. But, though she might be able to deny her fears, Gwen was in for a nightmare.

Abortion was now out of the question. Rebecca would not even consider bringing it up. Tears of shame fogged her eyes when she recalled her previous disgraceful behavior on that matter. *Oh, Gwen, how could I have been so cruel as to try to trample on you like that? I was so arrogant, so sure I was right. All I thought about was saving the program. I never thought of you. Forgive me. Forgive me.*

And whose program had she really been trying to save? NASA's. Send a crew to Mars and return them safely to Earth. For what purpose? For the purpose of gratifying the political needs of some Washington windbags? Was that a cause worth destroying Gwen for? Was that the cause to which she had dedicated her life?

Hardly. Nor was it exobiology. As important as such research was, Rebecca knew it was just a respectable cover for her deeper passion.

No, the real cause was—

Life to Mars, and Mars to Life.

The old Mars Society slogan had stirred her soul as a youth and recruited her to the movement. It was for *that* she had braved the freezing winds and falling scaffolds of Devon Island. It was for that she had poured out her spirit in a decade-long campaign to move a nation to reach for Mars. It was for that she had given up a life of security and privilege to take on the tough and risky career of an astronaut.

But when the chips were down, she had acted as if it were all a lot of hot air. It was Gwen—poor, uneducated Gwen—who had really accepted the challenge.

For the reality of the poetic-sounding slogan would be harsh. It would be a pain-ripped woman facing death on a blood-soaked table in an inadequate delivery room.

Gwen, forgive me. I betrayed you. I betrayed myself.

I'll do anything to help you now.

Alone in her bunk, the proud doctor cried.

"What's her status?" Townsend asked Rebecca.

In private conference with the colonel in the *Beagle*'s galley at night, Rebecca surveyed her charts. "Almost due. I'd say she has about three or four weeks to go."

"No sooner?" He gritted his teeth, as if hoping for a reprieve.

Rebecca had no choice but to disappoint him. "Two weeks at the earliest," she said with certainty.

The colonel slammed his fist down on the table. "Dammit!"

The doctor was taken aback by the violence of his reaction. "What's the problem?"

With effort, Townsend calmed himself. "Today is June 28. Our window for a fast-transfer trajectory return to Earth closes on July 8."

Rebecca shook her head. "She won't have given birth by then. And there's nothing I can do to induce labor. Those kind of drugs weren't in the standard medical kit for a Mars mission, you know. And as it is, first deliveries are notoriously late."

Townsend walked over to contemplate the wall calendar. "So, either we leave her here in the midst of labor, or stay to help out and miss our launch window."

Rebecca stared in silence for several significant moments. "Colonel," she said firmly, "we've got to stay."

His face a turmoil of despair and indecision, Townsend whirled on her. "Why? McGee will be here with her. You can instruct him on what to do. And Gwen is as tough and healthy a girl as ever was. If anyone can handle a natural childbirth, she can."

"Wrong," Rebecca was firm. "Tough's the problem. That tomboy build of hers will cause trouble when it comes to getting the baby out. I'm medically certain this is going to be a rough delivery, Colonel. She'll need professional assistance."

Townsend looked about the room as if seeking help. "Can you do a C-section and deliver the kid early?" he said, a hint of desperation in his tone.

The doctor was emphatic. "No way. The equipment for surgery here is completely inadequate, to say nothing of the problem of caring for a premature infant."

For several moments, Townsend remained silent. She could see something unspoken going on in his mind. She locked her eyes on him and waited, silently commanding him to come forth with the truth.

A few seconds later, Townsend offered in a quiet but tortured voice, "Mission Control wants us to take both of them with us by force."

"What!" Rebecca was shocked.

"That's right." Townsend lowered his furious eyes. "And I have orders directly from General Winters himself, representing both the Joint Chiefs and the White House. They can't afford having us abandon those two here, even if Gwen wasn't in labor. And under present circumstances . . ."

Rebecca cut him off. "Taking them is absolutely out of the question. Trying to deal with a birth in the zero-gravity environment of the ERV would be a disaster. And spending the first five months of its life in zero g would leave the child hideously crippled, if it survived at all."

Townsend looked at her. "I thought you were the one who wanted the baby aborted."

"That was then, this is now. That was abortion, this is infanticide. Ethically I can't allow it." Rebecca crossed her arms and returned the colonel's look with a level gaze.

"You realize what you're saying?" said Townsend, totally flustered. "After the sixth, the only way home is a slow transfer orbit that gets us home in May instead of January. Ten months in that little ERV cabin instead of six. It's only designed to provide life support for two hundred days at most."

"But there'll only be three of us instead of all five. We can make it."

"Maybe, except for one thing. Even the slow return window closes after July 21. What would you have us do if the baby hasn't arrived by then?"

"If that happens, Colonel, you do what you think best."

"And you?"

"I'll do what I have to do," the doctor said softly.

OPHIR PLANUM
JUNE 29–JULY 16, 2013

The concept of "launch window" in astronautics is a relative term. In principle, it is always possible to get from one place to another—if one has sufficient propulsive capabilities and sufficient time. However, if the propulsive system is fixed, and the flight time allowable is limited by available consumables, then the otherwise vague edges of the launch window during which it is possible to get from one planet to another can become very sharp.

Luke Johnson marked the calendar hanging in the galley with two important dates. On July 8 he wrote in green, "End of fast transfer window." On July 21 he marked in red, "Last chance to launch."

The first of these days was somewhat arbitrary; it was the last date during which the dynamics of the solar system would allow the ERV *Retriever* to make the transit from Mars back to Earth within the limits of the two-hundred-day flight it was rated for. A day later, the required trip time grew to 209 days; while outside specs, the returning crew might risk that much without too much fear. But if launch were delayed even one more day after that, they would need 218 days, and so on, until July 21, when a risky 306-day transfer was still possible.

But after July 21, no amount of time would do. The Earth would simply have moved too far for the ERV to make the trip.

As each day passed, Luke placed an X in one square after another. McGee questioned whether Townsend should have let this demonstration of anxiousness-to-leave continue, but he did, and the crew grew more nervous with each X. Finally the day came when Luke placed an X on July 8.

"Last chance for a quick flight," the geologist commented.

But Townsend just continued his reading.

Thus, the first critical day passed without incident.

Then another day was marked off, and another, and another, until July 16.

With nothing left to do but wait, the entire crew gathered in the galley. Gwen, Luke, and McGee were watching a Braves game. The TV sportscaster blared, "Bottom of the ninth, Atlanta trails 5:2. Two outs. Runners on second and third."

Sitting next to Rebecca, off to the side, Townsend whispered, "How much longer do you figure, Doctor?"

The sportscaster announced: "Coming to the plate for Atlanta is slugger Stan Slominski. Slominski, batting 342, twenty-nine home runs so far this season."

"Come on, Stan!" Gwen shouted. Stan was the man.

Rebecca shrugged. "I don't know. It could be today, could be tomorrow. Could be two weeks from now."

Townsend clenched his fist. "Dammit. We don't have two weeks. We don't even have one week. Isn't there anything you can do to push things along?"

"The pitch, high and outside. Ball one! Looks like Slominski's being given an intentional walk."

Rebecca briefly eyed the group watching the game with clinical interest, and then answered her commander. "No, nothing safe. At this point, Mother Nature's in charge."

Oblivious to the doctor's disdain, the sportscaster announced: "Two outs. Bases are loaded. Coming to bat for Atlanta is Carlos Gomez, a rookie who hasn't done very well this year. Gomez, batting 195, is at the plate. Here's the pitch, strike one!"

Gwen rose from her chair and turned away from the TV in disgust. "I don't want to see this."

"Strike two!" the sportscaster called.

Gwen walked to the refrigerator to get something to drink. She returned with a cup of juice and stood behind her chair, facing away from the TV to avoid witnessing the final debacle.

"And it's a powerful drive deep into left field!"

Gwen whirled in amazement. The sportscaster went on. "It's . . . it's . . . over the fence! A grand slam. Carlos Gomez has knocked the ball right out of the park! Atlanta wins, 6:5."

"Yes!" Gwen shouted.

Then she doubled over in pain, dropping her cup onto the floor. Stricken, Gwen clutched at her swollen belly. "Ahhhh! Help! I'm dying!"

Rebecca was up in an instant. "Quick," she shouted, "get her into the lab."

McGee tried to help his new wife walk, but her legs wouldn't work, so he put his hands under her arms and motioned to Luke, who lifted her legs. The two men carried her, moaning and screaming, into the lab. Rebecca slammed a cot mattress onto the table, and the men placed Gwen down on it. In a few moments, her screaming stopped, but her breathing remained agonized.

As Gwen's breathing slowly became more regular, Rebecca put on her doctor's coat and sterile gloves, and moved to unfasten Gwen's pants. "We better have a look—"

"Just what do you think you're doing?" Gwen angrily pushed the doctor's hand away.

Rebecca tried to be cool. "I'm going to deliver your baby."

Gwen's eyes went wild. "No you're not. No you're not! Do you hear me, Colonel. I don't want that atheist bitch to lay a finger on me!"

Flustered, Rebecca backed away before mustering her courage to try again. "Gwen, this is going to be hard. You've got to let me help."

Gwen shoved her away violently. "You stay away!"

Rebecca turned to her commander for assistance. "Colonel, she could die. I've got to find out what's going on."

Townsend didn't know what to do. "Try talking with her," he offered helplessly.

Rebecca took a deep breath to calm herself, then approached again, taking care to stay out of arms' reach of her wild patient.

"Gwen, listen to me," the doctor said softly. "I'm sorry about what I said. I'm sorry about trying to make you have an abortion. I was wrong. Now I want to help. Please let me help you."

Gwen glared at her. "Why should I believe that?"

"I'm a doctor. It's my oath."

Curiosity modified the hostile expression on the mechanic's face. "What good's your oath? You don't even believe in God, do you?"

Rebecca shook her head. "No, Gwen, I don't. But I believe in truth. Have you ever known me to lie about anything?"

Gwen thought for a moment. "No, I reckon not."

Rebecca knelt by the table. "Listen to me, Gwen," she whispered with a kind of passion. "I swear this to you on all I hold holy. I want you to have this baby. I want you to live, and I want the baby to live, and I want you and McGee to raise your child here on Mars. I believe in what you're doing, Gwen. I believe in it with all my heart. If I had the courage, I'd do it myself. I don't." She drew a breath. "But I have the skill to see you through this. Gwen, I can help you win. Let me help."

Gwen was bewildered. The doctor's outburst was honest, that was obvious. But still . . . She shook her head. "Do you have any idea how much I've hated you? I think I'd rather die than let you help me."

Rebecca looked her softly in the eyes. "And the baby, would you rather have her die?"

Gwen stared at Rebecca for several seconds. "*Her*. You called my baby a 'her,' not an 'it.' "

Rebecca nodded. "Yes, Gwen, your baby's going to be a girl."

Gwen was dumbfounded. "How long have you known?"

"A long time."

"But you didn't tell me."

"I didn't think you would want to know ahead of time."

"You were right." Gwen's expression softened a bit. "Thank you for considering my way of thinking."

"Sorry I let it slip."

"That's okay," Gwen smiled. "We all make mistakes. A girl. A baby girl!"

Rebecca leaned closer and whispered conspiratorially. "We're the only women within seventy million miles. Don't you think it's silly for us to be always, always . . ."

"Tearing at each other like cats?"

Rebecca nodded. "Precisely."

"You think maybe us behaving that way is giving women a bad reputation around here?"

Rebecca nodded again.

Gwen looked down at her swollen belly. "My daughter wouldn't like that."

Rebecca shook her head and smiled. "No."

Gwen regarded the doctor. "You know, Rebecca, I always thought you were a really fine person—for a damn Yankee atheist bitch, that is."

Rebecca grinned. "And I always thought you were super, Gwen, taking into consideration the fact that you're an ignorant Bible-thumping hillbilly, of course."

The two women exchanged smiles of recognition. Gwen slowly extended her hand to Rebecca, who clasped it warmly. "Go ahead, Doc. Do your stuff. Let's even up the odds around here."

For a moment Rebecca felt choked with emotion. *Oh, Gwen, if only we could have been friends sooner.* Then she mastered herself. "Okay, now let's have a look," she said clinically.

Rebecca opened up Gwen's pants. *What a mess.*

The mechanic saw her expression. "It's the bag of waters, isn't it?"

"Yes. Membranes have ruptured."

Gwen gritted her teeth in pain. "Uh-oh. It's happening again." Then suddenly she screamed.

The noise was startling, but Rebecca quickly gathered her wits. She looked at her watch. "That's five minutes since the last one. She's coming soon."

Gwen reached out. "Could I have some . . . privacy?"

Rebecca stood up and faced the three watching men. "All right, everybody out except the father."

For a moment, McGee and Luke looked at each other. Both women watched curiously, with similar thoughts. *Let's see who stays.* The confrontation didn't take long. McGee stood his ground. Luke hesitated and then looked to Townsend, who motioned the geologist to follow him out to the galley.

Seconds after the door closed behind the two departing men, Gwen screamed again.

The scream bespoke a pain that edged on death. McGee was terrified. "What's going on? Is this normal?"

Rebecca's voice was coolly professional. "We've got engagement, descent, and flexion. Internal rotation nominal."

"I'm cold," Gwen said with a violent shiver.

That, at least, was something he could deal with. McGee quickly found a blanket and covered Gwen's chest and arms.

"That's better." She smiled.

"Extension beginning, rotation complete," Rebecca recited.

Gwen yelled in pain. McGee's face went white, but Rebecca was all business. She placed her stethoscope to Gwen's swollen lower section and listened for a few seconds. A trace of alarm flashed through her eyes. McGee caught it and suddenly his fear changed to terror.

"What is it?" he asked.

"The heartbeat indicates fetal distress. That baby has got to come out fast." Rebecca hesitated for a bare moment.

"Okay, Gwen," she commanded. "You've got to push now. *Push!*"

Gwen tried her best, but the pain only increased. "It's no use."

Rebecca reached into the birth canal and felt around for the problem. "Dammit, there's some kind of blockage."

Gwen screamed again, but Rebecca kept probing. "It's the baby's leg. It's caught." She tried to move the small limb, provoking another horrible scream. The mechanic started to twitch wildly.

"Hold her still, Kevin. Hold her still!"

McGee clenched his teeth and pinned his wife as she screamed again, enough to set even Townsend's nerves on edge all the way out in the galley. Luke went deathly pale. Each of Gwen's cries was worse than before. Townsend started to pace. Luke put his hands over his ears.

Again Gwen screamed, telling of pain and agony beyond comprehension.

"I can't take much more of this," Townsend muttered.

Then the most horrible scream of all rang out. The commander looked wildly at Luke. "What's going on? She's dying!" There was no time to lose. Townsend ran and pushed open the door. Stumbling into the lab he was greeted by a new cry. The cry of a baby.

The colonel stopped, shocked. Rebecca held a blood-covered infant, which was crying lustily. Blood was everywhere. He looked at Gwen, but the flight engineer was alive. McGee was holding her sweaty hand. As they watched, Rebecca toweled off the baby, put drops in her eyes, then handed her to the new mother.

Gwen smiled at her tiny daughter, then announced to everyone, "Her name is Virginia Dare McGee."

"After the first English child born in America," McGee explained. "The first American. She is the first Martian."

Overcome, Rebecca broke into happy tears.

"Rebecca, you were great," McGee congratulated. "I guess all that delivery room experience never wears off."

"This was my first," the doctor sniffled.

Everyone was astounded.

Rebecca held her head up bravely. "But it won't be my last. I never saw it before. This is what biology is really all about. It's about life, and . . ." Rebecca hesitated for a second, glancing over at Gwen holding her baby. The others looked at her expectantly.

"And life's a miracle!" the biologist concluded triumphantly.

Gwen smiled at her child, and nodded in agreement.

OPHIR PLANUM
JULY 20, 2013, 09:00 MLT

The departing crew stayed for four more days, because they could. But July 20, Space Day, was time to leave.

Final farewells took place on the lower deck of the *Beagle*. Hands were shaken all around, and Gwen and Rebecca shared an emotional embrace, their differences resolved by much more than words.

Then the Hab's door closed. As McGee, Gwen, and baby Virginia watched through the windows of the *Beagle,* the departing trio trooped across the plain to enter the ERV. Townsend was the last to climb the ladder; as he prepared to enter the hatch, he turned to give a thumbs up, which Gwen returned. Then the hatch closed.

McGee, Gwen, and Virginia stood by the window and waited. A few minutes later, with the briefest of warnings, the ERV *Retriever* lifted off with a roar and disappeared into the Martian sky.

Returning upstairs after the departure, the castaways entered the galley. There on the table was a box, labeled in Rebecca's handwriting, "For Gwen."

The mechanic opened the cardboard container. Inside were two toy horses, fine models really, of the Tennessee Walking breed. Gwen could see that they had once been carefully hand painted, but the paint was worn, as if loving hands had petted the horses and played with them, many times over many years.

There was a note in the box. It read "Their names were Misty and Comet . . ."

With a tear in her eye, Gwen pranced the little horses before the fascinated Virginia.

CHAPTER 28

EXCEPT FOR THE SHORT RATIONS, THE JOURNEY BACK TO Earth began well enough. However, the ERV had never been designed for a three-hundred-day transit back to Earth, and during the final third of the flight, subsystems had begun to fail. That was when they really began to miss Gwen Llewellyn.

Fortunately, the ship's life-support system was built out of multiplexed sub-units, so they did not lose all capacity at once. But as one water-purification module after another dropped off-line, the crew had to increasingly put off the washing of clothes, kitchenware, and personnel, until by the 270th day they stopped washing altogether. The loss of water recycling also meant the loss of oxygen recycling, since oxygen makeup was provided by the water electrolysis units. By the final day of the return flight to Earth, even the compressed oxygen reserves on board had run out.

At his control console, Colonel Andrew Townsend drew shallow breaths of the foul cabin air. To his left, Luke Johnson was floating, peering out through the porthole at the Earth, which was now looming huge. Behind him, Dr.

Sherman drifted alongside some medical oxygen tanks, checking the gauges of these last reserves. Townsend assessed his two remaining crew members; both were short of breath, their eyes red, their faces and clothes dirty, their expressions taut with tension. *They've almost had it. Do I look that bad, too?*

"There it is. We're almost home," Luke mused out the window, but his voice was far from jubilant. The subtext was unspoken, but telling nevertheless. *Having come this far, must we die of suffocation now?*

The radio crackled with Phil Mason's voice. "ERV *Retriever,* this is Houston Control. We have you on radar. You are go for splashdown in South Pacific Quarantine Zone number three. ETA ninety-seven minutes."

Townsend picked up the microphone.

"Houston, this is *Retriever*. We copy. SPQZ 3. Laying in final descent program now." He began typing in the required commands, but was interrupted by a light touch on his shoulder. He turned to discern Rebecca floating behind him.

"Colonel," the doctor said, urgency in her voice, "the last of the emergency medical oxygen is gone. We don't have ninety-seven minutes."

"How long do we have?"

"Blackout . . ." Rebecca panted. "Blackout in no more than thirty."

The pilot clenched his fist in frustration, then a cool resolution set in his mind. He surveyed his instruments. *Very well.* He announced his decision with steel in his voice. "Then we'll just have to come in steeper. Fasten your seat belts folks."

Luke and Rebecca looked at each other in alarm. They barely had time to scramble to their chairs before Townsend hit the retros.

Kevin McGee sat in front of the camera in the *Beagle*'s galley with as many butterflies in his stomach as he'd ever experienced at his college tenure hearing. He had written his speech, rewritten it, practiced it a thousand times, until Gwen just told him to be himself.

The transmission had to be timed perfectly, so it would arrive at Earth just before the *Retriever* began its descent. He had learned not to leave well enough alone with politics on Earth. Despite the Administration's victory in the election, there was still a great deal of public hysteria over the bogus back-contamination issue. Wexler had filled him in on the deal the Administration had struck to mollify that sentiment, and the "contingency plans" that had accordingly been put in place—plans that could easily cost the lives of the returning crew. The only assistance the pair on Mars could give their former crewmates now was that delivered by the power of their words. It might not be enough, but they had to try. Townsend, Rebecca, and Luke were going to need all the help they could get.

Gwen set the recorder running before he even gave her a signal, and McGee had no choice but to start. "Hello, I'm astronaut Kevin McGee and this is my wife, flight engineer Major Guenevere McGee. I'm sure by now our faces are familiar to many of you."

Gwen sat next to him, holding the ten-month-old child in her lap. "And this is our baby daughter. Say hello to the people, Virginia." She waved one of the little girl's arms.

McGee cleared his throat, decided that sounded too stuffy, and continued. "As our crewmates approach Earth, we're making this broadcast to let all of you know why we have stayed behind. We understand some people have said that we've been abandoned here so the President can use us as an excuse to request funding for more Mars missions. Those stories are entirely false. In fact, the President both begged and ordered us to return to Earth with the rest of the crew, and we refused. Tonight, we're going to tell you why."

He looked at Gwen, then back at the camera eye. "I'm a historian, and I know that a society cannot have progress, or growth, or hope, unless there is an open frontier. That's what made America in its frontier days such a powerful engine of progress for all of humanity. It was a place where people could write their own rules, where stupid old habits could be thrown away, and newer and better ways could be tried. Before the discovery of America, the old world was like a play that had already been written, and all the leading roles assigned.

"But the American frontier created a stage where the actors could make up their own parts and their own script. We became the most creative nation in history, because we could see the infinite potential of the human mind, if only it's given a chance.

"Now, though, we're slowing down. We have bureaucratic regulations for everything. It's become much harder to find a place where we can try new things, so fewer new things get tried. In most fields that seem to involve risk, our technological progress is grinding to a halt. We don't build new cities anymore, and so we've begun to think of ourselves not as builders of our country, but as mere inhabitants.

"Our frontier has been gone too long, and now our nation is losing the spark. We can't let that happen. Here on Mars, we have a chance to open a new frontier that can breathe life back into our civilization. *That's* why I have to stay here, to make sure we don't lose this chance for renewal."

He turned to his wife, and the baby gave him a gushing smile in return. "Look, I'm a scholar, not a hero. What gave me the strength to put myself on the line for these ideas is the fact that I'm head over heels in love with the bravest and finest woman ever born—and she's staying."

Gwen blushed a deep red.

"It was Gwen who first saw the truth of why we can't leave Mars behind. I'll let her tell you in her own words why."

She handed little Virginia over to McGee, who bounced the baby on his knee. She seemed nervous as she started speaking. "Before I came to Mars, I thought this place would be a dead world, a big barren rock, like the Moon. And while the only living things we've found were little one-celled plants, the place didn't seem dead to me. Instead it seemed more like a place that was waiting, waiting for something.

"Kevin and I went out together on the first rover trip, and we drove all over the place and saw the most amazing things. We saw dry lakes and riverbeds, deep canyons, and towering mountains, and for a while it was hard for me to tell what it all meant. But on our second day out in the rover, we watched the Sun come up, the most beautiful sunrise you ever saw. The land lit up, and I *knew* that Mars wasn't just a rock. It's a world, a world that deserves to be filled with people and with life, with the birds of the air and the fishes of the sea. Why else would God have made such a wondrous place, if not to be a new home for all his creatures?"

The *Retriever*'s course change did not go unnoticed by the many radar stations of NASA's Deep Space Tracking Network or the Near Earth Tracking Network. Reports from these systems were rapidly relayed to Mission Control at the Johnson Space Center.

Within three minutes of Townsend's action, Alicia Castillo passed Phil Mason a sheet of paper. For a long five seconds, the flight director could only stare at the message in disbelief. Mastering himself, Mason picked up his microphone. "*Retriever,* this is Houston. Radar tracking has you way off course. You are coming in too steep. You could burn up. You are going to miss the quarantine zone."

After a few seconds of anxious silence, Townsend's voice came through crackly static. "No time for that. Out of air."

The crazy flyboy was going to try to evade quarantine! "No! Negative. You can't do that. Colonel Townsend, respond."

"What do you want us to do?" the radio voice responded. "Hold our breath?"

The Chief of Operations gripped the microphone. "You don't understand, Colonel. The President's deal with the opposition calls for shooting you down if you are off-target for quarantine."

This time, despite all the static, Townsend's voice came through loud and clear. "Let them try. We're coming in. *Retriever* out."

Mason slammed his fist down on the control console. "Dammit!" He stood staring at the huge map of the Earth displayed on the opposite wall. Across the map a light moved, showing the present and projected course of the *Retriever*.

All eyes in Mission Control were on the flight director. Everyone knew what he knew. Alicia was at his side. "What are you going to do?" she asked softly.

Mason swallowed the lump in his throat. "What I have to." As if in pain, Mason reluctantly picked up his phone. "Get me the White House."

The silence in Mission Control was like death.

Strapped in their chairs, the three returning Martian explorers endured significant g loads as the *Retriever* shook with the vibration of reentry. Rebecca wore a pair of headphones and turned dials.

"Colonel!" she shouted above the din, "I'm picking up a series of high-frequency radio bursts coming from the continental United States."

Townsend's gaze did not shift from his dismal control readouts. "Play it!" he yelled.

Rebecca threw a switch and a series of very high-pitched pings erupted from the loudspeaker in staccato repetition.

The pilot could not believe his ears. "That's BMDO targeting radar! The bastards are painting us."

Luke's depression instantly turned to panic. "What are you going to do?"

Townsend's voice was cool. "Make it interesting." With that, he jerked forward his control stick, and the *Retriever*'s nose pitched down, sending the craft on a deeper dive into the atmosphere. G loads increased, and an eerie red glow lit the porthole.

Trapped in the cramped metal vehicle, the crew began to perspire. Rebecca kept her eyes on the life-support readouts. "Cabin temperature 115. Hull temperature 1750 and rising," she recited in level tones.

Townsend did not reply, but noted the information internally, along with the reconfirmed observation, *She's a cool one, that Dr. Sherman.*

But Luke had completely lost control. "The hull's starting to ablate!" he shouted. "We're going to burn up!"

Townsend stared at his controls. The ship was not rated for this treatment, but it might survive . . . at least for a short time. "Come on, baby," he muttered. "Just a little bit longer."

```
            BALLISTIC MISSILE DEFENSE COMMAND
               CHEYENNE MOUNTAIN, COLORADO
                   MAY 16, 2014 10:45 CST
```

Deep inside Cheyenne Mountain at the Ballistic Missile Defense Command, preparations were being made for drastic action. The Chairman of the Joint Chiefs of Staff, General Bernard Winters, stood with other high-ranking officers in front of a huge illuminated map of the world. Blinking lights moved across it in various trajectories, and the assembled officers observed every movement with keen interest.

On a desk nearby, a small TV was playing the broadcast from Mars.

"General Winters, sir," said a colonel, approaching nervously, "we confirm *Retriever* well off course for quarantine. Heading toward populated areas at hypersonic velocity. Its trajectory is way too low for safety."

He handed Winters a sheet of data, which the general absorbed with a rapid glance. Winters stared at the situation map, and then looked over to the TV. A thirtyish woman with red braids was speaking, her dirty NASA coverall adorned with an American flag and a Silver Star. Her thin, lined face and bright eyes spoke of courage, matching that spoken for by the Star. "Our crewmates, who've been through the thick and thin of this place with us, are coming back today," she said. "They can tell you the wonder of this world, and of the new chance that God is giving us here. They can show you what we've seen. Please listen to them."

"Your orders, sir?" the colonel interrupted. "All defensive systems are armed and ready."

The general looked to the rows of weapons officers waiting at their consoles, then back to the brave young mother on the TV. He swallowed hard, then pursed his lips. "At that altitude, if we have to shoot, we'd better be accurate or collateral damage could result." He turned to the colonel and gave his order: "I want an immediate and complete systems check run on the targeting software for all anti-missile systems."

That was incredible. It took a moment for the colonel to find his voice. "But sir, that will disable the system for close to an hour."

In response, Winters gave the other officer a blank look. "Then you'd better get to it, Colonel."

Then understanding dawned. *Holy shit,* the colonel thought. *Disabling the system is precisely his intention.* Suddenly, the officer felt much prouder of the uniform he wore. A big knowing smile crossed his face. "Yes, sir. Right away, sir. A complete systems check." He rushed off to implement the order.

Moments later, a young captain approached carrying a red telephone. "General Winters, sir, it's the White House."

Winters paused to observe that the systems check was well underway. Then, wearing a mischievous grin, he reached out for the telephone.

When the Reverend Bobby Joe Stone entered his home, he found a group of middle-aged women gathered around the sitting-room television, watching a live broadcast from the three castaways stranded on Mars.

His wife sipped her iced tea and beamed at the image on the screen. "Oh, look at the baby! Isn't she cute?"

The minister came into the room, gave his wife a chaste kiss on the cheek, but the other women didn't even notice his entrance. "Hello, ladies. What's so interesting on TV?"

Charity Stone smiled at her husband. "It's those astronauts who are staying on Mars. See, there's the father, and the mother and the baby. Oh, what a cute little girl! And the mother is such a fine Christian girl. Just listen to her, dear."

Another woman munched daintily on a dish of mixed nuts. "Ooooh, look at that child's adorable little nose. What a cutie!"

Gwen continued to talk from the television. "Our family is going to stay here on Mars, because it's God's plan and because it's what the baby needs. Eventually, we hope that some of you will decide to come here and join us."

McGee leaned forward, picking up the thread. "Because we could use some friends here to help turn this planet into a home. Most importantly, though, don't feel sorry for us. We'll get by, the three of us, because we have love, we have each other, and a new and beautiful world to explore, live, build, and grow on."

Mrs. Stone gasped and turned to her husband. He had seen that fire in her eyes before. "Dear, we've got to do something to help them. It's a true mission you could take on."

The televangelist frowned uncomfortably. "I don't exactly see how. Those people are millions of miles away."

Charity Stone gave him a scolding look. "You saw them, dear. Look at them, look at that baby. We can't leave that family there all alone and in need. We've got to start raising money right now for a campaign for a second expedition!"

Now she had the Reverend's interest. "Raise money?"

"Why, yes! There isn't a Christian family in America that wouldn't give one hundred dollars tonight, right now, to help that poor brave little family. All you need to do is ask them."

The minister blinked. "You really think so?"

The woman with the mixed nuts reached into her purse. "In fact, let me start the ball rolling, Reverend. I'll pledge a thousand dollars right now. My husband will never even notice."

Bobby Joe Stone looked at the entranced women watching Gwen and baby Virginia on the television. "Hmm. I do believe you're right."

Smoky fumes filled the cabin of the *Retriever*. The entire ship vibrated massively with supersonic buffeting.

Rebecca coughed. "Cabin temperature 130! Hull temperature . . ."

"Firing drogue," Townsend announced. He opened two switch covers and then closed both switches. An explosion resounded, signaling that the drogue parachute had been mortared out. Suddenly an enormous jerk wrenched the ERV backward in the air, but then things quieted down as the vehicle dropped swiftly, but at subsonic velocity through the Earth's atmosphere.

Luke called off the altimeter readings. "Altitude forty thousand feet, thirty-nine, thirty-eight . . ."

Rebecca eyed the life-support monitors. Cabin temperature had begun to drop, but the air composition was lethal. "CO_2's off the scale. Take us down fast, Colonel."

Townsend's breathing was heavy. "Roger that."

The air whistled past the plummeting ERV.

"Twelve thousand . . . eleven thousand!" Luke cried. "You're coming in too fast. We're going to smash! For God's sake, Colonel, release the main chute!"

"No," Rebecca choked, "get us down."

Townsend armed the parachute release system. "Just a few more seconds."

Luke screamed, "Three thousand feet. Two thousand!"

"Firing main parachute." Townsend threw two more switches and released a huge parasail, subjecting the ship to another enormous lurch. He grabbed a stick to steer the sail. "We're coming in fast. Better brace yourselves, folks."

He called off the final approach. "Prepare for impact in eight, seven . . ."

Seconds later, the cabin shook as the ERV hit water at a terminal velocity of forty miles per hour.

The three explorers stared in amazement at the sight of hissing and steaming seawater splashing over the outside of the porthole. But there was no time to lose. In a blink, the crew was up, madly scrambling for the hatch. Rebecca reached it first and struggled to open the lock, but was too weak. When Luke got beside her, he added his muscle and cranked the wheel a little, but not enough.

Townsend joined in the effort. All of them were on the verge of passing out, suffocating only inches away from fresh, clean air. "OK, together on three. One—two—*three!*"

The three crew members shoved together, and the wheel rotated a quarter turn, after which the hatch popped open to reveal a patch of blue sky. A blessed whiff of sea air entered the cabin, bringing with it the promise of salvation. Then, as if mocking their renewed hope, the ERV tipped to bring sea level to the bottom of the hatch. Water began to pour in.

"Abandon ship," Townsend shouted.

Closest to the open hatch, Rebecca struggled to get through, but the onrushing water pushed her back. She felt a shove from behind, as the two men pushed her through the opening and into the ocean.

Thrown like a projectile, Rebecca landed headfirst in the sea, then struggled toward the surface. The doctor had once been a fair swimmer, but encumbered with heavy wet clothes, lack of oxygen, and weak from ten months on short rations in zero gravity, she could barely stop herself from sinking farther. She looked upward. Above, light shone on the surface. Air, all the air she could want, was only six feet away.

She kicked and clawed the water with mad desperation, her lungs about to burst. Then she broke the surface, and fresh air filled her stricken lungs. A wave crashed over her and forced her back down, but then she surfaced for another deep breath. She blinked in the bright light and stinging water, but could see nothing except sea and sky. Finally reorienting herself, she turned and saw the *Retriever,* its inflation collar beginning to fill.

Still gasping for breath, she swam wildly back to the ERV, and, with the help of Luke Johnson, who looked like a big wet Texas rat, hauled herself up on the inflation collar. Then she looked around and saw—the Statue of Liberty!

The ERV had landed in New York harbor on a beautiful spring day! She turned and stared in amazement at Townsend, who answered her with palms out and a self-satisfied grin. She laughed and shook her head, then took a deep breath of the fresh sea air and smoothed back her hair.

A forty-foot sailing yacht came tacking up. "Ahoy there, Martians!" the nattily clad sportsman at her helm called out. "Welcome back. Care for something to drink?"

Rebecca smiled. "A cappuccino would be nice," she said sweetly.

In seconds, the ERV was surrounded by pleasure boats, and a big floating party ensued. On one of the boats, a CD player blared out the song "New York, New York."

Rescue helicopters arrived overhead, instructing the civilian boats to disperse for reasons of quarantine, but were joyfully ignored.

Rebecca kicked off her boots and let them sink as she bathed her bare feet in the water. She sipped her cappuccino and gazed thoughtfully first at the Manhattan skyline, then at the soaring sea gulls, and finally at the infinite sky beyond.

EPILOGUE

AFTER TWENTY YEARS, BY NOW GRAYING AND SLIGHTLY pot-bellied, Kevin McGee sat in a chair in the galley looking at video footage on the monitor. Hanging on the arms and watching along with him were two kids, fourteen-year-old Caitlin and eleven-year-old Dylan. Gwen, her red braided hair also streaked with gray, was cooking, assisted by Virginia, who was now twenty-one.

McGee used the remote to zoom in on a series of video snapshots. "Well, we never saw them again, not in person, but we heard a lot about them. See, here's some footage of their landing on Earth. It was quite a show."

McGee pressed the button on the remote, and the video showed Townsend, Rebecca, and Luke clinging to the hull of the ERV *Retriever,* which, buoyed by an inflatable collar, bobbed in New York Harbor. The Statue of Liberty and lower Manhattan were visible in the background. Sailboats crowded around the ERV filled with people waving and snapping pictures. In the distance, rescue helicopters were waiting unheeded. Rebecca had taken her shoes off, and was bathing her feet while she leaned back to let her face take in the sunshine. Townsend sat grinning on the hull, returning the cheers with a thumbs up. Luke stood on the highest point of the floating ERV, waving his soaked cowboy hat in the air and whooping it up. Someone from a sailboat passed by and handed Luke a beer.

"They sure picked a dramatic place to make a splash," McGee commented. "The impromptu ticker-tape parade that followed kind of blew away the quarantine issue too." He switched to another image. "Now here's Townsend with his new general's stars, receiving the Congressional Medal of Honor."

Dylan broke in, "Who's the guy with the goofy-looking grin shaking his hand?"

McGee grinned. "That, Dylan, was the President of the United States."

The boy looked puzzled. "I thought Townsend was the President."

"He's the President now, Dylan. This other man was President then." McGee picked another image. "Now here's Rebecca getting her Nobel Prize."

Caitlin was dazzled at the vision of elegance that now filled the screen. "Wow, look at that dress . . . and look at *hers*."

McGee nodded. "That's the Queen of Sweden next to her. Now here's Luke on his big spread in Texas. He made a fortune importing industrial gems from Mars."

"Don't we know it," Virginia interrupted roughly.

Gwen scolded her older daughter. "Hush, child! His money has done a lot for this colony."

There was a knock on the lower deck door. McGee called out, "Come in, whoever you are."

To everyone's surprise, a pretty young woman walked in. She wore a doctor's uniform, including stethoscope, and looked very much like a young version of Rebecca.

The girl spoke. "Hi, I just arrived on the ship earlier today. My name's Rachel Sherman. I think you two knew my mother?"

"Well!" McGee stammered, "I thought I heard something about Rebecca having a daughter, but . . ."

"That's me. She met my father in Stockholm. He was a physicist, getting a Nobel Prize himself for discovering some new kind of particle. I think they were called tachyons, itsy bitsy little things that go faster than light. Mother says there really wasn't all that much to it. I wouldn't know, since I'm not glued onto physics, but anyway it got him to Stockholm. They met, married, and . . ."

"And you kept your mother's last name," Gwen interjected.

Rachel smiled. "You know my mother. Naturally, she made my father agree that any girls would get her name, and the boys could have his. But I was all they managed to hatch."

McGee nodded understanding. "It didn't last long?"

Rachel shrugged. "When Mother won her second prize for splicing Martian genes with Earth plants to make Arctic Wheat, Father just couldn't drink it, so he lifted off for England to take Hawking's old chair at Cambridge."

"And you?" Gwen asked.

Rachel toyed a bit with her stethoscope. "I spent my entire childhood flying around the world with Mother to conferences and laboratories and stuff, and since that didn't leave me any time for school, she educated me herself. She said school would be a waste of my time anyway. I guess she was right because here I am, eighteen years old, and I've passed all the medical boards."

McGee had to grin. "I'm not surprised. I'll bet you're the best doctor anyone could hope to meet."

"Yes, I am," Rachel continued in a matter-of-fact way. "But the problem is, on Earth they have all these asinine laws and regulations, and if you don't have a degree from an accredited medical school, it doesn't matter how good you are—the rhinos won't let you practice."

Gwen smiled warmly. "Well, I'm sure we can use you here."

Suddenly Rachel seemed to be hit by a new thought.

"Oh, I almost forgot. Here's a present for you from Mother." The young doctor reached into her pack and pulled out a bag of seeds. "It's her latest gene-splicing invention—'coldberries' she calls them. She says they should do fine growing outside on Mars."

Gwen gratefully accepted the seeds. "Thanks to both of you. But you haven't been properly introduced. These are our younger children, Caitlin and Dylan, and this is Virginia. Your mother delivered her, the first child born on Mars."

A teenaged boy wandered in and, without noticing the new arrival, started wiping greenhouse dirt from his arms.

"And this is our second, Brendan."

Brendan looked up and saw Rachel, who, pleased with her obvious effect on the boy, twinkled her eyes at him. "Hello, Brendan," the girl said.

A little embarrassed at being unexpectedly subjected to the study of a pretty girl, Brendan blushed. "Hello," he said awkwardly.

Rachel reassured him with a generous smile. "Anyway, I start work tomorrow, and I was wondering if there was any way I could get a chance to do a little exploring first? You know, have a look around the country?" She looked at Brendan to make sure the poor lad got his cue.

For a moment it seemed as if the boy didn't get it, then suddenly there was a light in his eye. "I've got a rover!" he blurted. "I know all the country around here. I could take you for a drive right now."

"That would be very nice," Rachel said.

Brendan gestured for the young doctor to follow and headed for the door. But Gwen stopped him with a restraining hand on his shoulder. "Now wait a minute, son, lunch is almost ready, and there's work . . ."

"Oh come on, Mom," Brendan pleaded.

McGee saw the stricken expression on his son's face and was reminded of the desperate and joyful hopes of his own youth. "Let him go, Gwen."

She nodded, as if understanding, and let go. In a flash,

Brendan was across the galley. Taking Rachel's hand, he was out the door.

Gwen called out after him, "Check the oil, transmission, and battery fluids if you're planning on taking out that old tin lizzie of yours."

Already downstairs, Brendan shouted his reply. "I will."

An instant later, the two young people were running down one of the translucent tunnels that now linked the *Beagle* to other habs and auxiliary buildings.

As they ran, Brendan held Rachel's hand in one of his, while using the other to point things out and make animated gestures. Rachel's eyes were wide.

"And this is my rover," Brendan explained, as they entered an inflatable garage. "It's the original one that landed with the *Beagle*. Everybody says it's too old for use, but I keep it in shape."

Rachel walked over and touched the machine. "You mean this is the very same vehicle that Mother used when she made her discovery?"

"Yep. And it's also the rover that . . ." Brendan leaned over and whispered in her ear, provoking a snicker from the girl.

Rachel regarded him coyly. "But if this rover is so old, how do we know we won't get stuck?"

"Yes, that would be awful, wouldn't it?" Brendan deadpanned.

Rachel gave him a playful shove. "Don't you even think of it, you . . . you, *Martian!*"

"Don't worry," Brendan reassured her. "Come on, let's go!"

They hopped into the rover, and Brendan cycled the airlock door and steered their way outside. As he drove, the young man kept talking animatedly with his hands, while Rachel looked at him, her smile alternating between interest and skepticism.

As they rode out, Rachel got a good view of the old Snoopy on the side of the *Beagle,* and then the emblems and flags on the dozens of other habs connected by inflatable tunnels. Oddly colored clumps of blue-green grass grew between the habs. Few from Earth had ever seen such grass firsthand, but Rachel had: It grew in the Mars simulation chambers of her mother's lab.

Then they were out of the base area and onto the planitia, whose endless expanse was beginning to be invaded by scattered tufts of tall blue-green grass spreading out from the base.

McGee and Gwen stood by the window of the *Beagle,* watching the two drive joyfully across the plain. He squeezed her hand, and she leaned her head on his shoulder. From the depths of his memory came a snatch of a song:

> *One spark of Reason thy life shall start.*
> *One spark of mind shall make alive thee.*

McGee flashed with feeling as he remembered the lyric. The hope had become real. Life, full of play and full of wonder, had come to Mars . . . and Mars was coming to life.

TECHNICAL APPENDIX:
THE MARS DIRECT PLAN

FIRST LANDING PRESENTS A HUMANS-TO-MARS EXPEDItion not as a venture for the far future, but as a mission for our generation. This is entirely realistic. As I explained in detail in my books *Entering Space* and *The Case for Mars,* the United States has in hand, today, all the technologies required for undertaking an aggressive, continuing program of human Mars exploration, with the first piloted mission reaching the Red Planet within a decade. We do not need to build giant spaceships embodying futuristic technologies in order to go to Mars. We can reach the Red Planet with relatively small spacecraft launched directly to Mars by boosters embodying the same technology that carried astronauts to the Moon more than thirty years ago. The key to success comes from following a "travel light and live off the land" strategy similar to that which has well-served terrestrial explorers for centuries. The plan to approach the Red Planet in this way is called Mars Direct. This is the plan used by the crew of the *Beagle* in the present novel.

Here's how the Mars Direct Plan works: At an early launch opportunity—for example, 2009—a single heavy lift

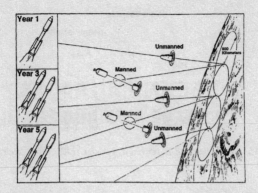

The Mars Direct mission sequence. The sequence begins with the launch of an unmanned Earth Return Vehicle (ERV) to Mars, where it will fuel itself with methane and oxygen manufactured on Mars. Thereafter, every two years, two boosters are launched. One sends an ERV to open up a new site, while the other sends a piloted Hab to rendezvous with an ERV at a previously prepared site.

booster with a capability equal to that of the Saturn V used during the Apollo program is launched off Cape Canaveral and uses its upper stage to throw a forty-tonne unmanned payload onto a trajectory to Mars. Arriving at Mars eight months later, the spacecraft uses friction between its aeroshield and Mars' atmosphere to brake itself into orbit around the planet, and then lands with the help of a parachute. This payload is the Earth Return Vehicle (ERV). It flies out to Mars with its two methane/oxygen-driven rocket propulsion stages unfueled. It also carries six tonnes of liquid hydrogen cargo, a 100-kilowatt nuclear reactor mounted in the back of a methane/oxygen-driven light truck, a small set of compressors and automated chemical processing unit, and a few small scientific rovers.

As soon as the craft lands successfully, the truck is telerobotically driven a few hundred meters away from the site, and the reactor deployed to provide power to the compressors and chemical processing unit. The hydrogen brought

Mars Vehicles

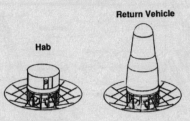

The Mars Direct hab and Earth return vehicles (ERV) within their aerobrakes.

from Earth can be quickly reacted with the Martian atmosphere, which is ninety-five percent carbon dioxide gas (CO_2), to produce methane and water, thus eliminating the need for long-term storage of cryogenic hydrogen on the planet's surface. The methane so produced is liquefied and stored, while the water is electrolyzed to produce oxygen, which is stored, and hydrogen, which is recycled through the methanator.

Ultimately, these two reactions (methanation and water electrolysis) produce twenty-four tonnes of methane and forty-eight tonnes of oxygen. Since this is not enough oxygen to burn the methane at its optimal mixture ratio, an additional thirty-six tonnes of oxygen is produced via direct dissociation of Martian CO_2. The entire process takes ten months, at the conclusion of which a total of 108 tonnes of methane/oxygen bipropellant will have been generated. This represents a leverage of 18:1 of Martian propellant produced compared to the hydrogen brought from Earth needed to create it. Ninety-six tonnes of the bipropellant will be used to fuel the ERV, while twelve tonnes are available to support the use of high-powered, chemically fueled long-range ground vehicles. Large additional stockpiles of oxygen can also be produced, both for breathing and for turning into water by combination with hydrogen brought from Earth. Since water is eighty-nine percent oxygen (by

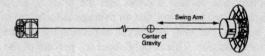

Tethered artificial gravity system requires two objects swinging around a mutual center of gravity. For Mars Direct, the Hab (on the right) is counterbalanced by the spent upper stage (on the left).

weight), and since the larger part of most foodstuffs is water, this greatly reduces the amount of life-support consumables that need to be hauled from Earth.

The propellant production having been successfully completed, in late 2011 two more boosters lift off the Cape and throw their forty-tonne payloads toward Mars. One of the payloads is an unmanned fuel-factory/ERV just like the one launched in 2009, the other is a habitation module carrying a crew of five, a mixture of whole food and dehydrated provisions sufficient for three years, and a pressurized methane/oxygen-powered ground rover. On the way out to Mars, artificial gravity can be provided to the crew by extending a tether between the habitat and the burnt-out booster upper stage, and spinning the assembly.

Upon arrival, the manned craft drops the tether, aerobrakes, and lands at the 2009 landing site, where a fully fueled ERV and fully characterized and beaconed landing site await it. With the help of such navigational aids, the crew should be able to land right on the spot; but if the landing is off course by tens or even hundreds of kilometers, the crew can still achieve the surface rendezvous by driving over in their rover. If they are off by thousands of kilometers, the second ERV provides a backup. However, assuming the crew lands and rendezvous as planned at site number one, the second ERV will land several hundred kilometers away to start making propellant for the early 2014 mission, which in turn will fly out with an additional ERV to open up Mars landing site number three.

Thus, every 26 months two heavy lift boosters are

launched, one to land a crew, and the other to prepare a site for the next mission, for an average launch rate of just one booster per year to pursue a continuing program of Mars exploration. This is only about ten percent of the U.S. launch capability, and is clearly affordable. In effect, this "live off the land" approach removes the manned Mars mission from the realm of mega-fantasy and reduces it in practice to a task of comparable difficulty to that faced in launching the Apollo missions to the Moon.

The crew will stay on the surface for one and a half years, taking advantage of the mobility afforded by the high-powered chemically driven ground vehicles to accomplish a great deal of surface exploration. With a twelve-tonne surface fuel stockpile, they have the capability for over 24,000 kilometers worth of traverse before they leave, giving them the kind of mobility necessary to conduct a serious search for evidence of past or present life on Mars—an investigation key to revealing whether life is a phenomenon unique to Earth or general throughout the universe. Since no one has been left in orbit, the entire crew will have available to them the natural gravity and protection against cosmic rays and solar radiation afforded by the Martian environment, and thus there will not be the strong driver for a quick return to Earth that plagues alternative Mars mission plans based upon orbiting mother-ships with small landing parties. At the conclusion of their stay, the crew returns to Earth in a direct flight from the Martian surface in the ERV. As the series of missions progresses, a string of small bases is left behind on the Martian surface, opening up broad stretches of territory to human cognizance.

Such is the basic Mars Direct Plan. In 1990, when it was first put forward by a Martin Marietta team led by this author, it was viewed as too radical for NASA to consider seriously, but over the ensuing years, with the encouragement of former NASA Associate Administrator for Exploration Mike Griffin and NASA Administrator Dan Goldin, the group at Johnson Space Center in charge of designing human Mars missions decided to take a good hard look at it. They produced a detailed study of a Design Reference Mission based on the Mars Direct Plan, but scaled up about a factor of two in expedition size compared to the original concept. They then produced a cost estimate for what a Mars exploration program based upon this expanded Mars Direct Plan would cost. Their result: $50 billion, with the estimate produced by the same costing group that assigned a $400 billion price tag to the traditional cumbersome approach to human Mars exploration embodied in NASA's 1989 "90 Day Report." If scaled back to the original lean Mars Direct Plan described here, the program could probably be accomplished for $20 billion. This is a sum that the United States or Europe or Japan could easily afford. It's a small price to pay for a new world.

In essence, by taking advantage of the most obvious local resource available on Mars—its atmosphere—the plan allows us to accomplish a manned Mars mission with what amounts to a lunar-class transportation system. By eliminating any requirement to introduce a new order of technology and complexity of operations beyond those needed for lunar transportation to accomplish piloted Mars missions, the plan can reduce costs by an order of magnitude and advance the schedule for the human exploration of Mars by a generation.

Exploring Mars requires no miraculous new technologies, no orbiting spaceports, and no gigantic interplanetary space cruisers. We can establish our first small outpost on Mars within a decade. We, and not some future generation, can have the eternal honor of being the first pioneers of this new world for humanity. All that's needed is present-day technology, some nineteenth-century industrial chemistry, a solid dose of common sense, and a little bit of moxie.

But history is not a spectator sport. Things happen because people make them happen. In 1998 an international organization called the Mars Society was formed. Its goal: Make humans-to-Mars a reality. We do public outreach, political work, and private exploration initiatives of our own. The first of these projects was to establish a Mars Arctic Research Station. Despite adverse weather, a failed paradrop, and a construction crew mutiny, this simulated human Mars exploration base was successfully built in the high-Arctic polar desert on Canada's Devon Island during the summer of 2000. If you want to find out more about what we are up to, you can look us up on our Web site at *www.marssociety.org*. Or write to: Mars Society, Box 273, Indian Hills, CO 80454.

The cause of the new world needs all types, from poets to pilots. Whether you are a McGee or a Townsend, a Rebecca or a Gwen, Mars needs you.

Join us.

On to Mars.